MICHAEL DRYSDALE

Michael Drysdale was born in London. A graduate of Essex University and Imperial College he had a thirty year career in computing. In 2010 he moved to South America to teach English. This provided the background for his first novel *The Banker*. He divides his time between London and Spain.

Visit https://michaeldrysdale.com

Praise for THE BANKER

Goodreads:

'I love this book, it is fun and easy to read but still smart and witty.'

'The story was easy to read, but still had a great story line and the author obviously did a great deal of research or has a very broad knowledge base.'

'It is so full of layers, twists, turns and even some climbs that it will keep you reanalysing what you thought was going to happen next. I don't think anybody will predict the ending from many pages ahead. And what a great finale!!'

'The novel is a clever multilayered twisting story of how Sir Phil Black got himself into a rather complicated space and the role of consequences in his life, some foreseen and others rather out of the blue.'

Amazon:

'The Banker moves forward at a breathtaking pace keeping the reader on the edge of their seat. The characters are so realistic you can almost feel the bad guys breathing down Sir Black's neck. Well the other bad guys anyway.'

'This book has so many layers of interest is it really hard to summarize in a few paragraphs. There are so many twists in the story line but I was sure I knew where the story was headed and then it would twist again. That to me, makes a very exciting read. The ending was original and perfect for the story and one that you will not be able to guess.'

'It is a contemporary tale set amongst the recent economic, and consequently, political crisis. It is a quick and easy read and a real page turner, a great book for the beach or a quiet afternoon in the hammock.'

'It is harder these days to write a good spy thriller, but Drysdale managed to accomplish it with his first novel. During the course of this adventure, we see some of the workings of the banking industry, some Russian mob stuff, some secret service stuff, some questionable China dealings, and all sorts of places around the world. This book will keep you hooked, as you try to figure out what is going to happen next. It will most likely not be what you had predicted!'

'A multi-layered plot which gets quite complex and yet it is not at all hard to follow. I enjoyed seeing some events turn out as I predicted but most events were complete surprises.'

LONDON 1972.
NAZI GERMANY HAS WON THE WAR.

SUCCESSION

MICHAEL DRYSDALE

Acorn Independent Press

PROLOGUE

"Mamungkukumpurangkuntjunya!" shouted Barry Johnston as he threw his boot with its scorpion occupant away from the 4x4. Barry liked to use Pitjantjatjara expletives while out in the bush. A lot of prospectors went native as far as tracking and water-divining skills were concerned; Barry just took it one step further than most.

He had parked his Toyota Land Cruiser about 50 yards from a mulga tree; any closer meant a risk of night-time visits from wildlife. He had slept on top of the car because it was cooler than inside – the ground was out of question because he didn't want to share his bed with creepy crawlies, whatever their intentions. During the night, he had managed to knock one of his boots off the roof. He now hopped to retrieve it, as the scorpion scuttled away to find a new home.

Reunited with his boot, Barry got the Primus going. He liked a full Australian breakfast – sausages, bacon, avocado, roast tomato, mushrooms, poached egg, biscuits and coffee – only this time, without sausages, bacon, avocado, tomato, mushrooms and egg. He was low on supplies so would have to make do with biscuits and coffee.

He was on his way home, having prospected for opal along Sergeant's Creek in the Musgrave Mountains. The hard sandstone meant it took over three weeks to dig a single shaft. So rather than digging new shafts, Barry had explored existing bores and tunnels left over from previous industrial mining operations. Often, opal could be found by sifting through the rock and debris created while making the tunnels. After six weeks, he had found nothing.

It was Barry's tenth year as an independent prospector. He spent the previous eight years as an employee of various Western Australian mining companies. So far, he had had enough success to eke out a living, but he had yet to strike it lucky and retire rich.

Rather than take the more direct Anne Beadell track home, Barry decided to go cross-country, taking a route parallel with and about 100 miles north of the track. This was new territory for him, and you never knew, there could be a gold field waiting to be discovered.

By seven o'clock, he had finished breakfast, started the 4x4 and headed west. The country was a bright red sandy plain with tussocks of spiny-leaved grass and woodlands alternating between mallee eucalyptus and mulga acacia. It was getting hot; by nine o'clock, it had reached a hundred and rising. There was little change in the scenery, until just after midday, a pink granite mound emerged on the horizon.

Could this be Lasseter's Reef?

It matched both the location and description for sure. In 1930, Harold Lasseter claimed to have discovered a vast, gold-bearing reef while prospecting some 20 years earlier. The gold reef hadn't been found since; half the prospecting community thought that Lasseter had been telling fairy stories while half, including Barry, thought there really was something in the tale. As Barry drove closer to the hill, he could make out a caldera at its edge.

Barry parked the car then walked towards the crater to take a closer look; he had stumbled on an open-pit mine. There were no signs of activity; it looked as if it had been completely excavated many years previously. He spotted a billboard announcing this to be '*Possum Hill Copper Mine*', and in smaller letters beneath, '*operational since 1931*'. Nearby was a shack with the remains of an electricity generator; it looked like the sort used in the 1930s. Inside the shack itself was one large room, largely bare; just a table, a few chairs and a filing cabinet. On one wall was a geological map of Western Australia, dated 1929; on another, a photograph of what looked like the mine's directors. Their clothing suggested the photograph was taken sometime in the 1930s. Nothing in the room indicated it was ever used later than that. Close by were the shells of a couple of huts that looked like workers' accommodation, but apart from the remains of bunk beds, they were empty.

Barry explored the area, took some photos, and then surveyed the scene with his binoculars. About two miles away, he could make out a level strip of ground with an adjacent building.

He drove to the spot; it was a disused airstrip and the structure was another shed. It was empty apart from a 1934 calendar attached to a wall, with incoming and outgoing flights and weather conditions marked. Barry felt a little deflated – not just because this was not Lasseter's Reef but also, because the copper price was low, there was little point scavenging around the mine.

Barry got back in the Toyota and drove off in a south-westerly direction, following a dry, shallow valley that would once have been a river or creek. It was Gibber terrain – a desert pavement of closely-packed pebbles, which meant he could step up a gear for a change. Barry would stop every now and then and check a stone sample, if it was a quartz-pebble conglomerate, which was often a good source of gold. Every now and then, a sample would have tiny yellow flecks embedded; he checked carefully that this was gold and not pyrite. He was beginning to feel good about the place. He collected the more promising specimens; back home, he would submit them to a metallurgical lab to check for any impurities, which would lower the gold's price.

The terrain got a bit rougher, which forced Barry to drive in first gear for much of the time. Fifteen miles from the airstrip, he was startled by the sound of a rattlesnake coming from his passenger seat; it was no reptile but the Geiger counter. Just after leaving Sergeant's Creek that morning, he had connected it to the Toyota's charging mechanism, but the counter had been silent up to that point. Could he have struck a uranium deposit? Barry got out of the Land Cruiser and walked around with his Geiger counter in one hand. Whichever way he went, the instrument showed readings way above background radiation. He reckoned he could well have stumbled on a quartz-pebble conglomerate uranium deposit. He was getting excited; this looked like it could be the best find in his 10-year career. He got back into his car and continued driving, stopping every now and then to check the area on foot with the Geiger. The readings were still good; it looked as if this was a large deposit.

The sun was getting low when he first sighted the tail fin. Then, a hundred yards further away, he could see the remains of an aircraft engine. Strewn along the valley floor were more parts of plane wreckage. He was no expert but he reckoned it was an aeroplane from the 1930s, and was probably taking workers to or from the Possum Hill mine when it crashed. The Geiger counter was still excited and, for a moment, Barry wondered if the plane had been carrying radioactive material. But as he walked away from the debris, he got some of his highest readings, so he ruled that out.

Barry was too short of supplies to stay longer and prospect the area thoroughly. It looked like the territory might be rich in both gold and uranium. So he took a few more rock samples, some photos of the terrain and the wreckage, and made a note of its location: 26°10'S 126°50'E. He would go back home and return as soon as he had restocked.

Chapter 1

She wasn't sure if it was the hard bed, the cold, or her headache that woke her up, but all seemed to be competing for her attention. As she turned over, she realised it wasn't a bed but a bench she had been sleeping on. As she sat up, a shiver shot through her body, so she rubbed her hands for a bit of warmth. The thumping headache was still there as she took in her surroundings. She was in a room measuring about 30 feet by 15, with half a dozen benches along the sides and strip lighting running along the length of the ceiling. A window almost filled one side of the chamber; next to it was a door. Otherwise, the place was bare. It wasn't her room, and she was certain she hadn't been here before. She looked through the window; she could see a huge hall. She got up and stepped outside, but it was even colder and she felt slightly giddy. She almost wanted to go back inside, but her curiosity was stronger.

The hall must have been a couple of hundred yards square, with shops placed along three of the sides. They were nearly all shut, but one or two were opening up. The ceiling was a mixture of iron and glass that let in daylight, but not much was getting in and the whole place was enveloped in a gloom. On the far side stood some train carriages, so she realised she must be in a railway station. She headed to the arrivals and departures board, still feeling unsteady on her feet. The station was very quiet with few people about; the departure boards announced trains to places like Brighton or Gatwick via Clapham Junction. The names meant nothing to her.

In the middle of the hall, a huge poster hung from the ceiling, showing an elegant, saturnine man in his 40s with a pencil moustache, wearing what looked like a fencing jacket, except that it was black rather than white. He must be someone famous, she thought, but she didn't recognise him.

A kiosk was positioned directly beneath the poster and a man in his late 20s, wearing a three-piece suit with a kipper tie and flared trousers, headed in her direction, clutching a newspaper in his hand. She thought she could trust him.

"Excuse me, could you tell me where we are?" Her own voice sounded distant, as if it was somebody else doing the talking.

"Victoria Station." He sounded even further away.

"Thank you." The name meant nothing to her. She took a step and almost lost her balance.

"Are you all right?" said the young man.

"Fine. Just a little faint."

"I can call for a doctor."

"That won't be necessary."

"Why don't you sit down for a while?" The man escorted her back to where she had woken up, which she could see, from a sign on the outside of the door, was a waiting room.

"Thank you. You've been most kind."

"I'd better dash or I'll miss my train."

She felt a bit better as soon as she entered the waiting room, although the headache was still bothering her. She sat down and tried to make sense of things. She must be in a dream. That would explain why it was so quiet, why the voices seemed so distant and muffled, and the strange names. After a while, she wasn't sure how long exactly, but it seemed like an hour, her headache eased and she felt more alert. She pinched herself. *This is no dream.* A lady in her 30s who looked like an office worker entered the waiting room. She could probably trust her. She asked where she was. She got the same reply – this time, loud and clear – Victoria Station. She felt the first stirrings of a mixture of fear and panic.

She tried to recall the last thing she did before going to sleep in the waiting room. Nothing – she couldn't remember. Had she got drunk? That would explain the headache. Surely, she wouldn't be drinking on her own. Maybe she'd been partying with friends. But they wouldn't leave her alone on a bench. But she had this feeling that she wasn't the sort of person who drank, or partied for that matter.

What did she do yesterday, before the supposed drinking or partying? She couldn't think of anything.

What about last week? Or last year? She couldn't answer.

Who was she with? She didn't know.

Did she have any brothers or sisters? She drew a blank. The breeze of fear and panic had turned into a storm of terror.

Who was she?

She looked at the clothes she was wearing: scuffed, low-heeled shoes, a blue skirt that reached just below her knees and could have been made from curtains, a cheap-looking white blouse, and a jacket that matched the skirt. She wore a beige plaid raincoat, but didn't have a hat. That seemed strange; she was sure she wouldn't go out without a hat. Maybe she left it on the train. She didn't have a handbag with her either. Maybe that too got left on the train. Or possibly it was stolen while she was sleeping.

She searched in her pockets, hoping to find something that would provide a clue where she'd come from or what she'd been doing. Her left jacket pocket was empty, but from the right, she pulled out a card. On it was a photo, so now at least she knew what she looked like. Next to the photo, she could make out:

Name: Mary Brown.
Address: 78 Kings Road, Hackney, London.
Age: 46
Occupation: Gardener.
Marital Status: Spinster.

Chapter 2

Apart from her clothes, the identity card was the only possession Mary had with her. She now knew her name and where she lived, so that was a start. She thought it would be best to go home, and that just being there might bring back memories. And even if she lived alone, her neighbours would surely remember her and could fill in some of the blanks of her past. She stepped out of the waiting room into the hall and felt dizzy again, although it wasn't as bad as her first walk round the station. It was a lot more crowded now, mostly with arriving passengers. She looked at her watch: it was a quarter to nine, so it seemed people were arriving for work. She found an information counter and got directions as far as Hackney. She'd have to walk, as she didn't have a penny on her. It would be a long walk too – Hackney was about five miles away.

As she left the counter, Mary spotted the woman who had just been with her in the waiting room. She was talking to a policeman, and both were looking in Mary's direction. So the woman couldn't be trusted after all.

What was all this trust business about, Mary wondered. Earlier, she'd thought she could rely on the young man with the newspaper. Did something happen to make her suspicious of people? Or was she always like that anyway?

She left the station and started walking along Victoria Street. It was overcast with an icy breeze, which made her shiver, but at least it wasn't raining. The street was a mix of shops and offices, and the pavements were crowded. The brisk, determined pace of the pedestrians suggested office workers on their way to work, rather than shoppers. Attached to lampposts were more posters of the man in the fencing jacket; these had *God Save The Leader* written on them. Occasionally, a lamppost would have a placard of an older man with a boyish face, inscribed with *God Save The King*. Both these men were important public figures, yet Mary hadn't recognised them; she'd have a lot of learning to do.

The same posters appeared on Whitehall, along with a third: a middle-aged man showing chiselled features, with piercing eyes and an aquiline nose. The accompanying message was *Britain Welcomes Germany's Führer*. Again, she didn't recognise the man, but that didn't worry her too much as she didn't expect to recognise foreign dignitaries. She passed the Whitehall Theatre, which was advertising a play starring Brian Rix. She made a mental note of that – he was obviously a famous actor. There were more theatres along The Strand; one proclaimed the 20th year of *The Mousetrap*.

Mary continued through the City of London, first being asked by a civilian to show her identity card, and at one point, getting lost. It was noon by the time she reached Mile End Road. It was still cold and gloomy and she felt tired and hungry. Ahead of her, a crowd blocked the pavement; facing it at intervals was a line of police. In the distance was some sort of procession. Mary stopped by the kerb to have a look; a few feet away, a film crew was recording the scene. The cameramen were dressed in leather jackets and wore dark sunglasses, although there hadn't been even a glimpse of sunshine all morning.

The procession was made up of a column of men, all wearing black fencing jackets. Ahead of the column was a policeman on a horse, holding the reins in one hand and a megaphone in the other. The parade was just a few yards away, when the mounted policeman raised his megaphone and called out, "Three cheers for the Blackshirts. Hip-hip."

A muted cheer rose from the crowd, then another. Mary kept silent. She felt an elbow nudge her ribs and a grey-haired woman, who was a bit older than Mary, whispered, "At least pretend, love."

It sounded like a friendly warning rather than a reprimand. The woman nodded towards the camera crew; they were filming the spectators, not the procession. Mary mouthed a hoorah.

The front of the Blackshirt column was now level with Mary. Apart from the jackets, they wore grey flannel trousers and black army combat boots. Some carried rubber truncheons; others wore knuckle-dusters. There were about 500 men in all.

"Think they're soldiers," said a voice from the crowd. "More like sheep."

"Baa Baa Blackshirts, have you any…" sang another, in tune with the nursery rhyme. The crowd burst out laughing then all starting looking at their shoes. A man emerged from the onlookers and darted into a nearby branch of Sainsbury's.

"What's the occasion?" Mary asked the grey-haired woman.

"It's no occasion. They do this every day, marching from Stratford to the Tower of London, causing all sorts of traffic problems along the way."

"What do they do when they get there?"

"They stop by Traitors' Gate and slag off the traitors."

"What traitors?"

"Reds, Jews, liberals, queers. There's a new lot every month, but always the Jews and the reds." The woman's expression suddenly appeared anxious, as if she'd spoken out of turn.

"But they're real lookers, our boys in blue, aren't they?" said the woman. "I do like a man in uniform, don't you?"

A policeman was pushing through the crowd towards them. "I was telling my friend, a uniform makes a man look so handsome," said the woman.

The policeman tried to supress a smirk. "Where did the subversive go?"

Mary supposed he meant the comedian.

"He popped in there," said the woman, pointing in the direction of a Woolworths.

Mary reckoned she must be near home so she asked the woman for directions to Kings Road.

"Turn left into Globe Road and carry on until you get to Vicky Park. Walk straight through; Kings Road is on the other side. It's a half-hour walk, or you can take a number 277 bus."

Mary thanked the woman and carried on walking, but it took her an hour to get to Kings Road. On the corner was a pub, The Bull, but it was closed. Except for the pub, the street was entirely residential, consisting of identical, three-storied, terraced houses. They were modest but well-maintained buildings, with each door clearly numbered; odd numbers on one side of the road, even on the other. Mary got as far as number 60, where the road came to an end; there was no number 78.

CHAPTER 3

Andy Deegan got into the Morris Marina with the children; Harry in the front and the twins, Jenny and Karen, in the back. As he drove off, he took a quick glance down Nelson Close; identical, pebbled-dashed houses on either side. Next to each top floor window, a flagpole protruded with a Union Jack fluttering in the breeze. One of the flags looked a little tattered; it belonged to number 17, Mrs Jones, who was getting on a bit. He ought to buy her a new flag before she got into trouble.

"What are you doing today, girls?"

"Ballet," the girls answered in unison. Aged ten, they were in their fourth year of primary school.

"Celia's coming too," added Jenny.

"Who's Celia?"

"She's our best friend," said Jenny.

"Then we've got rehearsals for the school play," said Karen. "I'm the milk maid."

"And I'm the shepherdess," said Jenny. "Horrid Diane wanted to be the shepherdess, but she's playing the witch. Serves her right."

"I'm sure she's not really horrid," said Andy.

"Oh yes she is," said Karen. "She had a bag of sweets, which she gave round class, but we didn't get any."

"Maybe there weren't any left?" said Andy.

"But she should have offered them to us first," said Jenny.

"What are you doing today, Harry?" said Andy. Harry was two years younger than the girls, in the second form of the same school.

"Cricket. Mr Fish says my bowling is almost as good as Fred Trueman's. I'm going to be in the England team when I grow up."

Andy thought it was far too cold and wet for cricket. It was more like November than April. Just when will this wretched winter end, he wondered. Still, it was the official start of the cricket season.

"Jimmy's in my team. He's my best friend. William's coming too."

"Who's William?"

"He's my very best friend. Even more best than Jimmy."

It took just 10 minutes to get to the London Road Primary School. Andy parked the car and piloted the children into the playground. They dashed off to be with their friends. A few parents were chatting in groups of two and three. Miss Miller, the headmistress, was present, and having spotted Andy, headed in his direction. She wore a black skirt, which almost reached the ground, and a turtle-necked grey blouse, with her hair tied back in a bun. She looked more like an Edwardian suffragette than a 1970's woman. The only modern thing about her was a British Union of Fascists lightning flash badge attached to her blouse. She was tall, thin, even gaunt, wearing wire-framed spectacles that only exacerbated her pale, stern face. Even Andy found her a bit scary.

"Mr Deegan. If I may have a word about Harry."

"Good morning, Miss Miller. Of course." They moved only just out of earshot of any parents.

"It has been brought to my attention that Harry hasn't joined the school's Cub group. All the boys join by the time they're eight. It's a shame, especially as Harry is doing so well in his lessons and in sport. He's well behaved too; we've only had to cane him once this year. But here at London Road, we believe in character development, and the Cubs are excellent in that regard. It's just two evenings a week and one weekend a month. Do think about it, Mr Deegan."

"I will. Thank you." There was nothing else for discussion so Andy quickly left. He wasn't in the mood for chatting with fellow parents.

As Andy continued driving towards his Fleet Street office, he thought about what Miss Miller had said. The headmistress' brother, Mr Miller, who seemed just as creepy as his sister, ran the Brentford pack. Maybe he was being over-protective, but Andy just didn't want Harry being supervised by someone like Mr Miller. Harry was strong and athletic so there was less of a problem in joining the Scouts in a few years' time; Harry could fend for himself then. On the other hand, the headmistress had made a thinly-veiled threat that Harry's schooling would suffer if he didn't join the Cubs. This was something he'd need to talk about with Jane.

Andy switched on the car radio to listen to the news headlines; the shipping forecast was still on. *Southeast Iceland, North 7 to severe gale 9. Finisterre, Southwest gale 8 to storm 10.* The news followed.

> *Buckingham Palace has announced that His Majesty the King has caught a cold. Engagements for today and tomorrow have been cancelled, but the King is*

expected to return to full duties later this week. Sixteen terrorists have been shot dead by security forces in Londonderry following an illegal demonstration by separatists. The Home Secretary, William Joyce, has upheld the death sentence on Doctor Whitworth, who last month had been found guilty of carrying out an abortion on a 12-week pregnant woman. In a statement, Mr Joyce said, "The Law must take its course." Foreign news. The German Olympics Minister, Albert Speer, has announced that black and Jewish American athletes will be given visas for the forthcoming games in Munich.

Andy switched off the radio. It was the fifth or sixth time this year that the King had been reported as being down with a cold. Andy had seen the King in person just the day before and he looked seriously ill; it was no cold he was suffering from.

Northern Ireland wasn't the only scene of illegal separatist demonstrations; these were regular occurrences throughout the British Empire, from Nairobi to Delhi. The news about the abortionist also came as no surprise. What had been a surprise was the Home Secretary's earlier decision to commute to life imprisonment the sentence of the woman who had had the abortion. William Joyce very rarely exercised his prerogative to commute a death sentence.

Andy parked the car in Shoe Lane and walked the short distance to the *Daily Citizen* building, where he had worked as a journalist for 13 years. In that time, he had had just one scoop, but it had been a big one, which boosted the paper's circulation and enhanced its reputation. Andy's investigative journalism had exposed notorious South London gangsters, the Darent brothers. Because he wasn't a Party member, Andy couldn't get promoted, but at least his scoop meant he couldn't easily be fired.

He went straight to his office on the second floor. At seven foot square, it was more a broom cupboard than an office, barely containing a desk with a telephone and a typewriter, a chair and a filing cabinet. But it was his domain, and he preferred it to the open-plan arrangement other newspapers were introducing. He started work straight away. Although Andy's specific beat was South London crime, much of the time, he worked as a general reporter. He had witnessed the German Führer's state visit to Britain the day before and he read back the notes he had made.

> *German Führer, Reinhard Heydrich, on his first overseas state visit, arrived at Victoria Station on a cold and wet morning, a mixture of sleet and rain. Sleet in April, for heaven's sake! Following the death of the German Führer, Adolf Hitler, from a heart attack last year, and a power struggle between Heydrich, Speer and Goebbels, all members of the Nazi Old Guard, Heydrich has come out on top. Goebbels is still propaganda minister but Speer has been demoted to Olympics Minister. Will life in Germany be any different now?*

The visit, originally scheduled for three days, had been cut to just six hours, presumably because of the Führer's fears of a coup in his absence. The Führer and his wife were met by the King and Queen and by Sir Oswald and Lady Mosley. The King seemed to have lost his voice; he could barely whisper, "Welcome." The party set off for Buckingham Palace in three horse-drawn landaus. King Edward and Heydrich led in the first carriage. The King looked grey-faced, hunched and gaunt, his admiral's uniform far too big for him. Heydrich, who speaks no English, remained silent, but he threw suspicious glances from side to side as if an assassin could be lurking in London's streets. Queen Wallis and Lady Mosley followed in the second carriage. Layers of make-up could not disguise the fact they were past their prime. They tried to smile in the pouring rain, but it was clear they'd both rather be somewhere else. Sir Oswald and the very plain Lina Heydrich sat in the final carriage. Sir Oswald, hyperactive as ever, was chatting away in German; Frau Heydrich's sour expression suggested she was bored with the whole show. On arrival at Buckingham Palace, the party stood to attention, raising their arms in Fascist salutes for the benefit of the photographers. The King could barely raise his arm halfway. After luncheon,

Sir Oswald and Herr Heydrich had a fencing match at the Lansdowne Club. Sir Oswald was thrashed. His limp, from a Great War injury, and the fact that he is eight years older than Heydrich, didn't help.

That just about summed it up, thought Andy; now, he'd have to write a version acceptable to the censors. At that moment, Paul Draper stuck his head through the door.

"Busy doing the Heydrich visit? Good show," said Paul Draper.

Paul Draper was not only an editor, but also a Member of Parliament, and a committed British Union of Fascists' activist. He was a chubby man of medium height, in his 40s with dark hair and a round, fat face, bulging eyes and small, thin lips. Despite this, he had a boyish appearance and would rush around the office with tremendous energy.

"We really should meet for dinner sometime. You and Jane could come round one Saturday evening. I'll come back to you later with some dates."

"That would be nice." Andy tried to sound enthusiastic. As soon as Paul Draper left, he continued with his revised draft.

German Führer, Reinhard Heydrich, on his first state visit, arrived at Victoria Station on a warm spring morning. The Führer managed to find an entire day in his busy schedule to visit Britain. The Führer and his wife were met by the King and Queen and by The Leader and

Lady Mosley. In his clear, commanding voice, the King welcomed the Führer, stressing the special relationship between our two nations. The party set off for Buckingham Palace in three horse-drawn landaus. King Edward and the Führer led in the first carriage. The King, looking 20 years younger in his admiral's uniform, could be heard telling the Führer that he had brought the lovely weather with him. The Führer himself, smart and handsome in his SS uniform, was the target of many appreciative glances from female members of the crowd. Queen Wallis and Lady Mosley followed in the second carriage. The Queen wore a stranded mink coat and a wide-brimmed silver birch felt hat. On her elegant wrist, an 18-carat gold ram's head bangle glittered in the sun. The Queen's couture was complete with a pair of tan leather court shoes with stacked heels. Lady Mosley looked so attractive in a tailored white silk coat and coral straw hat. Both ladies captivated the crowd with their dazzling film star smiles.

The Leader and Frau Heydrich sat in the final carriage; they could be heard animatedly discussing Goethe's Faust in German. The German First Lady wore a South West African Persian lamb coat-dress with square neckline, showing off her great beauty, with wide, three-quarter sleeves, edged in brown kid with matching kid belt. Her brown and camel velour hat displayed her exquisite taste. Dark-brown patent shoes edged in tan completed the picture of a lady with the most refined dress sense. Earlier, Frau Heydrich had charmed the crowd with her greeting, "Good morning my Britischer friends." On arrival at Buckingham Palace, a band of the Grenadier Guards played the two national anthems. The party stood to attention, raising their arms in Fascist salutes, keeping their salutes for the benefit of the photographers long after the anthems had finished. They looked like film stars at a Hollywood Oscars' night.

Luncheon was the occasion for the party to show off their finery; the gentlemen in white tie and tails. The Führer cut a fine figure, wearing the dark-red ribbon of the Order of the Bath, together with his numerous awards and decorations. The King himself wore the Grand Cross of the Order of the German Eagle in Gold with Diamonds, together with the accompanying crimson sash. Queen Wallis looked superb in a dress of pale orchid-mauve satin with the bodice and elbow-length sleeves embroidered all over in pearls and rhinestones. With it, she wore her beautiful pearl and diamond tiara with earrings to match, a diamond *necklace, and other lovely jewellery. After luncheon, The Leader and The Führer had a fencing match at the Lansdowne Club. The result in this most noble Anglo-German sport was a draw.*

Andy was happy with the result. Just about everyone in southern England knew how miserable the weather had been the previous day. After all, why would the ladies be wearing furs if it had been warm and sunny? So if readers spotted the lie about the weather, as they surely must, they would also wonder if the rest of the report was a pile of porkies. The next step was to submit the report to the censors. He wondered if there really was a need for censors; every experienced journalist knew what could get through them, and modified their reports accordingly.

Andy had just got up from his chair when Alice entered and handed him an envelope. Alice Greengrass was a trainee at the paper, who seemed to spend most of her time distributing mail or making tea and coffee. She was a slender girl with closely-cropped blonde hair and a fixed, slightly mischievous smile. He thought she would look a lot more attractive if she didn't have this tendency for wearing chunky turtle-necked sweaters. If he wasn't a married man, he could almost fancy her. Andy put the envelope in his in-tray; he wanted to get his report out of the way first. They left the room together, Andy opening the door for Alice. As she passed, she gave him a wink and Andy, more from a reflex action, winked back. He hoped Alice wouldn't misconstrue the gesture.

The censors' office was a middle-size room at the end of a corridor on the same floor. By law, every newspaper had to accommodate two civil servants from the Ministry of Information; at the *Daily Citizen*, these were Alan Hayman and Tim Wilson. Andy knocked and entered; Alan Hayman was in on his own, slouched in a chair with his feet up on a desk, about to throw a paper aeroplane. Andy had a good working relationship with Alan Hayman; often, they would share a few pints at the Ye Olde Cheshire Cheese. Once lubricated, Alan Hayman could be quite indiscreet and would share titbits about the goings on in the corridors of power. Andy handed him the report, turned and was about to leave the room.

"No need to go. We can sort this out right away," said Alan Hayman. He read through the report, from time to time nodding or murmuring his approval. "Good stuff, as usual. The only bit I'd change is the reference to Hollywood."

"Why? The Cold War is over," said Andy. "The policy of détente is more than two years old now. We've even got a McDonalds in London."

"Hollywood is still regarded as decadent. We've had a directive on that. Just change it to first night at the Royal Opera House."

Andy nodded his assent and headed back to his office. He picked up the envelope from his in-tray. It had no stamp and was addressed in handwritten capitals to MR ANDREW DEAGAN. His surname had been misspelled; it couldn't be anything official. He opened the envelope; inside were four passport-sized photographs of men in their 20s or early 30s. There was no letter or covering note. On the back of each of three photographs was a large red cross. The back of the fourth had no cross but all the photos had been partially stamped in their top corners. The stamps were illegible but looked like the sort that was entered in a passport.

Andy picked up the phone and got through to Alice. "Alice, where did you collect the envelope you just gave me?"

"It was with all the other mail in the front door letter box. I noticed it had no stamp, so it must have been delivered in person. And, in answer to your next question, no, I didn't see who posted it."

Andy thanked Alice and tried to make sense of all this. The photographs could have been sent by someone inside the building, but in that case, why the anonymity?

What could they mean?

One possible explanation was that these men belonged to some sort of criminal gang; a member of the public could have remembered Andy's role in bringing the Darent brothers to justice. Probably, there had been a covering letter, but the sender, possibly being elderly or absent-minded, just forgot to put the note in. They were also paranoid about the letter being lost in the post, so delivered it themselves.

Andy pulled out of his filing cabinet a folder of suspected gangsters operating in the London area. He opened it and compared photographs in the folder with the four that he had just received. He had just worked through the folder without success when the phone rang.

"Is that Mr Deegan?" It was a male voice that Andy didn't recognise.

"Yes it is. Who am I speaking to?"

"You can call me Mark. Have you seen the photos?" Mark sounded rather frightened.

"Yes I have. What is all this about?"

"The three are all dead; murdered. I'm in great danger; I'm sure I'm next on the list. Mr Deegan, can we meet?"

"Have you reported this to the police?" said Andy.

"No. It would be very dangerous if I talked to the cops. Please, can we meet?"

"Of course. Come to my office whenever is convenient."

"I think that's too risky. Can I come to your house this evening?"

Andy wasn't too comfortable with inviting a complete stranger, possibly a criminal, into his own home. "I don't think that's possible, Mark. We could meet in a pub or a café. Do you know Twickenham?"

"A little. What pub did you have in mind?" said Mark.

"How about the White Swan by the river? It's quiet weekday evenings so there'll be no problem us spotting each other. What time were you thinking?"

"Eight o'clock, say."

"That's fine. Mark, why were the three murdered? "

"I'll tell you all about it tonight. It's a much bigger story than the Darent brothers. Just be there, and not a word to the cops."

Chapter 4

"Hello gorgeous."

Andy stooped and Jane stood on tiptoes as they hugged. Jane was petite, flamed-haired, and some six inches shorter than Andy. Contrary to stereotype, she had a placid, sweet nature.

"Good day?" said Jane.

"So-so. I wrote up Heydrich's visit. Much of it was about how the VIPs were dressed; you could have done a better job yourself."

Andy had met Jane 15 years earlier on a journalism course. Jane went on to work for women's and fashion magazines, but after they got married, she managed only occasional freelance work.

"I spoke with Miss Miller this morning, or rather she spoke to me," said Andy. "In her unsubtle way, she said Harry ought to join the Cubs."

"You know what I feel," said Jane. "Mr Miller is such a creep."

"Maybe we should get Harry signed up with another pack. I'm sure we can think up an excuse for Miss Miller. Where are the children by the way?"

"The girls have gone to the Wilkinson's. Harry's here with Jimmy."

"I'll go and say hello." Andy went upstairs to his son's bedroom.

"Hello boys."

Harry was showing off his soldier action man to Jimmy; he already had the sailor and airman.

"Dad, can I have a Blackshirt action man?"

"No, I don't think that's a good idea."

Jimmy gave Andy a puzzled look. Andy was well aware that even eight year olds were being encouraged to report any so-called anti-social behaviour to the authorities. Refusing to buy your son a Blackshirt action man might just fall in that category.

"Not just now, but soon," said Andy.

"Before or after we go to McDonalds?" said Harry.

Shortly, the four, or five, including the action man, had supper. As they were finishing their apple pie and ice cream, Andy said, "I've got to be going now. It's to do with work; I'm meeting a contact. It could be a big story."

"Your story isn't how Andy Deegan won at darts or table football at the Rose and Crown?" asked Jane.

"It's work, honest; at the White Swan in Twickenham. Pub meetings are part of the job; you know how it is."

*

Andy got to the pub 10 minutes early. He liked the place. He walked past the bar at the front that looked out onto the River Thames, and headed straight to the bar at the back. There were four or five small tables with room for a dozen customers at most.

Andy bought a pint of Directors and found a free table in the corner by a radiator, which was a bonus this cold April night. There were just two other men standing at the bar, men in their 60s, neither of whom could possibly be Mark. As he glanced around for his mysterious companion, his eyes were drawn to the photos of rugby players and teams on the wall. In a casing by one of the windows was a collection of sporting items from the

1920s: tennis rackets, hockey sticks, cricket hats, and a pair of skates that seemed even older.

The ambience was only spoiled by a photograph of The Leader on each of the walls. Andy thought this was a bit over the top; just one photograph in every public room was all that was required by law.

He had mixed feelings about tonight's meeting. On the one hand, it would be nice to get involved in a major crime story. The Darent case had been four years ago; since then, he had reported on a variety of stories, but no real crime apart from shoplifting and house burglaries.

Andy knew that much of his reputation as a brave, fearless journalist was undeserved. In the course of his investigations, he found that Government Minister, Sir Reginald Corbett, was protecting the gangsters. Andy immediately dropped the case, realising he could get into serious trouble if he started sniffing too close to the country's rulers. Not long after, it transpired that The Leader wanted to get rid of Corbett, who was becoming just a little too popular. The Darent connection would provide an excellent pretext. Andy got orders from Paul Draper to continue with the story, but he was still reluctant. Only after The Leader had personally telephoned Andy did he write up his scoop and so earned his laurels. Andy was worried that Mark might have too high expectations of him.

An hour passed and there was still no sign of Mark. Andy checked the other bar where it was a bit more crowded. He asked around – but no Mark. He went back to his table and occasionally sipped from his second pint; he was reluctant to start on a third. After another half hour, Andy was on the point of calling it a day when a man in his 50s with dishevelled hair and a face that reminded Andy of a koala bear burst into the pub, accompanied by a black Labrador. The man looked pale and was trying to catch his breath.

"No dogs in here, sir," said the barman.

"Never mind that. There's a body just outside on the towpath. You'd better call the police."

The barman immediately dialled and handed the man the phone.

"I was walking the dog when I found this body; well, it was the dog that spotted it, by the river, about 50 yards from the White Swan in Twickenham. My name is Michael Roberts. The body is a male and he's definitely dead, that's all I know really."

Andy took out his journalist identity card and introduced himself to Michael Roberts. They both headed outside and walked along the towpath. A dense strip of trees and bushes bordered one side and the river the other. It was already dark but Michael Roberts had a torch, which he switched on when they were about 10 feet from the body. He stood still while Andy took the torch to have a closer look. The body was lying face down, half hidden in the bushes; only the head and shoulders were visible. He could make out a circular hole in the nape of the neck, about an inch diameter, surrounded by a ring of black speckled gunpowder residue. There was hardly any bleeding. Andy knew enough to recognise this as an entry wound. The bullet had exited from the top of the forehead, just above the hairline. The exit wound was twice the size of the entry wound, more ragged and still bleeding. A few feet from the head, spread among the bushes, was what looked like human tissue; Andy had a fair idea what it was, but didn't want to look too closely. The man was wearing a tracksuit and Andy would put him in his 30s. It was hard to tell because the man's face was only partly visible, but he could be Mark.

"I'll push off now if you're staying. Maurice needs his walk."

"I'd stay if I were you," said Andy. "The police will want a word with you. They shouldn't be long."

The police arrived 10 minutes later in two black Wolseleys, the party consisting of a plain-clothes detective and four uniformed policemen.

"Now you know where the body is, can I go?" Michael Roberts asked the detective.

"Not just yet. My boss should be here soon and he may want a word with you. He won't be long."

The police taped off an area about 50 feet in radius from the body and got to work, the detective examining the body while the uniforms searched within the taped-off area.

Half an hour later, more plain-clothes police arrived, among them, Detective Inspector Ron Cook of Twickenham Police Station.

"Good evening, Inspector. How are you? How's the wife?" Andy was professionally acquainted with the detective.

"Doing fine. The baby is due next month."

Ron Cook was a tall, thin, slightly stooping man, with a chiselled face and wearing a brown camel-haired overcoat. Inspector Cook had a brief word with the policemen who had been first at the scene, and then took charge of proceedings. He spoke to the detectives who had arrived with him, and they set about knocking on the front doors of nearby houses and interviewing their occupants. Meanwhile, a police doctor inspected the body.

"Who was first on the scene?" asked Inspector Cook.

"Me, sir," said Michael Roberts. "As I said on the phone, I was walking my dog."

"I'd like you to come to the police station and give a statement. It won't take long."

A uniformed policeman escorted Michael Roberts and his Labrador to the back of one of the Wolseleys.

"What were you doing here, Mr Deegan?" asked Inspector Cook.

"I was having a quiet pint on my own at the White Swan when Mr Roberts burst in minutes after he'd discovered the body. Of course, I immediately put my reporter's hat on and hung around so I can write something for my paper." Andy decided not to mention Mark's letter or his phone call; he had emphatically asked him to keep the police out of this.

"It's funny how you journalists always seem to have a quiet pint or whatever whenever there's foul play about," said DI Cook. "I'd like you to come to Twickenham Police Station tomorrow and give a full statement. Will nine o'clock be convenient?"

Andy nodded his assent.

"Good. You're free to go now, Mr Deegan."

Andy stayed on; an arc light was switched on and Andy sneaked past the tape to get a closer look. The body was now turned over and he was able to see the victim's face; it bore some resemblance to Mark's photograph. Andy got a bit too close before being spotted and shooed back behind the tape.

About an hour after the police had first arrived, an ambulance appeared on the scene. The body was put on a stretcher and loaded into the vehicle. Andy took what looked like the most junior policeman to one side and slipped him a fiver. "Is there anything I can tell readers of the *Daily Citizen*?"

"Not much. He was in his 30s and shot in the back of the head. Only a few hours ago, it's reckoned. There's nothing to identify him, no card or documents of any kind, although there was what looks like a telephone number on a scrap of paper he had. One other thing; he was whipped recently. There are at least 20 lashes on his back."

It was past half past 11 when the police began to disperse and Andy thought it was a good time to go home too. It was a brisk 20-minute walk and the curfew started at midnight. He puzzled over the phone number found on Mark. Could it be his number? It wouldn't take long for the police to check and, if the number was his office, he'd be in for a severe grilling in no time. Before going to bed, he telephoned in his report of the murder. It would be too late for the morning edition, but the *Daily Citizen* subscribers should read all about it in the afternoon.

*

The day after Barry Johnston returned home, he went to the Kalgoorlie Mine Office and checked out *Possum Hill Copper Mine*. It had been opened in 1931 and the copper ore malachite had actually been mined, but by the end of 1934, it was depleted and abandoned. More importantly, there were no stakes in the area and the

Possum Hill company's mining and exploration rights had long since expired.

With that news, he could treat himself to a few beers at the Exchange Hotel bar. He was on his third pint and lost in his thoughts so he was unaware of the man sitting down next to him.

"Hello sport, long time no see." It was Bob Birney, a reporter who worked for the *Kalgoorlie Miner*.

"How are you doing? Fancy a drink?"

"Thanks, mate. A pint of Swan Lager please," said Bob Birney.

Barry wasn't sure about Bob Birney. Barry himself was an Emu Bitter man, although he'd occasionally drink a Kalgoorlie Stout or a Hannan's Lager. Bob Birney's favourite tipple, a Swan Lager, was a drink strictly for Sheilas and poofters, as far as Barry was concerned. Although the way Bob ogled the barmaids, maybe he batted for both sides.

After a few more beers and a lot of small talk, Bob Birney said, "It must be a couple of months since you've been in town. What have you been up to?"

"Oh, this and that. Doing up my apartment. That sort of thing." Barry was always a bit reticent as far as his prospecting trips were concerned.

"Pull the other one," said Bob. "I can't see you spending more than a couple of hours on your apartment. You've been out in the bush. Where did you go and what did you find?"

"Yeah, well, I did go out to the Musgrave Range and prospected along some creek," said Barry.

"Was it a success?"

"Not bad. I got some opals," said Barry.

"Bullshit," said Bob. "You didn't find any opals. If you had, you wouldn't have told me you'd been to the Musgrave Range. After all, there aren't that many creeks there anyway. No, if you had found anything, you would have said 'Somewhere in Australia'."

"Have you done anything interesting in your reporting work?" said Barry, changing the subject.

"I flew in a private jet with some mining bosses up to Kimberley," said Bob. "We spent hours flying over desert. At one point, we had some engine problem; I thought we really wouldn't want to do a forced landing here. But the problem sorted itself out."

"I came across a plane wreck on my way back," said Barry. "It looked like an old one, 1930s, I'd say."

"There might be a story there," said Bob. "Did you take any photos?"

"Of course," said Barry.

"I'd be prepared to part with $50 for them," said Bob. "Deal?"

"Deal," said Barry. It was a good offer.

"I'll need to know the location as well," said Bob.

There was no way Barry was going to give that away. He didn't want other prospectors getting nosey; they might get to read Bob Birney's article and wonder what Barry was doing in the area. But Barry was good at mental arithmetic, even after six pints, so he calculated a position a good 150 miles from the true wreckage location of 26°10'S 126°50'E. He had memorised these co-ordinates; it was the location of a future gold and uranium mine, after all. He then took out a pocket diary and pretended to look for the information, making sure the diary contents were out of Bob's sight.

"There it is. 28°20'S 127°30'E," said Barry.

Chapter 5

Mary checked the numbers again, but there was no 78 on Kings Road. She made sure that the road was not one of those streets that came to an end in one place, only to continue a short distance away. Maybe there was an error on her identity card; a two could be mistaken for a seven, for example. She'd go to number 28 first. She didn't want to explain to strangers that she'd lost her memory, at least not until someone recognised her. She would tell people she was looking for a long lost friend, Mary Brown.

A young woman, wearing an apron with two small boys clutching at her skirts, answered her knock. No, Mary Brown didn't live here. She was fairly sure she didn't live in the street, as she knew most of her neighbours. There was a Mavis Brown at 54.

Mary tried there next. An elderly man answered. His wife, Mavis, was in hospital, but he didn't know of any Mary Brown. Mary tried the remaining houses and drew the same negative response. She got no reply at just four houses; she could try later but she wasn't hopeful. This was not the street in which she lived. She had hoped just being on her home ground might reawaken her dormant memory, but not so.

A thought occurred to her: maybe there was another Kings Road in Hackney? She continued to the end of the road, where it joined the busier Well Street, which had some shops. None of the shopkeepers could help her. She spotted a post office; they would know surely. As she entered, she reckoned if she did live in the area, surely she would have come here every now and then. Maybe the counter staff would recognise her. *Good afternoon, Miss Brown, how are you?* She hoped that's how the postmaster would greet her. There was just one person serving and Mary joined the queue.

Three people stood in front of her, none of whom she recognised. She looked around the office in the hope she might see something familiar; anything really that would tell her that she did indeed live near here. There were shelves with envelopes in different sizes, forms and a few stationery items. On one of the walls was a poster advertising holidays; it showed a beach with green wooded hills in the background. She glanced over the text:

> *Two weeks in Gotenland (former Crimea), Germany's Black Sea Riviera.*
> *Spend the day swimming or sunbathing on the most beautiful beaches in Germany.*
> *Visit German settlers and sample their excellent wines.*
> *Discover this land of milk and honey, formerly a Bolshevik wilderness.*
> *Visit the historic sites of Theodorichshafen (former Sevastopol), Inkerman and Balaclava, scene of the Charge of the Light Brigade.*
> *For Party Members and their families only.*

It all looked very nice to Mary but the poster didn't register anything with her. She was a bit puzzled about the Party Members reference; what Party?

But then, she did remember something:

> *Cannon to right of them,*
> *Cannon to left of them,*
> *Cannon in front of them,*
> *Volleyed and thundered;*
> *Stormed at with shot and shell,*
> *Boldly they rode and well,*
> *Into the jaws of Death,*
> *Into the mouth of Hell*
> *Rode the six hundred.*

She could recall an entire verse of a poem, *The Charge of The Light Brigade*, but she couldn't remember anything about her own past.

To the left of the holiday poster was another, captioned *Ten Ways to Identify a Jew*. Following the ten identifying traits was the exhortation: *If you see a Jew, keep calm and report the suspect to the nearest police station or Black House*. To the right was a third poster, titled *Ten Ways to Identify a Homosexual*.

Mary had still not reached the front of the queue so she started reading down the list of Jewish traits. *Jews walk with a bent posture*. Mary immediately stiffened; she felt her reflexes were telling her that being a Jew was not a good thing. She read down the list. *Jews cannot look you straight in the eye. Jews swivel their gaze from left to right. Jews don't smile but smirk or grimace. Jews continuously clasp their hands. Jews wear dark, dirty clothes. Jewish womenfolk wear wigs*. Although Mary couldn't remember, so couldn't be sure of course, but in her bones, she didn't feel she was Jewish. Besides, she didn't like dark, dirty clothes; she liked smart red, blue and green clothes. Not too bright but definitely not dark and dirty. She didn't think she wore a wig; she tugged on her hair just to make sure.

Mary then looked at the list of homosexual traits. *Homosexuals walk with a straight bearing. Homosexuals have a constant, direct gaze. Homosexuals have a fixed smile. Homosexuals have at least one wrist in a limp posture. Homosexuals wear bright, gaudy clothes.*

It seemed to Mary that homosexual traits were the opposite of Jewish ones. It was obviously impossible to be both Jewish and homosexual. Again, she didn't feel she was a homosexual; most definitely, she didn't like clothes that were too bright or ostentatious.

There was no "*Good afternoon, Miss Brown, how are you?*" from the postmaster when she reached the head of the queue. Mary asked about Kings Roads in the area and the official consulted a street guide and confirmed there was no second Kings Road in the borough.

Mary left the post office feeling very worried. She was cold, hungry, didn't know where home was, and could remember nothing before waking up that morning. To top it all, it had started to drizzle. She took another look at her identity card; apart from the address, there was nothing there that could help her. Her occupation was gardener; that didn't help very much. Then a thought occurred to her – maybe she worked around here. Parks and gardens were the obvious places to start. She had walked through Victoria Park earlier; it seemed big enough to have gardeners so she would try there first.

She headed back to the park, took a drink from a water fountain, and tried to find a gardening shed or office. The first building she came across was a closed tearoom, the second was the lido, also shut, but nearby was situated the park manager's office. Heading towards a side door was a middle-aged man, wearing wellington boots and pushing a wheelbarrow containing a spade, fork, axe and saw. She was in luck; he was obviously a gardener.

"Excuse me, I'm looking for Mary Brown. She's a gardener and I thought she might work here."

"You've got the wrong place, miss. There's four that do gardening jobs here and none of us are called Mary Brown."

"Are there any other parks around here?"

"Well, if you head along the Old Ford Road for about 10 minutes, you get to Bethnal Green Gardens," he said, pointing in one direction. "And down Grove Road, you've got Cemetery Park. All the gardeners will be packing up by now, mind. But we're all employed by the council. You should ask there."

"Where are the council offices?"

"On Mare Street. Not far from here, but the offices will be closed now."

Mary thanked the man and wondered what to do next. She walked aimlessly through the park, feeling desperate. Although she had another lead to follow – a visit to the council offices – that wasn't until tomorrow, and she had tonight to get through. She'd have to spend another night in a waiting room; she didn't fancy going all the way back to Victoria Station. It was early evening and the park was emptying, but she asked a passer-by and was told the nearest large station was Stratford, so she started to head in that direction. The drizzle had turned to rain, before she even left the park, so she took shelter in a marble alcove that conveniently had a bench to sit on.

The rain showed no sign of stopping – if anything, it was getting worse. Tired, cold, wet and hungry, Mary dozed off.

She was woken by a rough shaking of her shoulder.

"Get a move on, we close in five minutes." The intruder was a middle-aged man in a brown suit with matching shoes and trilby. He wore a yellow armband marked "Park Supervisor" and a lapel badge with a lightning flash.

She was still half-asleep and wasn't sure she'd heard the man correctly. "I'm sorry?"

"I said get a fucking move on. You dossers make me sick; get a job like everybody else. If you're not out in five minutes, I'll call the police."

"But I haven't got anywhere to go to."

"That's your problem." The park supervisor stood straight, red-faced, arms by his side and fists clenched. Mary remained seated. The man's expression changed from anger to indecision. It seemed to Mary that he couldn't make up his mind whether to get rid of her or report her to the police, with all the bother that might entail. The standoff lasted less than a minute. "There's a Salvation Army hostel in Mile End Road, near the ABC cinema. Now get out."

The hostel was about 30 minutes away and thankfully, the rain had turned back into drizzle. In the lobby, a lady wearing a grey skirt and jacket and a white blouse sat behind a desk. "How can I help you, my dear?"

"I need somewhere to spend the night." Mary showed her identity card and explained about her memory loss and the house number that didn't exist.

"You're too late for dinner, but I'll take you to the canteen and get you a cup of tea while we fix you up for tonight. I'm Lieutenant Pierce, by the way." They shook hands. "Your hands don't look like a gardener's; much too delicate," said the Salvation Army officer.

Inside the canteen, half a dozen long tables were positioned along the walls of the room. Each table had a bench on the wall side and about 10 chairs on the other. There was room for about a hundred, but Mary was on her own as she had her tea and a couple of Bourbon biscuits. The woman's last comment made her wonder whether she really could be a gardener. She certainly didn't feel she'd been one. Maybe the park manager was right and she was a tramp; except that she didn't feel she was one either. A few minutes after Mary finished her tea, Lieutenant Pierce re-appeared.

"Right, we've got a bed for you. There are sixty men here tonight, but just one other woman, Lily, so you'll be sharing with her. Breakfast is at seven, and after that, you can have a chat with one of our officers and we'll sort you out."

The bedroom was just big enough to fit three narrow beds, with only two feet spare between each bed. There was no other furniture apart from a single shelf, which ran head-high along the length of one wall. On one bed sat a plump woman of about 30, with a bloated, ruddy complexion and glazed eyes. She gave off a stench that caused Mary to recoil a bit; fortunately, there was an empty bed between the two of them.

Mary said hello to Lily and sat down. She thought she definitely couldn't be a tramp otherwise, she'd be used to the stink of others. Mary was learning a bit more about whom she was *not*, but she was none the wiser as to whom she *was*. As soon as Lieutenant Pierce left the room, Lily pulled a handkerchief from under her pillow, unfolded it and thrust it in Mary's direction. Mary could make out some sort of brown substance on the handkerchief.

"It's snuff," said Lily. "Like some?"

Mary declined then tucked herself into bed and fell asleep.

She was woken up in the morning by the sounds of the whole building coming to life; loud steps in the corridors, tables being laid, chairs being rearranged. She managed to get a shower before breakfast, which consisted of porridge, toast, jam and tea. She was beginning to feel a lot better, but her memory was still limited to the events of the previous day. She was on her second cup when another lady approached her. She was grey-haired and around 60, but dressed identically to Lieutenant Pierce.

"I'm Captain Hawkins. After breakfast, we always have hymn singing. You don't have to join in; it's quite voluntary. Afterwards, we'll have a chat in my office."

Breakfast finished and the tables were cleared by the officers, who all wore identical grey suit dresses, and by what looked like female volunteers. A few of the men helped, but most shuffled out of the room. Mary decided to stay; she had only her broom cupboard of a bedroom to go to. By the time they were ready for hymns, the congregation consisted of four Salvation Army officers, four volunteers and just three residents, Mary included. One of the officers sat beside a piano in the corner.

"The first hymn will be *Onward Christian Soldiers*," Captain Hawkins announced. The officers and volunteers sang the first verse with gusto:

*Onward, Christian soldiers, marching as
to war,
with the cross of Jesus going on before.
Christ, the royal Master, leads against the
foe,
forward into battle, see his banners go!*

"The next hymn will be…" Captain Hawkins stopped as Mary continued singing the second verse on her own:

*At the sign of triumph, Satan's host doth
flee;
on then, Christian soldiers, on to victory!
Hell's foundations quiver at the shout of
praise;
brothers, lift your voices, loud your
anthems raise.*

Chapter 6

It was Jane's turn to drive the children to school, so Andy walked the half-mile to Twickenham Police Station. It was a dry, overcast day; the weather forecast had called it anti-cyclonic gloom. Andy arrived 10 minutes early and reported to the duty sergeant at the reception counter. He was asked to take a seat. Shortly, a door marked *Staff Only* opened and the constable whom Andy had bribed the night before appeared.

"Tea or coffee, Mr Deegan?"

"Coffee, white with one sugar. Thank you, Constable Hadden." Now that it was light, Andy could read the constable's name on the epaulette he was wearing. Andy made a mental note to add the policeman to his list of contacts.

He had just started his coffee when Detective Inspector Ron Cook joined him.

"We won't be requiring a statement from you after all," said DI Cook.

"How come?"

"The case has been transferred to Thames Valley Police at Windsor. There are similarities with an existing investigation. Detective Chief Inspector Armstrong will be in charge. I'm sure the Windsor Police will contact you in due course if they need a statement."

The inspector left and Andy continued to sip his coffee whilst the duty sergeant looked on. DCI Armstrong was a name he was familiar with but didn't know in person. He had almost finished his drink when the staff door opened and a policewoman emerged with a black Labrador on a leash.

"Come on, Maurice, time for walkies," said the policewoman, although Andy didn't think the dog needed any encouragement.

As the policewoman and dog left the building, Andy said to the sergeant, "Inspector Cook just said the towpath murder case has been transferred to Windsor, so how come Mr Roberts is still with you?"

"It's nothing to do with the murder," said the sergeant. "Someone at the station thought Maurice was a Jewish name, so we decided to hold Mr Roberts and make further enquiries. We phoned the race department at Scotland Yard and found out it all boils down to spelling. If the dog is spelled 'Maurice'," the sergeant enunciated each letter of the dog's name, "it's probably not a Jewish name, and the man could be immediately released. However, if the spelling is 'Morris', it's more likely to be Jewish. In that case, we would need to do a full ancestry check on Mr Roberts."

"So it's 'Morris' with the two r's?" said Andy.

"Not exactly. Mr Roberts claims he has never written down the name of his dog so he doesn't know the spelling. When we asked him to try, he wanted to see his solicitor first."

"So you're still waiting for Roberts' solicitor to turn up."

"Oh no, absolutely not. That would defeat the whole purpose. It's Mr Roberts and not his solicitor that we want to find out whether or not is Jewish. Besides, the solicitor would very quickly suss out what the right spelling of the dog's name should be. So we're not letting Mr Roberts see a solicitor, or anyone else for that matter.

Sooner or later, he's going to have to commit himself." The sergeant paused for a few seconds. "It's a funny thing, fate. A little matter of how he spells his dog's name could change Mr Roberts' life forever."

Andy thought the business of the dog's name was all nonsense. He didn't believe Mr Roberts was Jewish, nor did he think that the police did for that matter. Mr Roberts must have rubbed the police the wrong way. He would have been angry at being held after curfew, and so having to spend the whole night at the police station. He probably spoke out of turn and the police were now getting their own back. Andy finished his coffee and handed the sergeant the empty cup, together with a fiver.

"That's my contribution for the coffee," he said.

Andy left and headed for the train station, situated just round the corner. He felt bad about the mess Michael Roberts had got into; after all, the man had wanted to leave the scene and it was Andy who had urged him to stay until the police arrived. Even if it turned out that the man wasn't Jewish, he would be in for a rather unpleasant experience. Andy realised this was not a politically correct thought to have. Instead, he should give himself a mental pat on the back for having being instrumental in the possible apprehension of a man of Jewish origin – someone who was, by definition, an enemy of Britain. However, Andy could not think of himself as a good citizen who had just done his duty, and he continued to feel guilty over the fate of Michael Roberts.

His plan had been to take the train to Central London and report to his Fleet Street office. But he changed his mind, phoned the office and bought a ticket to Windsor; he wanted to find out more right away, rather than wait until the cops decided to contact him. Mark had said that three of his colleagues had been murdered; possibly the existing investigation that DI Cook mentioned could refer to one or more of these.

Should he tell the police about the photos and the telephone conversation with Mark? Andy wasn't sure. Mark had been quite adamant not to contact the police. Maybe he had been in trouble with them, but now that he was dead, surely that didn't matter anymore.

The train was five minutes late; so much for The Leader's promise of making the trains run on time. Andy didn't believe Mussolini had managed it either. But as part of his vision of a classless society, The Leader had abolished travel classes on railways. However, each train had at least one considerably plusher carriage, *"chartered for private use"*; this was reserved for senior Blackshirt officials.

At Staines, the train passed close to the plate-glass offices of the European Aviation Safety Agency. Just above the entrance was a huge European Union flag: a cobalt blue background with a circle of a dozen gold stars that surrounded a bold, black swastika.

At Windsor Police Station, Andy showed his journalist credentials and asked to see Detective Chief Inspector Armstrong. He wasn't kept waiting very long.

"Mr Deegan, you needn't have come all this way," said DCI Armstrong. "The description you gave to Inspector Cook last night was quite satisfactory." The police officer was aged about 45, with a long, bald forehead, which receded back to dark hair on the sides of his head. He wore thick black spectacles and he looked more like an accountant than a detective.

"I've come here with both my witness and journalist hats on," said Andy. "Is there anything you can report? Have you identified the victim?"

"Not yet, no. He was in his late twenties and the time of death was sometime between five and eight o'clock last night. That's all we can say at this point."

"Are there any related cases?" asked Andy.

"Thank goodness, no. There's nothing to suggest we have a serial killer on our hands. At least, not yet."

"Then why are you dealing with this? Surely this is a job for the Met in Twickenham."

"They're busy at the moment and asked us to help them out."

Andy bought copies of *The Times* and the *Daily Citizen* from the Windsor station newsagent while he waited for the next train to London. He looked through the papers; the main headline in both was a report that six terrorists had been shot dead in Nairobi at an illegal pro-independence demonstration. On page four of the *Daily Citizen* was Andy's piece; it was largely unscathed by the censor – only the reference to the welts on Mark's back had been removed.

On the train journey back to work, Andy puzzled over the contradictory remarks from the two police officers about why the case had been transferred. Maybe the decision had been taken at a higher level than DI Cook and he had just been surmising. In the end, Andy had decided not to tell DCI Armstrong about the photos.

After all, if there were no related investigations, why complicate matters? If the Met wasn't busy, what could have triggered the transfer?

Andy mulled over this for a few minutes then remembered the telephone number found on Mark's body. It had to be a number in or near Windsor or for some reason, one that interested the Windsor Police. At least it wasn't Andy's or he'd be in real trouble by now.

Back at the office, Andy first looked through his own files on recent murders; there was nothing that resembled Mark's three colleagues. He then went to the *Daily Citizen's* own library and read the murder reports of rival newspapers, going as far back as six months. Most had given the age, or better still, had provided a photo of the victim, and Andy was able to rule all but two cases out. Of these, one related to an unidentified youth investigated by Lambeth police and the other, a 30-year-old man, Brian Smith, but without an accompanying photograph. Andy made a note of these two names to follow up later.

Back in his own cubbyhole, Andy phoned Detective Superintendent John Reidford of Scotland Yard and arranged to meet him for lunch the next day. Andy then took out the four photos delivered by Mark the previous day. He stared at the men's faces, hoping for inspiration. He could just make out letters and symbols on the passport-like stamps on each of the photos. The first had "*OK**", the second, " **LEF*", the third, "*UB**", and the fourth, "*ING*". He supposed these could be the markings of a photograph company or Government department such as the passport office, or maybe a place of work. But the letters on their own or in combination made no sense to him, so he gave up and put the photos back in their envelope.

He then turned to one of his on-going reporting projects. Andy hadn't been invited to report Adolf Hitler's funeral the year before; Paul Draper probably thought, correctly as it happened, that Andy wouldn't deliver a sufficiently hagiographic and respectful report. But as a consolation, he was asked to write a series of articles on the forthcoming Munich Olympics. He pulled from his file recent copies of *Der Stürmer* and the *Völkischer Beobachter*, two leading German newspapers. Andy had a good knowledge of German; since he was an eight-year-old, not only was German a compulsory foreign language in all British schools but also, it was a requirement as part of any vocational training such as apprenticeships or journalist college. So Andy was able to read the newspapers with little difficulty.

Although both papers reported that preparations for the games were going ahead of schedule, reading between the lines, Andy sensed that there were problems and officials were trying to pass the blame onto others. The assassination of another Nazi functionary was reported; since the death of Hitler, these killings were becoming a regular occurrence. Andy wasn't sure if this was the work of opposition groups or whether these were regime sanctioned murders as part of a power struggle. Andy put a fresh piece of paper into his Imperial typewriter and knocked something up that would keep both Paul Draper and the censor happy.

In the evening, before going home, Andy went for a few pints with Alan Hayman at the Ye Olde Cheshire Cheese. The pub was popular with journalists, and whichever of the pub's many rooms you picked, you were always sure to spot a reporter or two. Andy and Alan Hayman had picked the basement Johnson Bar; to get to it, you had to negotiate a very steep, narrow staircase, which could be a problem if this wasn't your first port of call in a pub-crawl. The Johnson Bar itself had a low ceiling and, apart from tables, chairs and benches, was quite spartan; there were no historic photos like the ones that adorned all the pub's other bars. Andy was halfway through his second pint of Samuel Smith bitter while Alan Hayman had started on his fifth. Andy was making sure Alan was well lubricated in the hope that he might be a little indiscrete.

"Alan, what's the most you've had to censor? Have you ever cut out half a report?"

"Half? Never. Occasionally a paragraph has to go but usually, it's one or two sentences at most. You lot are so well house-trained that most of the time, I don't change a single word." Alan Hayman paused. "Tell you what though. I know somebody who works in the cinema section. The other day, he was checking whether an American film, *Fiddler on the Roof*, was suitable for British audiences. After removing any Jewish references, the film was cut from one-hundred-and-eighty-one minutes to just three. It wasn't just that the characters were a problem; it was the music too."

"Will we see the three minutes?" asked Andy.

Alan Hayman gave him a dirty look. "What do you think?"

"While we're on the subject, in my last report, why did you remove the section mentioning whip marks on the victim's body?"

"Andrew, I didn't change a thing. Promise."

"I suppose Alice must have left it out when I dictated the report over the phone," said Andy. "It's not like her though."

"As you know, I have to read all reports a second time after they've been copy-edited and I'm fairly sure the whip marks bit was still in there. The typesetting team wouldn't have done it, so it must have been Paul Draper; only the editor would have the authority to change a piece that late in the process. I'd ask him, if it bothers you."

*

Barry Johnston was in a good mood as he nursed his Emu Bitter in the York Hotel bar. He had just about restocked and would be back prospecting around the Possum Hill mine in a couple of days. It had been a week since his meeting with Bob Birney. He had given him the photos and got his $50 cash in return. A couple of days later, Bob's article appeared in the *Kalgoorlie Miner*. It turned out that Barry's fake wreckage location was not too far from the Ilkurlka mine, and a plane carrying bosses to that mine had gone missing back in 1934. Despite extensive searching at the time, the plane and its occupants had never been found; Bob Birney now claimed Barry's photos were those of the ill-fated Ilkurlka flight.

After downing his sixth pint, he staggered back to his apartment, which was just five minutes away. This had been his home for the last seven years, but there was no way he would stay there if he did get rich and retired. Kalgoorlie was a mining town in the middle of the bush, hundreds of miles from anywhere else. No, he would move to Perth or the wine country round Adelaide. He climbed up the stairs to the second floor. His room was one of three on that level, together with a shared kitchen and bathroom. He opened the door, switched on the light and saw two men in suits sitting on his bed.

"Streuth, you nearly gave me a heart attack," said Barry. For a moment, he was confused then he realised. "I'm sorry, I thought this was my room. I'm Barry Johnston; I live next door." Barry started to back out.

"This is your room, Mr Johnston," said the suit closer to him. "We'd like to have a word with you."

"Then get the fuck out of here or I'll call the police," said Barry.

"We are the police," said the suit. "Or at least my colleague is," he said, pointing at the intruder furthest away from Barry. "He's Detective Inspector Hayes from Western Australia police. And I'm Dean Walsh from Air Accident Investigations." The man showed Barry a pass.

Barry took a good look at the men. Both were his age, around the 40 mark. Dean Walsh definitely looked like a civil servant, and probably drank Swan Lager. Detective Inspector Hayes had a harder expression, with heavy bags under his eyes that showed he didn't get much sleep in his job. But he didn't have the cruel, beaten-up features of a mining executive enforcer, a man that was prepared to break legs to find out about the latest hot prospect.

"Take a seat," said Dean Walsh.

Barry sat on the one chair he had in his room.

"We read Mr Birney's article about the plane wreckage," said Dean Walsh. "We sent spotter aircraft to the location mentioned but couldn't find any sign of the crash. The photo looks genuine enough so we reckoned there must have been a mistake in the location given. Mr Birney swears the co-ordinates are those given to him by you. We'd be grateful if you'd correct your mistake."

Barry dithered. The men seemed genuine enough but he wasn't happy about giving away his crown jewels, the true co-ordinates.

"Mr Johnston, may we remind you that failure to cooperate with a police investigation is a criminal offence," said Detective Inspector Hayes. "If you think it will be months before this gets to the courts, think again. We'll see your licence is suspended straight away."

"I've forgotten," said Barry. "There was nothing of interest from a prospecting point of view in the area around the wreckage so I didn't make a note of the location."

"In that case, we'll suspend your licence until your memory improves," said DI Hayes.

Barry felt the man wasn't bluffing and that he had no choice but to give the true location. He was regretting his decision to talk to Bob Birney; it wasn't worth $500, let alone the 50. Of course, it would be a while before news would get out about the wreckage's true location, so if he went out to Possum Hill in the next day or two, he would have a head start. But he would no longer be prospecting on his own.

CHAPTER 7

Mary Brown immediately intrigued Captain Sally Hawkins. Mary seemed different to the women who usually frequented the shelter. They nearly always belonged to one of three categories: prostitutes, women with alcohol problems or battered wives. It was soon clear that Mary belonged to none of these groups. Also, it was rare for residents to attend hymns in their first few days, let alone know some by heart.

Nevertheless, Sally Hawkins' interview with Mary Brown didn't last long. The poor woman had lost her memory and couldn't remember anything before she had woken up the previous day in Victoria Station.

"This is what we're going to do," said Sally, after Mary had said what little she knew about herself. "First, we'll go to a doctor to have your memory problem treated. Then we'll go to the council to have you registered; we have to do this for all homeless people. While we're there, we'll check if you've worked as a gardener for them. To be honest, I'm not that hopeful. I agree with Lieutenant Pierce, your hands don't look like a gardener's. I should know; before I came here, I was posted at our farm colony in Hadleigh and we trained residents in all sorts of farming skills, including gardening, before they left for the Colonies. We'll report you to Scotland Yard's Missing Persons Bureau and at the same time, we'll check with our own tracing service to see if you've been reported missing."

The doctor's surgery was located in a side street just a five-minute walk away. There were half a dozen patients already in the waiting room so they sat down for their turn. Mary briefly flicked through the magazines on a coffee table, wondering what she normally read. Sadly, *Country Life*, *Home and Gardens*, *Woman's Own* and *Action* didn't spark any recognition. Her attention then seemed to be drawn to the usual notices found in doctors' surgeries. On one wall was a poster showing a man and woman, internal organs displayed, with descriptions of illnesses associated with these organs. On another wall, posters listed diseases spread by Jews and homosexuals.

"Presumably, many of the patients here are homosexuals or Jews, seeing they have all these diseases," said Mary.

Sally was conscious of the murmurings of the waiting patients ceasing and all eyes staring in Mary's direction.

"Not exactly. I'll explain later," said Sally.

Sally realised that Mary had not only lost her personal recollections but had also lost her memory of some social matters. This made her even more vulnerable in the short-term. However, with some coaching from her, Mary could learn something about the world in which she lived and become more street-wise.

After 20 minutes, they were called to Dr Gordon's consulting room. Mary briefly explained her situation.

"It looks like you have a case of retrograde amnesia," said Dr Gordon. "Because you can recall most things since yesterday morning, at least you don't have anterograde amnesia; that's the inability to form new memories. But before I can treat you or refer you to a specialist, I need your SHS number."

"What's that?" asked Mary.

"The State Health Service," said Sally.

"I'm sorry?" said Mary, none the wiser.

"The SHS is one of the proudest achievements of Fascist Britain," said Dr Gordon. "It's a publicly-funded healthcare system where general practitioners and hospitals are all part of the same organisation."

"And all its services are free," said Sally.

"Except for the workshy and a few other anti-social groups," said Dr Gordon. "However, I still need your SHS number, which you can get from the Ministry of Health. I'm sorry."

As soon as they left the surgery, Sally said, "I don't think it's a good idea to have you registered with the council."

"Why not?"

"Mary, the way the system works is that once you are registered, we have a month to find you employment. What with the delay in getting your treatment started, I think there's a chance we may not get you work. Of course, if all goes well and we find your relatives then we don't have a problem."

"Surely you don't have to work if you're ill. Couldn't a doctor just sign a sick note?" said Mary.

"They could if they had your SHS number."

"Can't we go the Ministry and get my number?"

"We'll do that, but it's at least a two-month wait to get your SHS number."

"Ah, I see. So what would happen if I registered with the council and couldn't find work within a month?"

"You get sent to a retraining camp for two years, in theory, to learn a skill to make you more employable."

"Isn't that a good thing?" said Mary.

"Mary, you do not want to end up in one of these camps. All you'll learn is how to dig a hole one day and fill it up the next."

"But if I don't register and if after a month I haven't found out who I am and I'm not in work, I'll still be in the hostel. Wouldn't the authorities check the shelter from time to time to see if there are any long-term residents?"

"That's why you won't be staying at the hostel," said Sally. "You'll be a welcome guest in my home. We'll do all the things I mentioned this morning, apart from registration."

They headed to Hackney council offices and checked if a Mary Brown was employed as a gardener. The answer, which came as no surprise to Sally, was no. Sally's two-up two-down was just five minutes away, off King Edward Road. She led Mary to the upstairs bedroom; it was small but very tidy. The double bed was neatly made with crisp white sheets covered by a plain grey blanket and puffed-up pillows backing onto the headboard. On a small bedside table lay a bible and fixed to the walls were quotes from the scriptures. In a vase by the window was a bunch of freshly-cut flowers.

"This will be your room, Mary. Make yourself comfortable."

"Where will you be sleeping?" asked Mary.

"Downstairs, on the sofa."

"You've been very kind, Captain Hawkins, but I don't want to impose on you. I'll take the sofa."

"Very well. But there's no need for formality here; you can call me Sally."

Sally felt sorry for Mary. She felt it must be terrifying to lose your memory so completely. She seemed to be a decent person, but it was hard to know what she was like before her amnesia. Was she the sort of person she'd be friends with? But right now, Sally saw herself more as a teacher with one of their primary school pupils.

Sally and Mary went down to the kitchen and had some beans on toast. Mary enjoyed the snack, but the taste didn't bring back any memories. They took their coffee to the lounge. This was slightly larger than the bedroom and just as neat. A sofa and two armchairs, all upholstered in black cotton, took up most of the lounge. A television, coffee table, sideboard and small bookshelf occupied the remaining space. More quotes from the Bible were fixed to the walls. Sally noticed Mary looking at a framed photo, resting on the sideboard, of a 50-something man.

"That's my Jack," said Sally. "He passed away two years ago. It was cancer. We weren't blessed with children."

Mary picked up another photo; one of a young couple in their black and red striped uniforms.

"Is that you and Jack?"

"That's right; just after we got married."

"What are the uniforms?"

"In those days, we Salvationists wore uniforms. Then, in the 1940s, The Leader declared that we were a paramilitary organisation and we were banned; the Blackshirts became the only legal paramilitary force. But after a few years, The Leader reckoned he could do with our services and we were reinstated. Uniforms were still banned however; but all Salvation Army officers wear the same type of civilian dress so that we are easily recognisable."

They finished their coffee, and then Sally said, "I'll be going back to the hostel, but you can stay here, Mary.

Make yourself at home; feel free to watch TV or read a book. I'll be back about seven."

After Sally left, Mary stayed in the sitting room and took a look at the bookshelf. It contained mostly Salvation Army or other religious material. She glanced through a book of hymns; many of them were familiar. So that was something; it looked like she went to church, or maybe was part of a choir. Mary leafed through more of the books, hoping she might learn more about herself. She skimmed through an encyclopaedia and a cookery book. She didn't discover anything more, apart from being fairly sure she wasn't a professional cook.

Mary switched on the TV and watched a children's programme, followed by a documentary about an elderly lady who 50 years earlier was one of a team who discovered the tomb of an Egyptian pharaoh. Neither programme brought back any memories for her. The documentary was just finishing when Sally returned.

Supper was macaroni cheese, followed by a cup of tea and a slice of fruitcake.

What did she usually have for dinner, before she woke up at Victoria Station? Mary couldn't remember.

What sort of food did she particularly like or dislike? She was none the wiser.

Sally looked at her watch and said, "Time for *Coronation Street*; I don't like to miss it. In the last programme, Miss Nugent finally married Mr Bishop. Mind you, she should have married that nice Mr Swindley all those years ago. He was a bit pompous but a decent man all the same." Sally could see from the blank expression on Mary's face that she didn't know what she was on about. Nevertheless, Sally was sure Mary must have seen episodes of *Coronation Street* in the past; after all, nearly everyone in England watched the programme. She thought if they sat through tonight's instalment together, it might trigger some memories in Mary.

Sally switched on the TV; The Leader was still on.

"I think I do recognise him," said Mary. "I've seen posters of him all over London, although he looks much younger in them. Is he a famous actor?"

"He's The Leader, Sir Oswald Mosley, and he runs the country. A speech of his is always shown on TV just before a popular programme such as *Coronation Street* or a football match."

At times, being with Mary was a bit like being with a five-year-old, thought Sally. She reckoned she could be friends with Mary, although right now, she was more like the daughter she never had. The Leader shortly finished his speech, exhorting viewers to be vigilant. They sat through *Coronation Street* but nothing registered with Mary.

The programme credits had just scrolled by when the phone rang in the hallway. Sally left the room to answer it. It was a good 10 minutes by the time she returned.

"Sorry about that. It was my uncle David," said Sally. "He knows I'm a *Coronation Street* fan so he always phones me just after the programme's finished."

"I have an uncle called David too," said Mary.

Chapter 8

"Sprung from that soil for whose dear sake they bled," said Jenny from the backseat of the car.

"Against vested powers, Red Front, and massed ranks of reaction," said Karen.

There was a pause then both girls said together, "We lead the fight for freedom and for bread."

"We're being tested today," said Jenny. "Miss Miller said we can get one word wrong, but any more and it's one stroke of the strap for each mistake."

Andy wasn't sure if this was progress. He didn't have to learn the BUF anthem until he was 13, and now 10-year-olds would be strapped if they didn't know it.

"What does Red Front mean?" asked Karen.

"They're Communists," said Andy.

"Oh, we've been told about them. They're baddies," said Karen.

"And what does 'massed ranks of reaction' mean?" asked Jenny.

"The reactionaries? They're the enemies of The Leader," said Andy.

"So Communists are reactionaries," said Jenny.

"Not exactly. Reactionaries are people who don't like change, who are against progress." Andy felt he was walking on eggshells here. On the one hand, he wanted to be truthful, but on the other, he didn't want the girls to get into trouble.

"So a dad who doesn't take his children to McDonalds is a reactionary," said Harry.

That boy's growing up too fast, thought Andy, as they approached the school gates.

After dropping the children off, he drove down to Lambeth police station. On the way, he popped into Barclays Bank and changed twenty pounds for three fives and five one-pound notes. At the police station, he introduced himself to the duty sergeant.

"I'm Andrew Deegan, reporter from the *Daily Citizen*. I'm writing a follow-up article about the Baylis Road murder. Could you help me?" Andy took out his journalist's card, together with a one-pound note, and thrust them onto the reception desk. He then withdrew the card, leaving the note on the counter.

"You'll want to see Detective Inspector Bannister," said the sergeant. "He's on the case and, as luck would have it, he's in right now." The sergeant picked up the phone. "Inspector Bannister; you might find it worth your while talking to a journalist, a Mr Deegan, about the Baylis Road business. He's with me at reception."

Andy suppressed a smile; he knew very well the subtext in the sergeant's message. A few minutes later, Inspector Bannister appeared.

"I'm pleased to report we've made progress on the case," said the Inspector. "We've identified the victim and there's been an arrest. The victim was killed in a pub fight that got out of hand. His name is Colin Turner. The perpetrator goes by the name of John Palmer."

"Any chance of having a quick peek at the case files?" asked Andy.

"I'm afraid not. We've sent them on to the prosecutor. However, I've got Colin Turner's address in my notebook. You can contact his parents if that's any help to you."

Andy took down the details and then said, "You can't change a shilling for pennies can you? I need to make a phone call."

The Inspector obliged. Andy looked in his wallet. "I'm sure I had a shilling with me. Oh well, keep the change," said Andy, handing the Inspector a five-pound note.

Back at the office, Andy phoned Colin Turner's mother and the widow of Brian Smith, the second murdered man he wanted to investigate. Paul Draper stuck his head in. "How's it going?"

"I'm writing follow-up articles about some recent murders," said Andy. "I'm going to interview relatives of the victims and my reports will describe how families are affected."

"Good stuff. You know I mentioned coming round to dinner sometime. How about Saturday week at seven? You and your good wife."

"I'll check with Jane, but I'm sure we've got nothing planned for then." Andy paused. "My report on the Twickenham murder. Why was the bit about whip marks removed? "

"Was it? Oh yes, I remember," said Paul Draper. "Your piece wasn't enough for a full-page spread, but it was too long for half a page, so something had to go."

Andy wasn't entirely convinced by the explanation. The whip marks were an unusual aspect of the murder, and so very interesting from a journalistic point of view. Despite this, Andy's description had been fairly brief and if it really had to go to make space, something less significant could have been cut. Nevertheless, Andy decided not to push Paul Draper further.

Andy phoned the Windsor Police to see if Mark had been identified. He hadn't; in fact there was nothing further to report.

Lunch was with Superintendent John Reidford at Veerasawamy's in the West End. This was London's only Indian restaurant, with five-star prices; not somewhere Andy could get away with on his expense account, but Reidford was paying. Detective Chief Inspector Reidford, as he was then, had worked with Andy on the Darent brothers' case. The success of that investigation had led to his promotion and he was now in charge of Scotland Yard's Missing Persons Bureau. So Reidford felt he owed Andy one. Reidford had a military police background and it showed; he had piercing blue eyes, sat ramrod straight, and spoke as if he was dictating a telegram. Although still in his 40s, his hair was completely white, as was a neatly-trimmed pencil moustache. Their table was next to a window overlooking Regent Street. Andy had a Hyderabadi lamb biryani while Reidford chose steamed sea bass.

"This is delicious," said Andy. "Shame there isn't an Indian restaurant closer to home."

"What, an Indian restaurant in Hounslow?" said Superintendent Reidford. "It will never happen."

"Why not?"

"Two reasons. First, the British public will never accept the food. John Bull is used to his steak and kidney pie or roast beef and Yorkshire pudding; he'll never take to spicy curries. It's only the upper classes, a tiny elite really, that have such adventurous tastes."

It was the first time anyone had given him upper-class membership, but Andy let that pass. "I'm not sure I agree with you. When I did my National Service in Kenya, a lot of my fellow troopers, many of them working-class lads, would join me for a curry in town when we were off duty. I think there would be quite a demand for this sort of food throughout England. What was your second reason?"

"The Leader would never have it. He may well be prepared to have one Indian chef living in London, but he wouldn't allow two."

"You may have a point," Andy conceded.

They had started their coffees when Superintendent Reidford signalled it was appropriate to talk shop.

"How can I help you?" said Reidford.

"I'd like a list of men between the ages of 20 and 40 who have been reported missing in the last couple of weeks. The idea is to interview their families for a human interest story I'm writing."

"Hmm, if you say so," said Superintendent Reidford suspiciously. "I can give you that list, no problem. But don't go searching for the missing men. At least don't look too hard, if you get my drift."

Andy knew only too well what the Superintendent was saying. The Government had a habit of making its political opponents "disappear". They would either be secretly executed or spend years in detention. Andy's own father had disappeared on his way home one night, only to arrive 14 years later, having spent the intervening period in a labour camp on the Isle of Arran.

Andy was back at his desk when, shortly after four, he received a telephone call from one of his police contacts, Detective Sergeant Neil Toner from Surrey Constabulary's Egham station. A man's body had been found at Virginia Water, just off the A30. Andy drove straight down. It was easy to find the crime scene; just past Egham Wick, police had cordoned off one lane of the road where an ambulance and three police vehicles were parked. Oddly, they were marked Thames Valley Police, even though this was Surrey. By the time Andy arrived on the scene, the ambulance was driving away.

"Where's it off to?" he asked a police constable.

"Chertsey mortuary."

He showed the policeman his identity card. "Andy Deegan, crime reporter on the *Daily Citizen*. Is there anything more you can tell me?"

"You're a bit late. Your colleague from *The Globe* got here an hour ago. I'd ask him." The policeman nodded in the direction of a tall, bespectacled man with a lightning flash badge on his raincoat and a notebook in his hand. It was Richard Bartle, a fellow crime journalist who Andy knew professionally. Andy felt miffed. Now that the police were packing up and leaving the scene, it was going to be Bartle's story. He obviously had a better police contact.

"Who's your man at Surrey Constabulary?" asked Andy.

"Who said anything about Surrey Police?" said Richard Bartle.

"Who then?"

"A little bird," said Richard Bartle, tapping the side of his nose. "You know I can't reveal my sources."

"How come Thames Valley Police are here? We're in Surrey, after all," said Andy.

"Only just; the Berkshire border and Thames Valley area of operations is only a few hundred yards away."

"So what happened?" asked Andy.

"You'll find out all about it in tomorrow's edition of *The Globe*."

CHAPTER 9

The news that Mary had an Uncle David seemed like the first real break. All Sally had to do was telephone each David Brown and ask if he had a niece called Mary. Unfortunately, there were thousands of David Browns listed in the London telephone directory alone. Of course, it was possible the uncle was Mary's mother's brother, in which case he was likely to have a different surname; it didn't help that Mary couldn't remember if this was a maternal or paternal uncle. Nevertheless, each day, Sally picked 10 more David Browns from the directory and gave them a call. Each time, she got the reply: "No, we do not have a niece called Mary." Sally had hoped the revelation about Uncle David was a sign that the fog covering Mary's past was beginning to lift and that more would be revealed, but unfortunately, that didn't seem to be happening.

Over the next few days, Sally checked the Salvation Army missing persons file but couldn't find any matching Mary Brown. She'd also contacted Scotland Yard's Missing Persons Bureau, but got no joy there either. In the meantime, Sally thought it was important that Mary was active in some way and at the same time, learned more about the world around her.

Mary spent a lot of time helping out at the Mile End hostel and joining in the singing; Sally was impressed by the number of hymns she knew. Whenever they had free time, they would go for walks in the area in the hope that Mary might recognise something from her past: a school, church, workplace or shop. The fact she didn't made Sally believe that Mary didn't come from this part of London. They visited the Tower of London; if Mary was a Londoner, surely she would have seen it at least once before. But the visit didn't bring back any memories.

On Tuesday, they went to the British Museum to see the Tutankhamen exhibition as admission was free on that day. Mary had seen a couple of programmes about the exhibition on TV and seemed interested in going. They arrived two hours before opening to make sure they would get in, but the queue was already 200 yards long. They had to wait five hours before getting in but the first exhibit took their breath away. In a darkened room stood a life-sized blackened wood statue of King Tutankhamen dressed in gold, carrying a gilded mace and staff. Along the walls, panels described various aspects of life in Ancient Egypt. One panel explained that the Egyptians at that time were a white Aryan race quite different from the Arabs who settled later in the region. In the following rooms were a series of vases, chests, statues and jewellery – about 50 objects in all. In the seventh and final room, the climax of the exhibition was displayed; a gold funerary mask of the king with the rearing heads of a vulture and cobra. It took about an hour to get through the exhibition and they were running late, so afterwards, they only had time for a quick look at some of the permanent Egyptian exhibits.

They marvelled at the Rosetta Stone, which had a decree inscribed in three scripts and proved to be the key to modern understanding of Ancient Egyptian hieroglyphs. Sally reflected if only she could find a Rosetta Stone that would be the key to Mary's past.

Mary and Sally left the British Museum and headed down Great Russell Street towards Tottenham Court Road. They had been walking for only a minute when a convoy of Blackshirt motorcyclists, green tarpaulin-covered trucks and police Black Marias passed them, with sirens blasting out loudly. A few people who sensed what was about to happen dashed off down the side streets. The convoy stopped abruptly and scores of Blackshirts and police jumped out of the trucks and sealed off all exits to the road, bar one. It was a random identity card check; the trapped pedestrians were channelled towards one checkpoint where identity cards and bags were examined and people frisked.

Sally supposed the authorities picked this spot for an identity check because of all the additional visitors to the British Museum. They found themselves at the end of a 200-yard queue, but because of the thoroughness of the inspections, it was nearly two hours before they reached the checkpoint. One elderly lady just ahead of them didn't have her card. She explained that she only popped out to buy some milk and lived just a block away. Her pleas fell on deaf ears and she was escorted by a couple of Blackshirts to a Black Maria.

"What will happen to her?" asked Mary.

"Three years for a first offence, life for a second, and death for a third. Three strikes and you're out, as The Leader once put."

"Surely seeing it's life for a second offence, there will never be a third," said Mary.

"I've never thought of that. Maybe you need to carry an identity card with you, even in prison."

When their turn came, Mary tensed as she showed her card to the policeman. Of course, she was a long way from Kings Road, Hackney, so it was extremely unlikely that the officer would spot that number 78 didn't actually exist. Nevertheless, she held her breath until she and Sally were let through the cordon.

They had originally planned to have lunch at the YWCA off Tottenham Court Road, but as they were running five hours late, it was teatime when they arrived. They had fish and chips followed by apple pie and custard. They were halfway through their dessert when Mary said, "I've been here before. I can't remember the reason but I suppose it was to get a bite to eat. But something happened and I remember having to drive back home."

Chapter 10

Andy arrived at Chertsey Hospital bright and early at half-past seven. He had a job finding the morgue; there were signposts for Cardiology, Orthopaedics, Neurology, Haematology, Urology and Oncology, but nothing for the mortuary. Maybe the correct term was something like Necrology, but he didn't see that either. He supposed the hospital didn't want to advertise the mortuary's existence for fear of upsetting distressed visitors. He had to ask around, and was eventually told it was in the basement, access to which was through an unmarked door at the end of a long corridor. He climbed down the stairwell to the basement then followed a maze of dimly-lit passageways. Still no sign of the mortuary. He felt a distinct chill.

Is it really colder here or is it just nerves at the prospect of visiting a morgue?

He passed a door marked *Chapel of Rest* so he felt he was getting closer, and eventually, he came face to face with a pair of double doors marked *Mortuary*. Inside, a man with a white coat sat behind a desk reading a newspaper; Andy couldn't tell if he was a doctor, pathologist or indeed, just a receptionist.

"Good morning. How can I help you?" asked the member of staff.

"I'm Greg Parsons, I've come here to identify my brother, Tim," said Andy, picking names at random. "I'm a bit early. I'm supposed to be meeting Detective Chief Inspector Armstrong here at eight o'clock. My brother was found near Virginia Water and was brought here yesterday afternoon."

"Ah yes, I know who you're talking about. The police really should have informed us of your visit."

"Maybe they're just too busy," said Andy. "Or they tried to phone when the line was engaged."

"Yes, I suppose you're right."

"Look, it's another quarter of an hour before the Inspector will get here," said Andy. "Could I go and see my brother? I'd like to have a few minutes in silence with him, if it is my brother, that is. If that's all right with you?"

For a few moments, the man was silent sucking his lower lip, and then said, "I don't see any problem, come this way."

Andy followed him down a cold corridor bathed in an unearthly fluorescent green light. Then he became aware of that mortuary smell. Andy had visited mortuaries several times in his career so wasn't too put out by the atmosphere. However, someone identifying a relative and possibly visiting a mortuary for the first time would be very apprehensive, so Andy decided to exaggerate the nervousness he felt. He gulped audibly as the door was opened to the autopsy room.

"Your brother is in quite a decent state," said the man, pulling a drawer from what looked like an oversized filing cabinet. The body was lying face up and the sheet covering him was pulled down to the waist. The hole in the head was the same size and in the same place as Mark's. It was the same execution style that Andy had seen in Twickenham. The man had been very fit, more like an athlete. The expression on his face was neutral, if anything, slightly serene, despite the fact that he had been murdered. Andy had taken a good look at Mark's photos just before he arrived at the hospital; he was in no doubt this was one of the men.

Andy shook his head. "I'm quite certain it's not Tim." Andy wanted to check if there were whip marks similar to those on Mark's body. "Just to make sure, he had a birthmark on the back of his shoulder."

The man turned the body over; there was the same neat, circular entry wound at the nape of the neck and on the back were distinct welts, which could be from whipping, but no birthmark of course.

"It's not him," Andy confirmed.

They headed back to the reception area; Andy sat in silence while the man returned to his paper. At a quarter past eight, Andy stood up and said, "The police should have arrived by now. Is it all right if I phone them?" The man nodded towards a telephone and Andy dialled.

"DCI Armstrong, it's Greg Parsons. I'm at Chertsey Hospital," said Andy. There was a pause then he continued. "Oh, eight o'clock this evening. The corpse is definitely not my brother, Tim. Do I have to come here again?" Another pause. "Fine, Windsor Police Station, 11 o'clock this morning it is. Bye."

Andy put the receiver down and said, "There's been a misunderstanding; the police wanted me here at eight o'clock this evening. But seeing it's not my brother, the appointment has been cancelled. I just need to go to Windsor Police Station and sign some papers." Andy hoped the hospital official didn't spot he had been having a telephone conversation with the speaking clock.

"I hope you find your brother. Alive and well, that is."

"Yes, I suppose this is good news. Thank you," said Andy.

Back in his car, Andy took out the four photos. He wrote "*Mark*" on the back of the first victim's photo. He nearly wrote "*Victim B*" on the second, then realised he may end up showing the photo to a next of kin, so he just wrote "*B*".

Andy drove on to Neasden, not arriving until nine o'clock because of the traffic on the North Circular Road. He parked his car on a side street full of identical 1950's Fascist-style council houses, with their plain pink sandstone exteriors and a mixture of square and arched windows. Each house had a small porch with Roman-style columns, and above each door was a niche with a bronze bust of The Leader.

He knocked on number 23 and Heather Smith, Brian's widow, answered. He was shown into the sitting room, fashionably fitted with modern furniture. Alongside one wall was a Heal's co-ordinated wall storage system. A glass pendant lamp hung from the ceiling. There was no sofa in the room but four hammock-cushioned chairs with chrome frames, which looked like the sort you could get from Habitat, and a glass and brass coffee table on which lay an ashtray filled with a large number of cigarette stubs. As they sat down, Andy spotted a black folder on the coffee table with photos creeping out; if they were those of Brian then Brian was not one of Mark's friends. On one of the free walls was the usual portrait of The Leader, and along a window shelf was a full set of action men, including one in a Blackshirt uniform. Andy toyed with the idea of offering to buy the Blackshirt figurine from the woman.

"They're Tommy's, our little boy," said Mrs Smith, seeing Andy's gaze.

"And that's Brian," said Andy, pointing at the photographs. Mrs Smith nodded. Andy didn't want to be rude and leave there and then, so he spent the next 40 minutes chatting about Brian, with Mrs Smith bringing a family album and showing more photos.

Next, Andy drove to Wandsworth. He parked near the town centre and, walking along the crowded high street, he heard a sound of both clapping and jeering. A group of Blackshirts were frog-marching a couple of trouserless men who were otherwise fully clothed. It was the "*Jeans Police*". Andy couldn't tell if the jeers were aimed at the Blackshirts or their victims; he suspected it was a mixture of both.

Imported jeans were becoming increasingly popular among the young, but because of the Jewish origin of their American manufacturers, while not banned, they were disapproved of in Fascist circles. Recently, squads of Blackshirts throughout the country had taken it on themselves to arrest anyone wearing jeans in public, remove the offending trousers by force then march their owners to the nearest Blackshirt office where the victims would receive a thorough beating.

Harriet Turner lived in a third-floor flat. Andy was shown to the sitting room; it was cramped and dingy. A low, torn brown sofa, about nine feet long, took almost the entire length of the room. On it were strewn various items of clothing with only a tiny gap for Andy to sit on. In front of the sofa was a chipped black faux marble coffee table. It looked like the Turners got their furniture from a rubbish skip rather than Heal's or Habitat. On the coffee table stood a quarter-full bottle of gin and a pile of unwashed plates. In the corner of the room stood a table, on which were piled an assortment of papers, books and magazines; there was more junk beneath, creating a mountain that almost reached the level of the table.

Andy showed Mrs Turner Mark's photos and asked if any resembled her son, Colin. She shook her head. He then asked her if she had any photos of Colin. She showed an album of her son growing up, but the last photo was taken when he was 13 years old and still in school uniform. There was little similarity to anyone in Mark's photos. Andy asked if she had anything more recent. She rummaged through the pile on top and beneath the table but after 10 minutes, hadn't found a photo.

"Tell me what Colin looked like?" asked Andy.

"Well he was clean shaven and had dark hair," said Mrs Turner. "Quite good looking really."

"Would you say he was on the fat or slim side?" said Andy.

"Well not that fat, but a bit chubby is how I would describe him."

This didn't look good. "Did he do sports?" asked Andy.

"Not since leaving school. He was always in the pub, drinking and gambling. That's how he died; he lost a bet, couldn't pay up and got stabbed."

Andy had already written Colin Turner off when Mrs Turner recalled there was an article in the local paper about a year previously with a picture of him and his pub darts team. She raked through the table clutter for another 10 minutes before retrieving the newspaper report.

There was no doubt now; Andy could confidently cross Colin Turner off his list.

Back at the office, Andy got to work on his in-tray. The first item was an eight-page form with a note from Alice attached: *From the Ancestry Tracing Service, please complete ASAP.* The form asked detailed personal questions, not only of the respondent but his or her parents and grandparents. Andy wasn't going to waste time on this; he strode into Paul Draper's office, waving the form in his hand.

"What's all this about, Paul?"

"Ah yes. It's not just you; we all have to complete the form. It's a check on whether we have any Jewish ancestry."

"But that's absurd. All British Jews were deported in the 1940s."

"Resettled," Paul Draper corrected.

Andy was aware this was a taboo subject, so his tone became less aggressive, more cautious. "Nevertheless, that still makes this form redundant."

"The repatriations only applied to those with at least one Jewish grandparent. This new European Union directive prohibits people with *any* Jewish ancestry from employment or owning a business; in Britain's case, going back to Oliver Cromwell. It's perfectly reasonable to make this a Europe-wide standard. Why should someone who can trace a Jewish ancestor back to 1700, say, be banned from employment in Paris or Berlin, whereas a person with the same racial profile is happily working in London? It's not fair."

Paul Draper's tone was becoming more irritated, "Anyway, I'm not going to waste time arguing over this. Just do it."

By the time Andy had filled in the form and written his reports on the Smith and Turner murders, it was late and time to go home. He realised he hadn't seen Richard Bartle's article on the Virginia Water murder. He got hold of *The Globe* and flicked through the paper. There it was, taking up an entire page. Andy read the article carefully; there was nothing there that could help him, although oddly, the whip marks on the victim's body weren't mentioned.

CHAPTER 11

Alice came in with an envelope while Andy was having his morning coffee; it was the names of two more missing men from Detective Superintendent Reidford. He had already sent a list of twenty-one missing and Andy had spent the last two days checking them out. None matched. The first of today's names was Ben Wright. Andy phoned Ben Wright's wife, only to find out that Ben had got back home the morning after being reported missing. He had been drinking with friends, had fallen asleep on the train home and missed his destination, only to find the last train back had already left. The second was John Fox; Andy phoned Mrs Fox and found out that her husband was a 28-year-old tennis instructor who'd been missing a week. Andy arranged to visit Mrs Fox that afternoon.

The Fox family lived in a second-floor flat in Kingston, just a hundred yards from the River Thames. Mrs Fox had clearly been crying, and she spoke in a sniffling whimper as she led Andy inside. The hallway and lounge were stacked with cardboard boxes and crates. The only furniture in the lounge was a couple of armchairs.

"We are, were, planning to move house tomorrow. I'm not sure if I should postpone the move until John returns. If he returns, that is," said Mrs Fox between sobs.

"Tell me about John."

"John works as a tennis instructor in Esher, that's where we're relocating to be closer to his job. He didn't return from work about a week ago. I've rung all his workmates and friends and told the police, but I've heard nothing."

Andy showed Mark's photos to Mrs Fox; she picked out her husband straight away. He was one of the two men who had not been found yet. Mrs Fox struggled to say more about her husband, bursting into tears every now and then. She offered to show a photo album of John and started pulling household paraphernalia out of a crate. She emptied half of it before Andy stopped her. He arranged to see her again in a few days, after she'd moved and unpacked. Mrs Fox gave Andy her new telephone number and agreed to him writing a piece in the *Daily Citizen*. As soon as he left, Andy wrote "*John Fox*" on the back of the photo.

The next day was the 20th of April – the anniversary of Adolf Hitler's birth and a holiday throughout Europe. Andy decided to take the whole family to visit his parents, Peter and Fiona Deegan. They lived in a one-bedroom flat in Leatherhead.

Andy had grown up really without a father. Peter Deegan had been an accountant with Leatherhead Council, and when Andy had just started primary school, had been asked to swear allegiance to The Leader, Sir Oswald Mosley. Peter refused; a few weeks later, he was arrested by the secret police on his way home from work and disappeared. Fiona was not told of his arrest and all her attempts to find out what had happened to him were stonewalled.

She heard absolutely nothing for five years, until one afternoon, when she was taking Andy to the local swimming pool, a gaunt, dishevelled, middle-aged man approached and asked if she was Fiona Deegan. The man was Charles Jackson and he had been released from a labour camp on the Isle of Arran a few weeks earlier. He had shared a bunk with Peter Deegan and had been asked by Peter to let her know he was alive and well.

Fiona had two more such encounters over several years until, fourteen years after his disappearance, without any warning, Peter returned home. He was still blacklisted and couldn't get work as an accountant, so had to make do with a job as a janitor at a nearby school on a meagre wage and 20 hours a week. But now, in 1972, Andy had been making a good living for several years and was able to help his parents out.

Andy brought two record albums with him: Cliff Richard's *Live at the Talk of the Town* for Mum, and *Tom Jones' Greatest Hits* for Dad. After lunch, the girls sang the BUF anthem; not only did they know the words by heart now, but they were top in the school choir and wanted to show off. Peter Deegan managed to smile and clap but his eyes showed the pain he felt.

In the afternoon, they headed back home, stopping off at Hampton Court Palace. In the gardens, a Blackshirt brass band from Halifax was playing *On Ilkla Moor Baht 'at*. Andy listened to the band while Jane took the children to the maze. The youngsters wanted to have a go on their own; the girls got to the centre and back in good time but Harry got stuck, burst into tears and had to be rescued by his mother.

They drove home through Bushy Park, Harry still whining in the back of the car. As soon as they passed the perimeter of the Ministry of Defence Research Station, situated at the northern edge of the park, Andy took a right turn towards the centre of London instead of heading straight home.

"Are you feeling hungry?" asked Andy. The children nodded. "Then I have a surprise for you," he said. Harry's whining stopped and he gave a broad grin.

It was dark when they got home from their West End trip to McDonalds. They put the children to bed then sat down to watch the moon landing. This was the first American-manned lunar expedition, although the Germans had flown men there four times previously. However, this was the first time the event was being transmitted live, and it was a sign of détente that it was being shown on British television. The landing was scheduled for 9.40p.m. British time. When Andy switched the TV on, the lunar module, named Orion, with two astronauts inside, had already detached from the command module, named Casper, which was orbiting the moon with the third astronaut inside. By 10 o'clock, Orion had still not touched down, although pictures were still being transmitted from both Orion and Casper as the landing area was on the near side of the moon. Shortly, it was announced that there was a fault with the control system in Casper. At 11 o'clock, the TV transmission finished for the night. There was now doubt, not only whether Orion would be able to land, but also whether it would be able to re-dock with Casper, with the prospect of two men being stranded in space. It had made for gripping viewing. Then the phone rang.

"Andrew Deegan? It's Detective Chief Inspector Armstrong from Thames Valley Police."

"How can I help you, Inspector Armstrong?"

"You've been reporting on the Twickenham and Virginia Waters murders."

"I have indeed. Anything wrong with that?"

"I want you to stop. You're interfering with a police investigation."

"But I'm just doing my job."

"And I'm doing mine. You wouldn't know anything about a Greg Parsons. He was seen a few days ago at Chertsey mortuary."

"No, never heard of him."

"You have been warned. Goodnight."

*

The revelation that Mary had previously been to the Tottenham Court Road YWCA suggested to Sally that at least she was a Londoner after all. The YWCA was not the sort of place people from outside London would go for lunch. Mary had said that something had happened and she had had to go back home. Mary couldn't remember what the incident was, but she thought she left in either a car or a taxi. So it seemed that Mary came from a rather well-heeled, middle-class family. Mary had been with Sally for three weeks now and was becoming a friend. She was learning fast; Sally no longer thought herself to be Mary's mother but more like her big sister. Mary had made hardly any progress with her memory though; they should visit some more West End attractions to see if further memories could be rekindled.

On the next free day, they visited the Science Museum. They took a lift to the top floor and started with the history of medicine exhibition, which included a special section on the life and career of the German Nobel Laureate for Medicine, Josef Mengele. Mary didn't seem too enthusiastic; Sally didn't think she was a doctor. They worked their way downwards until they reached the huge hall on the ground floor.

Here were displayed some 18th century steam engines, including one by James Watt. Early 19th century steam locomotives followed, including the *Puffing Billy* and Stephenson's *Rocket*. The next section showed exhibits of early aircraft, culminating in the display of the actual command module, *Zeus*, of the 1969 German moon landing. An information panel explained that the lunar module, *Hera*, which actually landed on the moon, was exhibited in the Deutsches Museum in Munich. A panel displayed the first words spoken on the moon: *Ein kleiner Schritt für das deutche Volk, ein riesiger Sprung für den Führer*, together with a translation – *One small step for the German people, one giant leap for the Führer.* Additional panels described the history of the *Ares* project, as the German space mission was known. There was much on the career of the *Ares* project director, Oberst-Gruppenführer Wernher von Braun.

"Well, what did you think of it?" said Sally as they left the museum.

"I suppose it was quite interesting," said Mary. "I'm fairly sure I never liked science. *Multiplication is vexation, Division is as bad; The Rule of Three doth puzzle me, And Practice drives me mad.* Funny how I can remember that."

Chapter 12

At first, Andy took heed of DCI Armstrong's warning. He kept himself busy writing articles about how various communities had celebrated Europe Day, and about the American moon landing. The fault in the control system had been fixed and touchdown had been six hours later than scheduled. There followed three drives in a lunar roving vehicle then it was time to return. The return journey was also exciting, with one of the astronauts performing a spacewalk. Andy had initially written that the Americans seem to be catching up with the Germans in the space race. However, this caused problems with the censors so the final version pointed out that this was just a first step for the Americans and Germany still had a commanding lead in space technology. Nevertheless, there was far more public interest in the American mission and Andy put it down to it being shown live, in contrast to the German endeavours, which weren't announced until after their astronauts safely returned to Earth.

After a few days, Andy found he couldn't stay off the case of Mark and his three colleagues any longer. He started by writing a piece about Mrs Fox and her missing husband, John. He avoided approaching Thames Valley Police, but phoned contacts in the Surrey and Twickenham forces; they were still approachable, but had no more news on the case. Finally, he got Alice to telephone Thames Valley Police, pretending to being a trainee at *The Globe*. The police were polite but had nothing to report, other than all lines of enquiry were being pursued.

What linked the four? They were youngish and fit looking. Could they be army, Blackshirts or police? If that were so, surely they would have been reported missing by their colleagues.

What if they were all members of Thames Valley Police? In that case, the force would know their identities, but for some reason, the police authorities didn't want to make them public. That might explain Inspector Armstrong's warning. It would also explain the decision to take Mark's case off Twickenham Police's hands. Andy didn't think there was much he could do if that were so.

Andy took yet another look at the markings on the photos: "*OK**", "**LEF*", "*UB**" and "*ING*". He was trying to make sense of them when Alice Greengrass came in with the mail.

"What do you make of these?" said Andy, showing Alice the stamps on the photos.

Alice stared at the photos for a minute then said, "I reckon the asterisks mark the start or end of a word. So we're looking for one word starting with '*LEF*', another ending '*UB*', and a third ending '*OK*'. The fourth word could have '*ING*' at the start, end or middle." They both tried thinking of possible words but nothing came to mind, so after a few minutes, Andy thanked Alice and put the photos away.

After lunch, Andy was writing an article on British athletes hopeful of competing in the Munich Olympics when the phone rang. It was one of his contacts, Detective Constable Hindson of Ascot Police; two bodies had been found in Windsor Great Park. Andy was a bit surprised to have received the tip-off; Ascot was part of Thames Valley police, as was Windsor. It looked like the decision to warn Andy off the case was made locally by the Windsor Police and not any higher.

An hour later, he met Detective Constable Hindson by the side of the A332 in the middle of Windsor Great Park. A group of boys, looking very pale and nervous, were talking to one of half a dozen policemen who were at the scene.

"What happened?" asked Andy.

"The bodies were discovered by three boys looking for a lost ball. The men were found in that thicket," said Detective Constable Hindson, pointing to some trees about a hundred yards distant. "Both men were in their 20s or 30s, I'd say, and dead for at least a few days."

"Can I take a look?"

"Go ahead. Just don't touch anything. There's a bit of a smell, so don't say I didn't warn you."

A couple of men from forensics were inspecting the naked bodies, which were only a few yards apart. They were lying face down and had whip marks on their backs, and had been shot in the nape of the neck. Andy watched as the bodies were turned over; although he wasn't absolutely sure, one looked like John Fox and the second bore a resemblance to the fourth photo, which he then marked "C". There was something impersonal referring to the victims as "*B*", and "C". He ought to give them provisional names. In the end, he crossed out the letters on the photos and wrote down "*Luke*" and "*Matthew*", together with Mark and John, the four evangelists.

At that moment, a black police Wolseley arrived; Detective Chief Inspector Armstrong and Richard Bartle from *The Globe* stepped out. DCI Armstrong had a few words with Detective Constable Hindson then headed towards Andy with Richard Bartle in tow. Armstrong glared furiously as soon as he spotted Andy.

"Clear off," Armstrong shouted. "Do I make myself understood?"

It must be something personal, thought Andy as he drove back to the office. DCI Armstrong was happy to have reporter Richard Bartle around but not Andy. Had he done or said anything in the past to upset Windsor Police? He didn't think so. Maybe Andy had stumbled onto something that Richard Bartle hadn't, which Armstrong wanted to keep under wraps. He tried to think what that could be. He had met Mrs Fox, John's wife, or rather widow. Maybe the answer lay there.

As soon as he got to the office, he phoned Mrs Fox's new Esher number. He got a disconnected tone; it looked like she hadn't moved in yet. He tried her Kingston number; there was no reply.

Chapter 13

After visiting the Science Museum, Sally and Mary took a tube to Oxford Street to do some window-shopping. The rain had only just stopped so the street was less crowded than usual. Outside Selfridges, they were stopped by a middle-aged lady carrying shopping bags, who had just left the store. She asked to see their identity cards; Sally and Mary complied.

"Was she a police detective?" said Mary after the woman had waved them on. "This is the second time this has happened to me. On the day I left Victoria Station, I was stopped and had my pass checked by a man dressed as a civilian."

"No, she was probably an ordinary citizen," said Sally. "You see, we're all supposed to check each other's identity cards. 'Just one check a day keeps the subversive at bay', as The Leader put it."

"I've never seen you check anyone," said Mary.

"I get to see far more than one identity card with each day's new arrivals at the hostel."

"What happens if a person refuses to show his or her card?"

"Then you are obliged to perform a citizen's arrest and hand the individual over to the nearest police officer or Blackshirt."

Near Oxford Circus, there was some kind of commotion; a throng some 50 strong had gathered, so they went to have a closer look. A 60-year-old man was leaning on a bus stop, holding a handkerchief to his nose, which was bleeding profusely. Assisting him was a woman of the same age.

"Are you all right?" asked Sally.

"We're fine, thank you," said the woman. It looked as if she was his wife.

"I tried to stop them," said the man. "But they're all half my age."

A few yards away was the action the man had tried to stop: a Blackshirt "haircut". These were becoming quite common occurrences in London in the last few years, and Sally had witnessed one such "haircut" before. She didn't want to see another.

Sitting uncomfortably on a bench was a youth in his early 20s. He wore a suit with flared trousers and a flowered shirt. His arms were stretched behind him and over the back of the bench, and held in position by two Blackshirts. Another Blackshirt stood with his boots firmly on the young man's feet, while a fourth was administering the haircut with a large pair of scissors. The hair on the youth's left side was already closely cropped, while on the right, it still reached his shoulder. Another half-dozen Blackshirts were witnessing all this.

"I think we ought to leave," said Sally.

They turned only to find more people had gathered behind them. They tried to push their way out, only to find their exit blocked by two middle-aged men dressed in dark suits, beige trench coats and black bowler hats. They were both of similar height, but one was thin and the other heavyset; they reminded Sally of Laurel and Hardy.

"Ladies, I don't think it's a good idea to leave," said Laurel. "Please turn around and watch."

"Turn around and watch," said Hardy.

Sally stopped in her tracks; there was no mistaking who these men were: secret police.

"It's important not only for justice to be done, but to be seen to be done," said Laurel.

"Seen to be done," said Hardy.

Sally and Mary turned and watched the rest of the spectacle. At intervals from within the crowd, they could hear, "Why doesn't someone call the police?" or, "I think the police have been called", or, "A fat lot of good that will do."

The Blackshirts, having cropped the youth's hair all over, then produced a can of shaving foam and sprayed it over his head. Then, with the aid of cutthroat razors, the Blackshirts took turns to roughly shave the man's head. The result was not only a bald head, but a bloody gash across the man's head, from which blood trickled down the sides of his face like an octopus's tentacles.

"Make way. Police," a voice barked from behind.

The crowd parted to form a corridor, down which a uniformed police sergeant and six of his men proceeded.

"Well done lads," the sergeant spoke to the Blackshirts. "We'll take care of the hoodlum now." The Blackshirts released their grip on the youth and stepped aside. The sergeant unclipped his truncheon and lifted it above his head. The youth raised his hands to protect his head but failed to deflect the blow.

"Constable, we can nail him for resisting arrest as well as hooliganism," said the sergeant. "Take a couple of witness statements."

While the constable nearest the sergeant proceeded to do this, the sergeant clipped his truncheon back in place and retrieved a pair of handcuffs, which he attached to the youth's wrists. Two of the constables seized the man by his elbows and frog-marched him down the street. As they passed the elderly man with the bleeding nose, Laurel stepped forward and showed the sergeant a pass.

"I think you might also be interested in questioning this man," he spoke, pointing at the older man. "He seems to be an accomplice of the hooligan."

"This way, sir, just a few routine questions," said the sergeant.

"But he's done nothing wrong," said the wife.

"Madam, mind your own business," said the sergeant. "Obstructing the police is a serious offence."

The police led the two arrested men to a waiting Black Maria and drove off.

After the crowd dispersed, Mary said, "Was the young man really a hooligan?"

"Probably not," said Sally. "He was just unlucky enough to have long hair and run into this group of Blackshirts. The man's hairstyle is not actually illegal, but some Blackshirts and police think it should be."

"Are the police always so strict?"

Sally noted that Mary used the more politically correct term of "strict" rather than "rough" or "brutal". She was becoming more streetwise. If only her memory could show similar signs of improvement.

"They were less strict when I was younger," said Sally. "In those days, before The Leader came to power, you could ask a policeman for directions. Now, if you tried that, you'd be arrested for wasting police time." Sally realised she may have gone too far. "And quite right too. The police are far too busy catching criminals or subversives who want to harm The Leader."

They turned into Regent Street and nearing Piccadilly Circus, they came across a man in his 30s, holding a street map and looking confused.

"Can we help?" said Sally.

"Bond Street Station. Where is she please?" said the man in a foreign accent.

"Go straight down Regent Street until you get to Oxford Circus," said Sally. "Then turn left along Oxford Street and in another five minutes, you'll reach the station."

"Please repeat. I am French. My English is not so good."

"Vous allez tout droit vers Oxford Circus. Tournez à gauche et cinq minutes plus tard vous arrivez à la gare," said Mary in fluent French.

Chapter 14

"We like to say grace before meals," said Paul Draper. He was hosting a dinner at his mansion in Horsley, a well-heeled commuter village, 30 miles south-west of London. He had invited Andy and Jane Deegan to join him and his wife Louise, but Jane couldn't arrange a babysitter. He had pressed Andy into coming regardless; Andy wondered why Paul Draper was so keen to request the pleasure of his company. Paul Draper wasn't in the habit of socialising with humble employees such as Andy; in fact, the last time Andy had been invited for dinner was four years earlier after his Darent brothers' scoop. To make a foursome, Alice Greengrass had been invited in Jane's place. Alice wore a sleeveless, knee-length black silk cocktail dress that was held up by straps not much wider than spaghetti strands. It was quite a change from the chunky sweaters she wore at work. The party stood behind their chairs round the dinner table.

"For what we are about to receive, we thank The Leader," said Paul Draper. "We give thanks to our Leader for providing food at the table of every law-abiding Englishman. We are grateful to The Leader for keeping safe our streets and homes." He paused for a moment then gave a raised arm salute. "The Leader."

Louise Draper and Alice Greengrass immediately followed suit, but Andy paused long enough to receive a glare from Paul Draper. Slowly, three seconds later than everyone else, Andy raised his arm and murmured, "The Leader."

Andy felt he was being a bit of a fraud; he hadn't wanted to give the salute and it seemed deceitful to have concurred. He also thought it was rather cowardly; the brave, intrepid Andrew Deegan, recipient of the Military Cross, exposer of the Darent brothers, had been afraid to make a fuss. He could have said, "Sorry Paul, I think this is going too far." But he didn't.

The party sat down to eat and drink.

"The beef is absolutely delicious. Exquisite," said Andy. On offer was fillet of beef Prince Albert, accompanied by Krug Grand Cuvee champagne. "This is quite a contrast with the McDonalds burger I had with my kids a few days ago."

"I didn't think you would stoop so low, Andy," said Paul Draper. "You know I don't like this idea of détente at all. Still, there's probably no harm in just one branch opening. I suppose The Leader wants to keep the plebs happy. What on earth made you go there?"

"Harry kept on nagging me to go. So I finally took the family as a Europe Day treat. They advertise themselves as a fast food restaurant and it's true; once you place your order at the counter, you only wait a couple of minutes before it's ready. But we had to queue for an hour just to get in the place. But, brace yourself for this, Paul, what do you think they call their largest beef burger?"

"I haven't the faintest idea."

"A McLeader."

Paul Draper's face went puce and he almost knocked over his champagne glass. "The cheek. This wouldn't happen in Germany."

"I suppose it's a McFührer over there," said Alice.

"I don't think so," said Paul. "I'll report this to The Leader; it's my duty as an MP."

"I'm sure The Leader has been informed," said Andy.

"You're probably right, Andy," said Paul after his anger had subsided. "Talking about my duty as an MP, can I count on your support in the forthcoming elections? You can be sure I'll be fighting against this pernicious American influence that has been creeping into our society. They can't wage war on us as our German ally has the nuclear bomb, so instead, their tactic is subversion. They want the people of Europe to lose respect for their leaders and this burger product name business is one small but good example of what I mean. I'm sure the Jews are behind this; it's a shame Lindbergh failed to win the US Presidency."

Andy thought Paul Draper was attaching far too much importance to his role as MP. The lower house, or House of Commons, as reformed by The Leader in the 1950s, had elections every five years on a vocational constituency basis. This meant, for example, that Andy, as a newspaper journalist, could only vote for a candidate who worked in, and represented, the press. To stand for Parliament, one had to be a member of the British Union of Fascists and usually, there was a choice of two candidates for each seat. To critics who suggested this all smacked of a one-party state, The Leader replied that as the British Union of Fascists was no longer a political party but a movement, Britain was a no-party state. Requiring a candidate to be a member of the BUF was no more restrictive than the stipulation that he or she was a British citizen.

Parliament was limited to a purely advisory role. It could not initiate any legislation; that was the Government's job. So if the Government decided to pass more laws on newspaper censorship, for example, an MP such as Paul Draper could only advise on how, and not whether, the censorship should be implemented. Parliament could constitutionally call a vote of no confidence in the Government; in that case, the King would ask The Leader to form a new Government. The Leader would only need to replace one member of his cabinet for it to be deemed new. Such a vote of no confidence had never been made. There was no upper house in Britain, the House of Lords having been abolished in the 1940s. Given how powerless Parliament was, Andy decided to humour Paul Draper.

"Of course, Paul; you can be sure of my vote."

"Alice, if you don't mind me asking, do you have a boyfriend?" asked Louise Draper.

"No, I split with Steve a month ago. He failed the Tigger test."

"What's that?"

"Tigger's my pet kitten and it turned out that Steve didn't like cats."

"I must admit, I'm not a cat person myself. What do you plan to do tomorrow? When I was your age, an ideal Sunday would be a walk in the countryside with the Young Fascists."

"Well, my idea of a perfect Sunday is relaxing with a good book and Tigger on my lap. I like historical novels and I'm halfway through one about Mary, Queen of Scots."

They were just finishing dessert, spotted dick with custard, when Paul Draper said, "There's another matter I'd like to discuss with you, Andy. You know as well as an MP, I'm also chairman of the Surrey Young Fascists. However, I am required to stand down when I reach 45, which will be later this year. Andy, you're a young man in your 30s."

"Only just," Andy interrupted.

"You can easily pass for a 30-year-old." Alice flashed a wide smile.

"Nevertheless, I think you'll make a suitable successor," said Paul Draper.

"But I'm not a member of the Surrey Branch. I'm not even a Party member."

"We can get round that; you'll have to join the Party, of course. But with your Military Cross and a character reference from me, that will be a formality and we'll be able to parachute you straight in as chairman."

Andy wondered why Paul Draper wanted him to take up the post. After all, it was common knowledge at the *Daily Citizen* that Andy cut quite a non-political figure. *Was it the prestige of the Darent brothers' scoop? Or, more likely, having won a Military Cross?* That was part of it, but there was another reason, Andy concluded. It was precisely because he was apolitical that Paul Draper thought he could remain the power behind the throne and easily manipulate Andy.

"Well, I'm not sure," said Andy.

"Think about it," said Paul Draper.

"That's enough talk of politics," said Louise Draper. "Let's go and see our holiday photos."

"Yes, let's," conceded Paul Draper.

Alice made a face and Andy quickly grinned back when the Drapers weren't looking. He too wasn't looking forward to the ordeal of being showed someone's holiday photographs.

They all moved to the lounge, where a colour television was still on, showing *Come Dancing*.

"Bruce Forsyth looks so much better in colour," said Louise Draper, before switching the TV off.

Andy was sure the box had been left on just to show him that the Drapers were the owners of a colour television. Colour TV had only been introduced at the beginning of the year, and a set would cost Andy three months' salary. Furthermore, colour sets could only be bought by Party members. This was in contrast with black and white sets that cost a tenth of the colour price and were available to everyone. Andy surmised these were subsidised by the Government so that the whole population could listen to The Leader's speeches in the comfort of their own homes.

Paul Draper offered his guests generous measures of Glenfiddich then set up a slide projector and screen. He gave a little cough when he was ready.

"Last year, just before Christmas, we went for a week's holiday to the Petschoragau region of Northern Germany," said Paul Draper. "In fact, the trip was organised by the Surrey Young Fascists. We stayed in a lovely lodge in the middle of a huge forest." He then showed a few slides of the interior and exterior of the chalet.

"It was very cold; so cold that if you poured a glass of water from your balcony, it would freeze before reaching the ground," said Louise Draper. "And because it's so far north, near the Arctic Circle in fact, the days were very short. But it really was a beautiful winter scene with all the snow, just as it should be at Christmas."

"We went on a sleigh ride one day," said Paul Draper, clicking through photos of the expedition. "As you can see, our sleighs were pulled by reindeer. And here you can see us standing by a brazier in a forest clearing, drinking mulled wine." A few more clicks. "And here we have our meeting with Santa."

Alice yawned and Andy tried hard to suppress a grin. He felt there was something almost subversive in his and Alice's behaviour.

"We all got presents, not just the children," said Louise Draper.

"Often at night, we would have a good view of the Northern Lights," said Paul Draper. He clicked through a series of photos of the night sky; the Northern Lights took the shape of arc-like wisps, vertical streaks, waves or halos. The colours of the lights varied; they could be green, red, violet or yellow. Andy was impressed.

"And here are some of our youngsters cross-country skiing with a group of Hitler Youth," said Paul Draper. "Note the black armbands they are all wearing; Adolf Hitler had died just four weeks earlier.

"On another day, we visited what is officially the coldest place in Europe," Paul Draper continued, clicking through the slides all the while. "There's a monument and a small museum. Inside the museum, there's a café that is actually inside a freezer."

"What does that sign say? That's in German, isn't it?" said Alice, trying to sound interested.

"Yes, I'll translate it for you," said Paul Draper. "It reads: *Escape the cold and come into our cosy, warm, little freezer for a drink*. The temperature inside the freezer was minus 20 and it was minus 35 outside on the day we were there, so it was a lot warmer in the cooler."

Alice was on the point of yawning again so Andy gave her a gentle poke in the ribs.

"On our final day," Paul Draper continued, "we visited the Gulag museum in Eichmannstadt, the main town in the area. Before the Germans liberated the region, it was part of Bolshevik Russia and the centre of a complex of slave labour camps known as the Gulag. The museum is actually a former camp built next to a coal mine."

"We were shocked at the descriptions of conditions there," said Louise Draper. "It's just as well we saw the place on our last day; it would have soured the mood of our holiday if we had seen it at the start of our trip."

"Yes, it's truly shocking what the Judeo-Bolshevik regime got up to," said Paul Draper. "You know, there's something satisfying about Hitler's decision to create a Jewish homeland in the Petschoragau. It's quite fitting that the Jews should be resettled to the scene of one of their crimes, as it were."

"Did you manage to visit a Jewish reservation?" asked Andy.

"No," said Paul Draper. "The Jews seem to run their enclaves as mini Soviet states. To visit one of these places, you first need an invitation from a resident. Then you need to be vaccinated against a whole host of diseases. Finally, you need to apply for a permit at the reservations office in Eichmannstadt. It takes about six weeks for the permit to come through."

"I've never heard of anyone who's visited one of these reservations," said Andy.

"I've never heard of anyone who'd want to," replied Paul Draper, icily.

Andy thought these Jewish areas didn't exist. He wondered about his boss's position: *Did Paul Draper really believe that the reservations existed, or did he just pretend to believe in them?*

The slideshow over, Paul Draper topped up his guests' glasses with whisky.

"Tell us about some of the crimes you've come across," said Louise Draper. "Any juicy murders?"

"Well, there've been four murders recently, which I think are all linked," said Andy. "The victims are fit men in their 20s who have been shot in the back of the head, gangster style. No identification was found on them, nor have the police been able to name them since. What's also puzzling, and further links the cases, is that all the victims had been whipped, but there was no other evidence of beatings or torture."

"Maybe they all liked to visit a dominatrix," said Louise Draper.

"What, a lady who canes or whips you for a fee?" said Andy. "I thought that sort of thing wasn't allowed."

"Not at all," said Paul Draper. "Although prostitution is illegal, dominatrices are free to do business. The Leader's view is that regular physical chastisement is good for character building. It's believed that, even at the age of seventy-six, he starts each day with six of the best."

Louise Draper yawned, from tiredness rather than boredom, Andy supposed. He looked at his watch; it was past 11 – time to go. Because he knew there would be a fair amount of booze on offer, Andy had taken the train with Alice rather than drive. Random breathalyser tests had been introduced a few years earlier and the penalties were severe. Anything more than the equivalent of half a pint of weak beer resulted in a minimum of 12 months' imprisonment.

Alice had checked the time of the last train, a quarter-to 12, so the pre-booked taxi arrived just before half-past

11. Curfew started an hour later, at one, on a Saturday night, so they had plenty of time to get home.

"What a dreadful couple," said Alice as soon as they got into the taxi.

"Oh I don't know," said Andy, "I suppose they were trying to be friendly, in their own way."

"If you say so, future Young Fascist chairman." Alice slipped her arm through his.

They arrived at the station just five minutes later, only to find the last train had been at a quarter-past 11. The taxi driver was still talking on his radio so hadn't driven away, but he wasn't prepared to take them all the way to London. It was the end of his shift and it was just too far. He was ready to drive them to Guildford, just a few miles away, where they were sure to find a hotel for the night. They took up his offer and ended up at the Wey View hotel.

"You're in luck, we've just one room left," said the receptionist, a middle-aged lady with a Dusty Springfield beehive hair-do. "A double bed with en-suite toilet and shower."

Andy realised they had no other choice. He looked at Alice; she nodded. "We'll take it," he said.

"Could I have your passport or identity card please?" Beehive asked. Andy complied and his details were checked. "Your identification too, please, Mrs Deegan."

"Actually, I'm Alice Greengrass." She handed over her passport.

"Oh, we may have a problem," said Beehive. "We don't approve of any funny business in our hotel."

"We're reporters, here in Guildford as part of our work," said Andy, showing his journalist card. "We're used to roughing it regarding accommodation."

"There's nothing rough about my hotel, Mr Deegan." Her tone was still suspicious.

"My boss is Mr Draper, member of Parliament and chairman of the Surrey Young Fascists. Here's his phone number, you can check with him."

Beehive pondered for a moment then her demeanour changed. "That won't be necessary," she said, handing him the keys. "It's room eight on the first floor. Have a pleasant stay."

Beehive's summary of a double bed with en-suite toilet and shower was an almost full description of the room. There was little furniture, apart from a Queen-size bed and a wardrobe. But the room was clean and they had been provided with two towels. There was a smug air about Alice; Andy wondered if all this had been engineered, that Alice had known all along that the last train ran at a quarter-past 11 and not a quarter-to 12.

"Is it OK if I use the shower now?" asked Alice.

"Go ahead."

Alice locked herself in the bathroom, and there was quiet for a few minutes. The door opened and Alice stepped into the bedroom, stark naked. "Andy, I can't get the shower to work. Can you help?"

Chapter 15

"What are you thinking about? You're grinning like a Cheshire Cat," said Alice. She and Andy were on the train heading back to London.

"Just looking forward to a relaxing Sunday; it's nice to have the day off," Andy lied. It was the image of a naked Alice straddling him the previous night that was on his mind. It was his ego that was also on a high: he could still bed a 21-year-old.

"So how will you spend your day?" said Alice.

"There are always jobs that need doing around the house or garden. Then I'll take the children to the park. If there's time, I'll relax, listening to some music."

"What kind of music do you like?"

"Mostly classical stuff such as Mozart or Wagner. But I do like popular music as well. Jane and I both like Val Doonican and often watch his TV show."

"My dad likes Val Doonican," said Alice.

Ouch, thought Andy, and mentally flinched. He didn't need Alice to remind him that at 38, he was just about old enough to be her father.

"What type of music do you like?" asked Andy.

"Rhythm and blues. My favourite band is The Rolling Stones."

"Never heard of them." Andy did know that blues with its American Negro origins was disapproved of by the authorities and could not be played in public.

"That's not surprising," said Alice. "They're an illegal group."

Andy turned his head in all directions to see if there was anyone else in the carriage. He knew this was not the sort of conversation to have in public.

"If they're illegal, how do you get to listen to their music?"

"The way illegals work is like this," said Alice. "You get a phone call about nine o'clock on a Saturday evening about a performance that's about to start at a place near you in just an hour's time. You then telephone one or two of your trusted friends and spread the news. The show only lasts half an hour, so that if neighbours report the event, by the time the police or Blackshirts have arrived at the scene, it's all over and the performers have left. Most illegal bands only last a year or two because they get caught in the end and get sent off to labour camps. But The Rolling Stones have been going for over six years."

"How come they've lasted that long?"

"A couple of reasons. First, they're very good on logistics. The band members all arrive separately at the chosen locale, as does their equipment, such as guitars and drums. But they also play in the nicer parts of South London, where a lot of Blackshirt officers have their homes. And when these Blackshirts go to a Wagner or Val Doonican concert on a Saturday evening, their sons or daughters invite The Rolling Stones to play in their homes. Of course, the neighbours would be far too scared to report a Blackshirt to the authorities."

Andy was going to object at the connotation that being a Wagner or Val Doonican fan made you a Fascist supporter, but he let it pass. It seemed to him that people like Alice were losing their fear of the authorities. The whole system of Government was based on fear and if people were no longer afraid then the Government's grip on power would weaken. He wondered if there was a generational aspect to this; older property-owning citizens were afraid to report a Blackshirt, whereas youngsters like Alice had not only no qualms about attending illegal concerts, but were also prepared to talk about it. Although maybe after last night, Alice had placed Andy in the category of "trusted friend".

Just who are you kidding? Pulling a 21-year-old?

It had been Alice who pulled Andy. But was it the real Andy Deegan she was after? Or was it the hero Andrew Deegan MC? If so, it was one more case of getting something under false pretences. Andy's euphoria diminished a bit.

The euphoria ebbed away completely as he contemplated the consequences of the previous night. He was sure there would be repercussions. There was no free lunch. That's what Paul Draper always drilled into his staff in the context of their professional activities. Reporters often entertained their contacts, but the expectation was that they would get a lead or story in return. There would be no free lunch as far as last night's tryst was concerned either.

He didn't think Jane would find out; he had phoned her the night before to let her know he'd missed the last train. But she didn't know that Alice had been invited to the dinner. There was hardly any social contact between Jane and the Drapers so she wouldn't learn anything from them. There was no reason for Jane to be suspicious; this was the first time in their marriage that he had strayed. He began to feel just a bit uncomfortable about that; would he experience more guilt with time or would he forget the whole business?

He thought there might be ramifications at the office. Working with Alice might get complicated, or his own prospects might be damaged if the boss found out; Paul Draper didn't countenance any "hanky panky" among members of his staff.

*

On Monday, Andy was back at the office, going through the yellow pages of telephone directories and making a list of dominatrices to question. He spent less than an hour on this when Paul Draper burst into the room, brandishing a newspaper and looking furious.

"Have you seen this?" he said, thrusting the paper on Andy's desk.

It was an article in *The Globe* about Mrs Fox. She didn't know where the *Daily Citizen* had got the story that her husband John was missing. He was a travelling salesman who often spent weeks away from home on business. There was a picture of Mr and Mrs Fox, both with broad smiles; the husband didn't have the least resemblance to Andy's photo of John Fox or any other of the evangelists.

"This makes us look like idiots," said Paul Draper. "You're to immediately drop all work on those murders. You can write about the Newfoundland visit, as well as continuing with the Munich Olympics series." He then stormed out of the room.

As soon as Paul Draper left, Andy picked up the phone and dialled Mrs Fox's Kingston number; it was disconnected. He tried the Esher number and got an invalid number message. He then phoned Detective Superintendent Reidford, who'd provided him with

Mrs Fox's name in the first place; he was told he was unavailable.

Andy was almost as angry with himself as with Mrs Fox and Superintendent Reidford. He had been taken in too easily. Mrs Fox had divulged nothing about herself at all. Her flat had revealed nothing; her belongings had all too conveniently been packed away in boxes. Andy should have insisted that Mrs Fox show a photo of her supposedly missing husband. He had been taken in by her very convincing act of a distraught wife.

"Bad day at the office?" said Jane, as soon as Andy was over the doorstep. Andy thought he could hide his feelings from most people but not from Jane.

"You can say that again."

He then told Jane all about how he had been set up by Detective Superintendent Reidford and a Mrs Fox.

"Obviously, the authorities don't want you looking into these murders," said Jane. "You're probably getting in their way."

"Or could I be getting close to uncovering something the establishment wants hidden?" said Andy.

"Oh, I forgot to mention," said Jane after a pause. "The Wey View hotel in Guildford phoned earlier. You left your scarf behind when you stayed the other night."

CHAPTER 16

Charlotte was wearing her school uniform, although it was a quarter of a century since she'd left Chelsea Ladies' College. She also had a nurse's, Girl Guide's and secretary's outfit in her wardrobe. In fact, she had nearly 20 costumes; a police woman's and Blackshirt's were the only uniforms she could think of that she didn't have. Her client, Roger, a man of about her own age, was tied naked to a Saint Andrew's Cross. It was a classic role reversal game, a teacher being punished by one of his pupils; one she'd played many times before, and not just with Roger.

She picked up a bullwhip and lightly brushed it against Roger's back. His body started quivering; anticipation was just as important as the punishment itself. This was the climax of the session and she was now on a high that would last until her next client. Roger was quite an attractive man; he had a nice, firm bum. At least, he had an hour before; since then, it had been at the receiving end of a paddle, cane, riding crop and cat of nine tails. After the bullwhip, his backside would be a bloody mess, bearing little resemblance to what it looked like when he'd arrived.

"We'll finish with 20 lashes. You'll count each stroke." Charlotte paused for a few seconds then delivered the first blow.

Roger screamed then managed to blurt out, "One. Thank you, mistress."

Charlotte continued with the punishment, Roger's yells getting louder; after the twelfth stroke, the screams got fainter and were more like whimpers. After the nineteenth lash, Roger was reduced to whispering.

"I didn't hear that," said Charlotte. "We'll have to start all over again."

Charlotte meted out another 20 strokes then untied Roger. As he crawled towards the corner of the room where he had left his clothes, Charlotte gave him a kick in the backside. "If you misbehave again, you'll get detention."

Roger left; Charlotte had another half hour before her next client, a new punter by the name of Sam. He hadn't specified any uniform, so she changed into her leather gear. She lit a cigarette, put on a cassette of *Nessun Dorma* and sat back on the sofa; right now, she was overwhelmed with bliss.

*

Andy parked just outside Chastisers, the seventh S&M establishment on his list. This one, in the centre of Slough, had a reception area with a couple of sofas and a well-dressed, middle-aged lady behind a desk. Andy explained he was a journalist and wanted just a couple of minutes with the dominatrices. Andy showed the receptionist the evangelist photos, but she didn't recognise any of them.

"Usually, we have two mistresses in residence," said the lady. "Denise's got a cold, but Charlotte is in and I think she's free." She made a quick phone call then said, "You can see her now. She's on the first floor, second door on the right."

As he headed up, Andy wondered if this S&M scene was something he should try with Jane. If she found out about Alice, she would be more than happy to give him a good caning, he reckoned. He knocked on the door and entered.

The chamber was the size of a sitting room, with padded walls of red leather pouches. It was dimly lit, but Andy could make out a St Andrew's Cross at one end, flanked by a cage on one side and stocks on the other. Alongside another wall was what looked like a dentist's chair, but with restraints for the occupant's hands and feet. Next to the chair was a bench of the sort Andy used in the gym for sit-ups or tricep dips, although he was sure that wasn't its purpose here. From the middle of the ceiling hung a set of chains, and on shelves and racks throughout the room were cuffs, spiked collars and dozens of canes and whips of different sizes.

In the middle of the room stood a woman, about an inch taller than Andy. She was about 40 with long black hair and dressed in a tight-fitting leather miniskirt and thigh-high boots. She stretched out her hand. "Mr Deegan, how can I help you? I've a client arriving shortly, so I can only spare you a few minutes." Her voice had a pleasant tone and her body language was calm and reassuring; Andy had been expecting her to be more strident, barking out commands.

Andy gave her a bit of background before showing the photographs; she looked at each for a few seconds and shook her head. Then she came to Mark's photo and took a longer, closer look; her eyes narrowed then widened. She bit her lip and looked puzzled; Andy was sure she'd recognised Mark. Her expression changed to neutral as she handed back the photos.

"No, I haven't seen any of these men before. I'm quite sure. Sorry I haven't been able to help you."

Andy had the feeling she was lying; nevertheless, he thanked her and left. He returned to his car from where he had a good view of Chastisers' entrance. A nervous-looking man in his 50s entered then left after an hour. Ten minutes later, a taxi drew up by the entrance and Charlotte got in. She was wearing slacks and an overcoat but Andy was quite sure it was her.

Quite spontaneously, Andy decided to follow the taxi. It was nearly 10 o'clock and at that time, there wasn't too much congestion so he could easily tail it. There was just enough traffic so that it wasn't obvious that he was following the cab. They drove through the suburbs, with Andy about 200 yards behind. The taxi just passed a pedestrian crossing when the lights turned red; Andy would have driven through, but there was a Vauxhall Victor between Andy and the taxi, which decided to stop. The cab took the first turning left, so was now out of sight. As soon as the lights turned green the Victor stalled so by the time Andy got moving he was worried he might have lost the taxi completely.

The left turning was Kilmorey Close, a no-through road. He soon spotted the taxi at the far end of the close; it performed a U-turn and headed back towards Andy. He drove on to where the cab had stopped but there was no sign of Charlotte. He reckoned there were three or four houses that Charlotte could have entered; all were lit up inside so he couldn't narrow down her address any further. Andy waited on the off chance Charlotte might pop out again; after half an hour, he gave up and drove home.

*

Charlotte closed the door and stepped into the lounge; Lucy was sitting watching TV with a mug of tea in her hand. She was an out of work actress; frankly, Charlotte didn't think much of Lucy's acting abilities, but she could sing like an angel.

"Good day?" asked Lucy. "Fancy a cuppa?"

"Not bad. I'll skip the tea, thanks. I'll have a bath and make it an early night." Charlotte went upstairs, ran a bath, stepped in, and tried to relax. She had had a good day, at least until Mr Deegan turned up. She wondered how she should handle that. She'd been about five minutes in the tub when Lucy, naked, walked in. She held a bottle of champagne in one hand and two glasses in the other.

"Mind if I join you?" Without waiting for an answer, she stepped into the bath. She was a head shorter than Charlotte, with a slim build and firm breasts that Charlotte liked to nibble. "You didn't ask me how my day was."

"I didn't; something at work *did* crop up that's bothering me, that's why," said Charlotte. "Anyway, how *was* your day?"

"I've just got my big break," said Lucy. "I got offered the part of Eva Braun in a new musical, *Adolf Hitler, Superstar*. We start rehearsals next week."

"A musical about Hitler? Sounds controversial; surely, the authorities won't allow it."

"The censors have seen the script and passed it, with a few amendments here and there. The whole tone is very respectful, starting with Hitler's struggles as an artist in Vienna and ending with him unifying Europe. A lot of the music is similar to the *Merry Widow*, Hitler's favourite operetta, so that helped. Of course, the censors will want to take another look at a full dress rehearsal before we go into preview. But it will happen; fame at last."

"Lucy, that's wonderful. That deserves a celebration."

Chapter 17

On a Sunday afternoon, Sally took Mary to listen to a Salvation Army brass band, playing in Hackney Downs. Sally had by now found out a little about Mary: she was a middle-class Londoner who could speak French, but didn't like science. But otherwise, there was no progress in discovering Mary's identity. Sally had phoned more David Browns without success. Nothing had been found in the Salvation Army missing persons file. That was a bit odd; the Salvationists' Missing Persons service was used far more than Scotland Yard's equivalent. Political opponents of the Government frequently disappeared, but relatives and friends were wary of reporting such disappearances to the police for fear of bringing the authorities' attention to themselves. Instead, they would come to the Salvation Army; even if there was little reason to believe the missing person was a political dissident, the relative would still play it safe and report the disappearance to them rather than the police.

Sally had come to regard Mary as more of a friend than a little sister. They both liked watching *Coronation Street*, even though Mary could still not recall any of the earlier episodes. Mary enjoyed the fundraising activities, and was happy to chip in with the chores at the Mile End hostel. Sally, for a moment, thought that Mary might have been a Salvation Army officer before she lost her memory, but that was absurd, as her fellow Salvationists would have immediately reported her missing.

While the band played, Sally and Mary mingled among the spectators, collection boxes in hand. After an hour, the Salvationists were chased away by a rival Blackshirt band, despite having booked the bandstand for the whole afternoon.

A funfair in the northern corner of the park was attracting a lot of custom, so they headed there. Sally was upset about losing the bandstand, but her mood lightened when they were let in; not all funfairs were keen on Salvation Army personnel fundraising on site. Mary started handing out copies of *The War Cry* while Sally accepted donations. It was the noise that assaulted them; children laughing and shrieking, and the music from the rides clashing to form a jarring sound. The first stall they came across was a ball in the bucket stand. For a shilling, you could throw three tennis balls into a bucket, positioned about 10 feet away; the bucket was placed horizontally so a ball thrown too hard would bounce out. If one or more balls stayed in the bucket, the prize was a teddy bear or other furry animal. Sally didn't approve of this sort of gambling, for that was what it amounted to, but she lingered anyway. There was always the chance a winner might make an extra-large contribution to her collection box.

The warm, sunny weather had brought in the crowds; Sally's collection box was soon half-full.

In the centre of the fair were a number of carousels, all catering for three to five-year-olds. One had a mixture of fire engines, buses and ambulances. A second had swans, a third, open cockpit aeroplanes. A fourth had spinning teacups, in which the children sat, with a teapot in the centre. Mary seemed to be enjoying herself just watching the little ones have fun. Sally thought there was just a chance the funfair might trigger some childhood memory in Mary, but so far, there was no response.

Next to the carousels was a dodgem car attraction, popular with older children. They wandered over to the far side of the funfair, gingerly stepping over heavy power cables snaking across the grass, then passing the ghost train, helter-skelter and big dipper. The last was popular with grown-ups as well as children, but both Sally and Mary felt they were too old for that. Still, the sunshine and the sight of happy funfair-goers put them in a good mood and made them forget the business with the Blackshirts at the bandstand.

It was quieter around the doughnut and candyfloss stalls, but neither Sally nor Mary were tempted by the sweet and sticky smells. Behind were two tents, the smaller one a fortune-teller, the larger, a hypnotist stage show. Outside was a poster displaying:

> *The Amazing Abra Cadabra*
> *Conquer Your Phobias*
> *Grown-ups, Relive Your Childhood Memories*
> *Hypnosis Shows Every Hour on the Hour*

"Are you thinking what I'm thinking?" said Mary.

"What, seeing if hypnosis can bring back your memory?" said Sally. "I'm not sure if I believe in this sort of thing, but I suppose we could go in and see if this Abra Cadabra is any good."

They paid their shillings, entered and took their seats; the show was just beginning.

"Does anyone here have a fear of spiders?" asked Abra Cadabra. The man wore a black suit, studded with silver sequins, and his dark hair was brushed back, just reaching his collar and covering his ears; there was something of the spiv about him, Sally thought.

Half the audience put their hands up and the hypnotist picked a 12-year-old girl from the middle of the third row. She stepped up onto the stage and sat in a chair facing the audience.

"What's your name?" said the hypnotist.

"Rosie," said the girl.

"Well, Rosie, how afraid are you of spiders?"

"I'm really scared of them. I won't go into the bathroom if there's a spider inside. Mum will have to remove it first."

"Do you like picnics, Rosie?"

"Yes."

"Well, you're going on a picnic and when I snap my fingers and say 'Abracadabra', you'll be back here in the fairground." The hypnotist pulled out a chained gold watch out of his pocket and let it swing like a pendulum a few inches away from Rosie's face.

"Now, Rosie, just keep looking at the watch and relax but keep your eyes open all the time. You're leaving this tent and you're going to walk out of the fairground and follow a path across the park. You keep on the path as it winds through some woods until you get to a clearing where you decide to have your picnic. Now, Rosie, I'd like you to stretch out your arm with your palm face up."

Rosie complied.

"Rosie, do you have a pet?" asked the hypnotist.

"Yes, a kitten."

"What's its name?"

"Sooty."

"Well, you're having your picnic with Sooty and a fly starts bothering your kitten. Then a spider arrives and chases the fly away. You have your picnic in peace now. Are you glad the spider chased the fly away?"

"Yes," said Rosie.

"Is the spider a nice spider?"

"Yes."

The hypnotist walked to the side of the stage and picked up a jar from a stand. He went back to the girl and took out a wolf spider from the jar, placing it on her palm. There was no reaction from Rosie; she seemed just as relaxed as before.

"Now, Rosie, you've finished your picnic and it's time to go home." The hypnotist snapped his fingers and said, "Abracadabra."

For a few seconds, the girl didn't react, then she looked at her palm and saw the spider. Her eyes widened and she gave a piercing scream. The hypnotist quickly put the spider back in the jar.

The show over, the audience left the tent, impressed with the performance. Sally and Mary walked over to the stage where the hypnotist was clearing up.

"Mr Cadabra," said Sally, "I'm Mrs Hawkins. The poster outside has 'Relive your Childhood Memories'. Does that mean you can bring back memories you've forgotten?"

"Indeed it does, madam. Indeed it does. One of my acts has adults recalling something naughty they did as children. When they come out of hypnosis, they admit they actually committed the naughty deed they had quite forgotten about."

"So, would it be possible to recall exactly what my friend, Miss Brown, did the day before she met me?" asked Sally.

"Of course," said the hypnotist.

At that moment, a curtain behind the stage was pulled open and a girl's head appeared.

"Dad, can I have my ice cream now?" It was Rosie.

"Mr Cadabra," said Sally, "we've all been taken in by you; you're no hypnotist. You're a fraud, although I must admit your daughter is a very good actress. We'd better be going, Mary. I shall report this to the fairground management."

"Please don't do that," said the hypnotist, putting a hand on Sally's sleeve. "I am a qualified hypnotist. It's just that on stage in front of a large audience, a subject is rarely relaxed enough to get into a trance. Let me refund your entry fee and give you a demonstration of what I can do. Gratis, of course."

The hypnotist put two shillings in Sally's collection box.

"The Salvation Army is always willing to accept donations," said Sally, giving the collection box a shake.

"Of course." The hypnotist coughed and put a 10-shilling note in the box.

Mary then took her place on the stage chair while the hypnotist gave Rosie sixpence for her ice cream.

"Please relax as if you're going to sleep, but keep your eyes open." The hypnotist took out his gold watch.

"Take slow, deep breaths and keep looking at the watch." He stood four feet in front of Mary and slowly swung the timepiece like a pendulum.

"Miss Brown, you're going to leave this tent and go on the helter-skelter next door. It's a bit of a climb to the top but take it nice and slowly. You're on the top now; take a mat and let yourself go down the slide. This is no ordinary helter-skelter; it's a time machine. Each turn round the helter-skelter takes you back in time. So you go round and round until you reach the bottom. You land with a bit of a bump and when you get up, you realise it's the day before you met Mrs Hawkins. Tell us what you did that day."

"I woke up at Victoria Station," said Mary. "I walked to Hackney, but I couldn't find my home. I tried sleeping in a park but I was chased off by a warden, then I moved on to the Mile End hostel where next morning I met Sally."

Sally realised that she hadn't asked the right question to the hypnotist. Mary lost her memory not the day before meeting her but the day before that. "Can we go back a day more, Mr Cadabra? It's that day Miss Brown is a little forgetful about."

"If you insist," said the hypnotist. He continued in his somnolent voice. "Miss Brown, you love the helter-skelter so much you want to have another go. You climb up the stairs but this time, you stop at the first level. You take a mat and slide down. It's now a day earlier. What did you do that day?"

Mary said nothing. Then the pupils of her eyes expanded and her Adam's apple started throbbing. "I'm walking," Mary finally said. "No, I'm running."

"Why are you running, Miss Brown?" said the hypnotist.

"I'm running away from people who want to harm me."

"Where are you running from?"

"I don't know. A building of some kind, I think."

"Where are you running to?"

"I don't know."

"A police station perhaps, seeing as bad people are chasing you?"

"No, not the police." Mary seemed to be even more agitated.

"Why not?"

"Because it's the police who are after me," said Mary.

"I think we had better end it there," said the hypnotist. He snapped his fingers and said, "Abracadabra."

CHAPTER 18

Early the next morning, Andy drove down to Kilmorey Close in Slough. He parked his car about a hundred yards from the end of the road and kept a watch on the half-dozen houses he thought Charlotte could have entered the night before. It was an attractive area in the northern suburbs of Slough; an estate agent might call it South Stoke Poges, Andy supposed. The houses were all detached mock-Tudors; clearly, Charlotte did well out of her chosen profession. Any one of numbers one to eight could be her address. Around seven o'clock, a door opened and a middle-aged man in a business suit stepped outside, turned and waved back at the opened door before getting into a Mini Cooper and driving off. Andy wrote down the house number, seven, in his notebook; he probably could rule this one out. Of course, it was possible that the man had been waving to Charlotte who had remained inside. By nine o'clock, apart from numbers six and four, at least one occupant had left each one of the houses under surveillance; two of these were women, neither of whom resembled Charlotte. By this time, it was more than half an hour after anyone had left home so Andy decided to give up and drive to work. He was about to start the car when a post van arrived and a postman got out, holding a bunch of letters. Andy got out and, showing his journalist card, told the postman he wanted to know the names of people living there for a newspaper article he was writing. Showing his identity card worked, as it often did, carrying almost as much authority as a police pass. There were letters for numbers one, two, five, seven and eight. Andy made a note of the names and drove off.

Back at the office, with the aid of a directory, Andy worked through his list of names and called each one. Three answered, all women, but none was called or even sounded like Charlotte. After lunch, he phoned Chastisers, only to find that Charlotte wasn't coming in that day. Andy didn't want to push his luck after the previous day's warning from Paul Draper, so he started to write his piece about the Newfoundland visit.

The Canadian ship, Newfoundland, was due to make a goodwill visit to Britain the following month, with ports of call at Plymouth, Portsmouth and London. The plan was to invite a senior British naval officer at each of the first two ports to travel as a guest to the next. But it was the history of CS Newfoundland that was interesting; it was a shame the censors would not like it.

The ship had started life as the British *HMS Belfast* and, in 1940, was refitting in England so was not able to sail when Winston Churchill, in one of his last acts as Prime Minister, ordered the entire British Fleet to move to Canada. Consequently, *HMS Belfast* was one of the few ships that Britain was allowed to keep. By 1943, Britain had become a Fascist country and in that year, the ship set sail for South Africa, a Fascist ally. In the course of the voyage, the crew mutinied, seized control of the ship and sailed instead to the nearest Free British territory, Trinidad in the Caribbean, where it joined Churchill's Free British forces.

Churchill had, in 1940, set up a government-in-exile, the Free British, headquartered in Canada and recognised by both the Canadian and United States governments. Initially, the only territory controlled by

Free Britain was a few islands of the British West Indies in the Caribbean, whose governors had declared loyalty to Churchill. But by the end of 1941, Free British forces had occupied those remaining islands in the British West Indies, who had earlier declared for Mosley. Although the Free British Army and Air Force was fairly small, its Navy was one of the largest in the world, as the majority of the British Navy had made it to Canada in 1940. The Free British Navy, at the time of the *HMS Belfast* mutiny in 1943, was engaged in the Pacific, fighting alongside its allies, the United States, Canada and Australia, against the Japanese. Consequently, in 1944 and 1945, HMS Belfast took part in several battles in the South Pacific until, in 1945, Japan surrendered after the United Sates dropped two atomic bombs on its cities.

The United States had never declared war on Nazi Germany and when, in 1946, Germany exploded its atomic bomb, a nuclear stalemate resulted the start of the so-called Cold War. From 1947, Free Britain started selling off its ships. Because of its prestige, *HMS Belfast* was the last ship bigger than a frigate to go; sold to the Canadians in 1956. They renamed the ship *CS Newfoundland*.

Andy wondered how much, if any, he could write about this history. He was safer with the last few years, starting in 1969. In that year, US President Richard Nixon made his famous "I'm a Berliner" speech in the German capital, signalling the thawing of relations between the New World and Europe. By 1972, relations between Canada and Fascist Britain had improved to the extent that this goodwill visit by *CS Newfoundland* was now possible.

By lunchtime, he had written enough for a half-page spread.

In the afternoon, Andy had an idea. When he got home that evening, he would first fill Jane in on the latest of his investigations into the four evangelists, then he would ask her to telephone the five Kilmorey Close numbers he had. Jane would request to interview the lady of the house for an article that would appear in the *Daily Citizen*, regarding living in Slough from a woman's point of view. If she got the interview, she would take a photograph of her subject to appear in the paper and ask about any female lodgers matching Charlotte's description.

*

After Jane had dropped the children off at school, she went shopping , cleaned up around the house, made herself a small salad then sat down to write her article. Although, as a married woman, she was banned from most full-time employment, she was able to do occasional freelance work for a number of magazines. This time, she was writing a feature on Ancient Egyptian jewellery for *The Lady*; the Tutankhamen exhibition had set off a craze for all things Egyptian. She had finished her first draft then switched on the TV to see a programme about the Pharaohs; she thought it might provide more material for her article.

It was The Leader again; he obviously was aware how popular the Tutankhamen fad was. He explained how the roots of Fascist civilisation went back to Ancient Egypt. There were a few wrong turns along the way, such as the Ancient Greeks' experiment with democracy, and the two centuries following the so-called enlightenment. But that apart, civilisation was on continuous upward trajectory, culminating in the Fascist world of today. The schools, hospitals and motorways are the modern equivalents of the pyramids. The Leader's broadcast lasted only a few minutes but it meant the following documentary was abruptly cut short so as not to disrupt subsequent schedules.

The programme had just finished when the phone rang.

"Is that Mrs Deegan?"

"Yes, who's calling?"

"That's not important. Let's just say a concerned parent. I just wanted to say how sorry I am about your son Harry's injury at school today." The caller immediately put the phone down.

Straight away, Jane phoned London Road Primary and got through to the headmistress. "Miss Miller, this is Jane Deegan. What's happened to Harry?"

"What are you talking about?" said Miss Miller. "Nothing has happened to Harry; he's in his geography class right now."

"He hasn't been hurt in any way?"

"Of course not."

"When was the last time you saw him?"

"At assembly. Mrs Deegan, I don't like your tone. You are not a member of His Majesty's Police."

"Could you check how he is now? I've just had an anonymous telephone call claiming Harry has been hurt. It could be a hoax of course, but I think it's best to check. Please."

Miss Miller let out an audible sigh, "Very well, if you insist." Jane heard her slam the phone on her desk and the sound of her footsteps as she stormed out of the room. The footsteps faded, there was silence for a couple of minutes, and then the footsteps got louder again. "Mrs Deegan, Harry is fine; I've just seen him face to face. Now if you excuse me, I have important work to do."

The relief Jane felt lasted only a few minutes. The phone call seems to have been from a crank, but this crank knew her son was called Harry and had gone to the trouble of finding out her telephone number.

Heavy traffic caused Jane to arrive at London Road Primary 10 minutes later than usual. Miss Miller was waiting by the entrance. "Harry's had a slight injury. He's in the sick bay; this way." Jane followed her upstairs and was shown to a small room where Harry was drinking orange juice and reading a copy of *Dandy*. He had a one-inch cut on his cheek, which was the centre of a much larger bruise.

"When did this happen?" asked Jane.

"At playtime, after you'd phoned," said Miss Miller. "One of the boys threw a stone at Harry."

"Did you see who it was, Harry?" said Jane. Harry shook his head.

"None of the boys admitted guilt," said Miss Miller. "So they've all been given an hour's detention. If no one still confesses then they will all receive a caning until the culprit owns up."

"That won't be necessary, Miss Miller," said Jane.

"You are not a school inspector, Mrs Deegan. That being so, may I remind you that I am responsible for classroom discipline."

"Could you show me where it happened?"

Miss Miller took Jane to the playground. School buildings surrounded three sides, but the fourth bordered on Northumberland Park, separated by a five-foot high fence. Someone standing on the park side of the fence could easily have taken a shot at Harry with a catapult, say.

As soon as she got home, Jane phoned Andy and told him about Harry. Andy would come over straight away. Jane and the children were still waiting for Andy when the phone rang.

"Good evening, Mrs Deegan, this is Concerned Parent speaking. Please tell your husband to keep his nose out of police matters. I wouldn't want Harry to come to more serious harm, or Jenny and Karen for that matter."

"What's going on, Andy?" said Jane the moment he was through the door. She repeated the details of the anonymous telephone calls and Harry's injury.

"After DCI Armstrong's warning the other week," said Andy, "I've been very careful not to do anything that could be construed as interference. The only time I broke that rule was when I arrived in Windsor Great Park where the last two bodies had been discovered. But that was because I got tipped off by Ascot Police, who didn't know I was persona non grata. Armstrong arrived a few minutes later and chased me off the scene. I suppose that must have been the trigger for this latest threat."

"Look Andy, this has got to stop. It's one thing sticking your own neck out, but quite another endangering your own children. Are these four nobodies really worth it?"

"Of course, Jane, you're right. I'll drop this business right away. They crossed a line with what they did to Harry."

"Do you promise?"

"Of course."

"Because I know you, Andy. You'll stop for a day or two then your curiosity will get the better of you."

"Don't you think I'm just as upset about Harry as you are?"

"If you do go back to the case and there's the slightest threat to the children, I'll take them out of school and move in with Mum and Dad."

Chapter 19

Andy wondered if he should drop his investigations altogether. It looked like the police were involved with the murders in some way. If this involvement was with the regime's backing then not only would Andy get nowhere but he could get into serious danger. If the police were acting in some way against the regime, did Andy really want to be the one to have saved the Government from a police conspiracy?

For a whole day, Andy did nothing, then thought at least it was safe to phone Charlotte at Chastisers. He wanted to interview her again; he was sure that Mark had been one of her clients. He was told she had taken a day off. He tried phoning the next day and got the same reply.

Jane had been right: it had taken him just one day before he had returned to the case. He had decided he would be careful though and avoid contact with the police. But for the time being, he would keep Jane out of the loop. He would have to tell her eventually, but now was not a good moment, so soon after the assault on Harry. This meant he had to drop the idea of Jane interviewing residents; instead, Andy would go back to Slough and keep Charlotte's address under surveillance. The next morning, he was parked at the end of Kilmorey Close. He already had names for five of the properties so his plan was to follow whoever left one of the remaining three, namely numbers three, four and six. If any left early, he might get back to intercept the morning postman and get another name to an address.

The first to leave was a man in his forties from number six. He got into a Triumph 1500 and drove off in the direction of London, with Andy following about a hundred yards behind. They got as far as West Drayton Secondary School for Boys, where the man parked his car and went in. He had to be a teacher, thought Andy, but he waited outside, just in case the man was a parent or just visiting. After half an hour, schoolboys started arriving so Andy decided it was time to leave. He drove back to Slough, only to find the post van leaving. He waited another hour in case someone left number three or four, but without success. He then drove back to West Drayton, found the local library and asked for any material on West Drayton Secondary School for Boys. In the school prospectus, he saw a photograph of the man, Mr Allen, the headmaster. Andy didn't think he would have a dominatrix for a wife or lodger, but you never knew. At least he had one more name to an address; only numbers three and four were left.

The following morning, he staked out even earlier in Kilmorey Close, while it was still dark. The first light appeared on the horizon when a policewoman left number four; it was Charlotte. He didn't recognise her at first because of the uniform and her hair being tied up in a bun, but it was her all right. He supposed a client wanted her to dress up as a policewoman as part of her dominatrix act. She got into a black Jaguar XJ6 and headed west out of town, rather than to Chastisers. That didn't surprise him; it was too early for that establishment to open. More likely, a client wanted her to visit him at home before he set off to work. Twenty minutes later, she drove into the reserved parking area of Maidenhead police station.

Charlotte wasn't role playing; she was a police officer for real.

Andy reckoned it wouldn't be too difficult to identify her; there couldn't be too many policewomen working there, after all. Andy had a second breakfast at a café while he waited for Maidenhead library to open. As soon as it did, he went straight to the reference section and in few minutes, found an article that, with an accompanying photograph, identified "Charlotte" as Superintendent Pauline Young of Thames Valley Police.

Although at first, it looked as if Andy was making progress, he quickly realised he had reached a dead end. It was clear to him that Superintendent Pauline Young was connected in some way with Mark's murder, and possibly had given orders to Inspector Armstrong to harass Andy. But it was far too dangerous for him to pursue this line of investigation.

The following morning, Andy needed to go to the British Museum Reading Room as part of his Munich Olympics research. He went straight to the Pornography and Restricted Items section.

The official at reception was a man of about 50, wearing a white shirt and a black suit, with a lightning flash lapel badge. He had black hair, coated with Brylcreem and parted down the middle. He wore the standard round State Health Service spectacles.

"What item of pornography would sir like to access?"

"*The New York Times*," said Andy. "The latest Saturday edition."

"For what purpose?"

"I'm a reporter on the *Daily Citizen*. I'm writing an article about American athletes hoping to participate in the Olympics."

"Can I see your identity card please?"

Andy complied.

"And your Party card please, Mr Deegan."

"I'm not a Party member."

"I'm sorry, Mr Deegan. Access to the pornography section is restricted to Party members only."

"That's news to me," said Andy. "I've been allowed in the Reading Room before without problems. Besides, it's only the sports section I want to consult."

The receptionist opened a drawer of a filing cabinet by his desk and searched through its contents before pulling out a card.

"So you have, Mr Deegan. But you have only five minutes of your allowance left."

Andy had forgotten about that. He had a standard two hours a month quota for the restricted section. The thinking was that prolonged exposure to pornography was likely to deprave and corrupt; furthermore, all newspapers from non-Fascist countries were classified as pornography. Two hours a month was regarded as a safe limit for Party members and other trusted individuals.

"I really need half an hour," said Andy. "Could you not deduct that from next month's allowance?"

"I don't know about that," said the receptionist. "I need to consult my superior."

He lifted a phone and spoke in a whisper that Andy could barely make out. The receptionist put the phone down.

"You can have 20 minutes, supervised of course, 15 of which will be deducted from next month," said the receptionist. "Please take a seat." He pointed to a bench some 20 feet away.

Andy had to wait for about 10 minutes before another official appeared from the entrance to the restricted section. He was identically dressed and of similar appearance to the receptionist, except the newcomer wore white gloves.

"Wilkins, 20 minutes supervised for Mr Deegan here. He wishes to consult the sport section of Saturday's *New York Times*," said the receptionist.

Andy followed Wilkins into the Reading Room. There were four men at separate tables, slouched over their periodicals or newspapers. On each of their tables stood a large stop clock and behind the readers stood officials, who all looked like they were Wilkins' twin brothers. Had the authorities found ways to clone censors, Andy wondered. A fifth reader was next to a table in the corner, reading unsupervised; someone very senior in the BUF hierarchy, Andy surmised.

Wilkins ushered Andy to a table, brought a copy of *The New York Times*, opened it at the sport section, set the stop clock counting down from twenty minutes, and stood three feet behind Andy.

Andy browsed through the paper, skipping articles on football and baseball, and concentrating on athletics and swimming. He wanted to write a profile of an individual athlete from the United States team, expected to do well at the forthcoming games. He soon found one; swimmer Mark Spitz was expected to win several gold medals. Andy made some notes and turned a page.

He was immediately drawn to an article about Albert Speer, the German Olympics minister, which had found its way to the sport section and took up a quarter of a page. The report mentioned the power struggle between Speer, Goebbels and Heydrich, and argued that although Speer's current position looked like a demotion, at least it meant he was safe for the time being. Heydrich would not want to jeopardise the Munich Olympics by arresting the minister responsible for its delivery. The article also claimed that in the six years since Nazi Germany had been awarded the games, up to 200,000 forced foreign labourers had been press-ganged into Olympic construction projects. The nearby Dachau concentration camp had tripled in size to accommodate the additional workforce, half of whom were estimated to have perished from overwork or simply shot when failing to meet deadlines.

A white gloved hand suddenly covered the Speer article.

"I'm sorry, sir. You're only authorised for sport," said Wilkins.

Wilkins' hand remained in place while Andy read the remaining articles on the page before turning over. The following pages contained just sport and a few advertisements. Andy's eyes were drawn to one particular advert. It took the form of an oval in which was written *"TRIBECA"*. Above the oval were the letters: *" *RIGHT HOOK*"*. Below were the letters *" *BOXING CLUB*"*.

Andy had a feeling of déjà vu; he had seen this before, possibly in a different context. It didn't take long to click. One of the photos had *"UB*"* stamped, while a second had *"ING"*; surely part of *"BOXING CLUB*"*. Although, *"SWIMMING CLUB"* or *"FENCING*

CLUB" were also possibilities. But what clinched it were the markings on the third and fourth photos: " *LEF" and "OK*" respectively. " *LEFT HOOK*", surely, he was looking for the LEFT HOOK BOXING CLUB.

On the opposite page was another article detailing Mark Spitz's background. Andy saw he had a big problem with his proposed report. The swimmer was Jewish; there was no way an article about a Jewish athlete would get past the Daily Citizen's censors. Andy had to find another athlete; no sooner than he started, his 20 minutes was up.

The moment Andy returned to his office, he looked through a directory and found only one matching boxing club in London; the Teddington Left Hook Boxing Club. He would visit it the next day; meanwhile, he had his article about American Olympic hopefuls to deal with.

He was in a bit of a predicament because he had only made notes about Mark Spitz. Would the Daily Citizen's censors know the swimmer was Jewish? Andy decided to go ahead with his profile, omitting any Jewish references. If the censors were subsequently to reject the report, Andy would claim ignorance regarding the athlete's race. Would the Germans really give Spitz a visa, despite what he'd earlier heard on the radio? Andy recalled Hitler's refusal to shake Jesse Owens' hand during the 1936 Olympics after the black athlete had won four gold medals. Spitz could well better that score. Andy supposed Heydrich would be skipping the swimming events.

Alice didn't bring him his afternoon tea as usual, so he went to the kitchen to make some himself. He had sensed remoteness from Alice over the last couple of days. Andy had made it clear to Alice that he had regarded the night in Guildford as a one off. Maybe she had expected more, and was annoyed that he wasn't prepared to get into a relationship.

He found Alice in the kitchen with a mug in her hand, looking a bit awkward.

"Is that my tea?" said Andy.

"No, it's Larry's," said Alice. Larry Featherstone was the *Daily Citizen's* home affairs editor.

"How come? You don't usually do his," said Andy.

"Well, only that…" Alice seemed embarrassed.

"Well, only what?" said Andy.

"Paul Draper told me I'm no longer your assistant."

"Since when?"

"Half an hour ago," said Alice.

"We'll see about that."

Andy stormed out of the kitchen, went straight to Paul Draper's office, knocked and entered. There was nobody in. Andy hung around for a couple of minutes then, his temper having cooled, gave up.

As Andy made his way back to his office, he wondered if Alice's reassignment was due to Paul Draper getting wind of the Guildford affair, or had she asked for the transfer herself? It wasn't good, of course, but at least there had been no consequences regarding the one-night-stand at home. There had been a close shave, however, with the scarf business; the hotel could have mentioned to Jane that Andy had shared a room with Alice, but didn't.

He decided to focus on his Mark Spitz article, and had written the opening paragraph when Paul Draper entered.

"You're fired," he said.

"I'm sorry?" Andy wasn't sure he'd heard right.

"You're dismissed. You must leave immediately."

"But why? There have been no complaints about my work."

"You've been wasting time on those murders, despite my instruction not to. You've come in late every day this week."

"I've been visiting libraries as part of my research," said Andy. "Besides, I've met all my deadlines anyway."

"I'm not wasting any more time arguing over this. Just collect your personal belongings and Saunders will escort you out of the building. I've notified the Ministry of Employment."

It was only then that Andy noticed the security man hovering in the doorway. It took him only a couple of minutes to gather a few family photos and a diploma, hand Saunders his pass and leave the office. He didn't even have time to finish his tea.

Andy was in a state of shock as he left the building, and only after a few minutes did he start speculating on how Paul Draper had known about his activities. He had been to Slough three times; he couldn't see how Draper had known about any of that. He had phoned Chastisers several times from the office, so it was possible that Draper had bugged his telephone. The other possibility was that the police leant on Draper himself, but how would they know what he'd been up to recently? Maybe he was being followed; Andy hadn't noticed anything untoward, but now that he was aware of that possibility, he would have to take care he wasn't being tailed.

There was an upside and a downside to his new situation. He could now spend all his waking hours on the case if he still wanted to. However, as Draper had already notified the Employment Ministry, he had only a month to find a job or be arrested under the Workshy Act. He didn't want to go straight back home, given the mood he was in, so he turned round and headed along Fleet Street to the Punch Tavern to down a few beers.

The pub, popular with Fleet Street journalists, had a Victorian décor with huge wood panels framing etched mirrors and frosted glass. Andy went up to the large marble-topped bar and ordered a pint; it was the only drink he had to pay for. He was soon joined by fellow reporters from the *Daily Citizen* and other newspapers, who on learning of Andy's fate, offered their commiserations and bought him a beer. Even Richard Bartle from *The Globe*, usually a competitive professional rival, turned up and seemed sorry about Andy's situation.

"How come you managed to report on the Virginia Water and Windsor murders and still remain in Inspector Armstrong's good books?" asked Andy.

"Well, it was actually Armstrong who tipped me off on both occasions," said Richard Bartle. "He had to have final editorial control over anything I wrote; in particular, there could be no mention of the whip marks on the bodies."

Andy stayed in the Punch Tavern, not just to drown his sorrows, but to delay the inevitable; telling Jane. She sensed something was up as soon as he got home.

"What's happened?"

"I got fired."

"Why?"

"Paul Draper didn't approve of me investigating the four evangelists' case."

"So what are you going to do?"

"Look for a job, of course, although I may not get one as a journalist." It was only half-true; he would spend some time looking for a job, but he felt it was still too early to tell Jane that he would continue looking into the murders of Mark and his three colleagues.

"Well you'd better find one, because it doesn't bear thinking about if you don't. What do you think will happen to us if you get sent to a retraining camp for two years? I might be able to scrape by on my freelance earnings, but if I can't, it will mean the children being taken into care."

*

The next day, Andy went straight to the Left Hook Boxing Club located on Teddington High Street. The manager recognised the men in the photos straight away.

"Ah yes, the four musketeers, as they were called here. They usually came in pairs and would run to the club already in their boxing kits and have a workout. They're regulars, they'd come at least once a week, but I haven't seen any of them for a few weeks."

"Do you have their registration details?" Andy asked, passing the manager his precious photos.

"Let's see. That's Bob Thomas," said the manager, looking at the photo of Mark. He opened a filing cabinet and pulled out a card. "That's funny, the photo's missing," he said.

There were staple holes on the card and part of the club's registration stamp was visible. Andy placed his photo on the card and the two parts of the registration stamp matched. Mark, or Bob Thomas, as Andy now knew him to be, had taken the photo from the card.

"As you can see, we only have Bob Thomas's name," said the manager. "He's left his address, phone number and employment details blank."

The remaining evangelists had also had their photos removed from the club's membership file, and these were now in Andy's hands. He made a note of the remaining names: Gavin Baker, Frank Parker and Max Kitson. As with Bob Thomas, their addresses, phone numbers and employment details had been left blank."

"Did they say anything about where they lived or the sort of work they did?"

"No, they were always rather tight-lipped about that. I think they mentioned they had some kind of Government job. Hush-hush sort, if you ask me. But it couldn't be too far from here as they always ran from work then back again."

"Did they always come on the same day or the same time?"

"No, the days varied. Sometimes weekdays, sometimes weekends. And just as likely to be early evenings as lunchtimes. It looks as if they work shifts."

Andy thanked the manager and left. At least he had names now, although he wondered if they were genuine. He supposed there couldn't be that many government establishments within running distance. *What was running distance?* He reckoned it was possible to run three miles, have a boxing session and run three miles back. The thought of checking out all Government offices within a three-mile radius depressed him. But if they boxed during their lunch break, they would have to work a lot closer than that. He would start with Government buildings closest to the club and work his way outwards.

It was noon, so Andy decided to head home and have lunch with Jane. A black police Vauxhall Victor was parked just outside his house, and as Andy drew level with the car, two uniformed policemen got out.

"You're wanted for questioning," said one of the policemen. Andy was then handcuffed and bundled into the back of the car with the policemen sitting either side of him. The whole operation had taken less than 20 seconds. A third policeman was sitting in the driver's seat and the car sped away as soon as the doors were closed.

*

"Did I say anything about my past?" said Mary, as soon as they were out of the hypnotist's tent.

"No," Sally lied. She didn't like lying, especially to someone like Mary, who she regarded as a friend. But she could see no point in Mary knowing the truth; it could only frighten her. "Absolutely nothing. I never believed in this hypnosis stuff; it's all trickery, as we saw earlier."

But Sally did think about what Mary had said; she was on the run from the authorities. Sally didn't think Mary was a criminal type. *Could her memory illness suddenly have changed her criminal character to the obviously decent person she now was?* Of course, Sally had seen many villains reform themselves, but that was a slow process over months and years, not overnight.

No, Mary had never been a wrongdoer. But then why would the police be after her?

Maybe she was Jewish, but on the other hand, she knew a lot of Christian hymns. Of course, in an attempt to disguise one's Jewishness, a fugitive might make a special effort to learn some hymns. But the songs of praise seemed so deeply embedded in Mary's memory that Sally felt she had learned them as a child and had sung them over and over again.

No, Mary wasn't Jewish.

Maybe Mary was a political? She might have escaped from prison or internment camp, in the course of which she could have received some sort of injury, to the head say, which caused her memory loss. That would explain why nobody had reported her missing.

The thought occurred to Sally that Mary's fleeing from the police might not be a real memory. Only a couple of days earlier, Mary had seen the Blackshirts and police at work with one of their "haircut" victims. She seemed to be upset by the incident. Maybe that had stuck in Mary's subconscious and the hypnotist merely retrieved a dream rather than a memory.

Whether it was a dream or a real memory, Sally knew she should report the incident to the authorities. There was a risk that Mr Cadabra might do that anyway; although given the dodgy nature of his stage shows, it was unlikely. Finally, Sally made a decision: she was not going to report the hypnosis incident to the authorities. She felt a bit uncomfortable about that; it was one thing for shifty characters like Cadabra having a cavalier attitude to the law but quite another for a respectable Salvationist like Sally. She had always regarded herself as a law-abiding citizen, even if she didn't agree with many of the country's laws. But now that she had made up her mind regarding Mary, her conscience was clear.

There still remained the longer-term problem of what to do with Mary. In many ways, Mary was quite self-sufficient and could be left to her own devices without getting into trouble. Given she knew French, Sally supposed she could get work as a tour guide, but there was a lot about London she would have to learn first. Sally still thought Mary had the potential to become a Salvationist. Then she had an idea.

"Mary, our William Booth College in Denmark Hill can always do with more hands. Would you like to help out?"

"Would they put me up?"

"You can still stay with me. It's just a half-hour bus ride away. Interested?"

"Yes. Why not?"

CHAPTER 20

"What's all this about?" asked Andy.

"You'll soon find out," said the policeman on Andy's left.

"What am I charged with?"

There was no response. Andy didn't recognise any of the policemen, but decided to try some small talk. "How's Detective Inspector Ron Cook doing? His missus is due to have their first child any day now."

The policeman on his left replied again. "Mr Deegan, let me give you some advice. Do us a favour and keep your trap shut. You'll have plenty of opportunity to talk later."

The rest of the journey was made in silence. They headed west out of London along the A4, and in half an hour, reached Windsor Police Station. Andy was taken straight to an interview room where he was handed over to two new police officers. His handcuffs were removed and he was ordered to strip. When he was down to his underpants and socks, the handcuffs were put back on and the uniforms left the room, taking Andy's clothes with them.

The windowless room was empty, apart from a large table with two chairs on opposite sides. Andy was left there for the best part of an hour, which he spent pacing up and down the room, wondering what was going to happen next. He tried opening the door, but unsurprisingly, it was locked. Suddenly, DCI Armstrong burst into the room, stopped for long enough to land a fist on Andy's right eye then strode towards the table, on which he placed a folder.

"Sit down."

"I'd rather stand." Andy didn't mind sitting, but felt with this tiny act of resistance that he had an element of control over his situation.

Without warning, DCI Armstrong punched Andy's jaw. "Sit down."

Andy complied. Armstrong remained standing on the opposite side of the table. He opened the folder and pulled out Andy's photos of the four evangelists.

"How did you get these?"

"They were posted anonymously to the *Daily Citizen*." Andy decided his strategy should be to tell the truth as far as possible; besides, he couldn't think of a credible alternative explanation as to how he got the photos.

"You were at the White Swan just yards from where this victim was found." DCI Armstrong pointed to the photo of Mark, who Andy now knew to be Bob Thomas. "Don't tell me that was just a coincidence."

"No. The victim phoned me earlier and we agreed to meet at the pub."

"What else did he say?"

"Nothing."

Armstrong's fist struck Andy's nose, causing it to bleed. "You are the prime suspect in this man's murder. I can detain you without charge for 90 days, but I'm just going to hold you for 30."

"But this is absurd. I want to phone a solicitor."

"No, that's not possible."

"Can I phone my wife, at least?"

"No." Armstrong then left the room. Ten minutes later, the constable who had arrested Andy outside his home entered.

"This way." The constable led him out of the room and down to the basement, along a corridor of cells. The constable opened a door and removed his handcuffs. "In here."

"Can I have my clothes back?"

"I'll see what I can do. For the moment, you're going to have to share."

The cell door clanged shut. Andy looked at his surroundings with a mixture of disgust and horror. The room measured just seven feet by four and had just one item of furniture, a bed that took up most of the cell's space. On top of the bed lay a dirty mattress that stank of urine and there were no sheets or blankets. Beneath the bed was a bucket. The only saving grace was the absence of The Leader's portrait.

But there was another occupant, a fully-clothed civilian in his 50s. He had a gaunt appearance, with an untrimmed, two-week-old beard and a white checked shirt. At least it had been white once; now it looked it belonged to a two-year-old who had decided to feed himself, rather than let Mum do the job. The shirt had stains of varying sizes and colours, and it looked as if a few bits of food had landed as well. The man had been lying on the bed but he got up and sat on the end furthest from the door as soon as Andy had entered.

"Welcome, take a seat. I'm Philip Chapman."

Andy sat down and introduced himself.

"What are you in for?" asked Philip Chapman.

The man could easily be a stool pigeon, thought Andy. He decided not to lie to the man, but all the same, be economical with the truth.

"Murder," said Andy. "Of course, I didn't do it. There's been some sort of misunderstanding. I'm sure they'll drop the charge fairly soon. How about yourself, been here long?"

"Since the morning after Europe Day. I've been arrested for not smiling."

"I don't understand. How come?" said Andy.

"I hadn't even wanted to go to the procession," said Philip Chapman. "You see, there was a Blackshirt march from the river to Windsor Castle on Europe Day. It was announced earlier so most people decided they had better things to do and tried to keep clear of the route. Seeing it was the first nice day in months, I decided to relax in my back garden. Then the authorities reckoned there weren't enough spectators and decided to press gang more civilians to get the numbers up. Two policemen knocked on my front door and escorted me and some of my neighbours straight to the procession. There was the usual film crew, interested in the crowd rather than the marchers. It was the next day I got arrested for not smiling during the march."

"I know you must have been annoyed at having your day off disrupted," said Andy, "but you must have known you were being filmed. Didn't you at least try?"

"That's the problem, I can't smile. I've got Parkinson's. Funny thing is, they didn't get me for my raised arm salute. I can do one but it's a bit shaky."

"I'd have thought you'd be given a bit of leeway; it's not as if Parkinson's is classified as an anti-social disorder. After all, Adolf Hitler suffered from it."

If Parkinson's had been regarded as anti-social by the authorities then Andy, as a journalist, would have been first to know. He recalled how Down's syndrome had been handled. First, there was a newspaper and television campaign showing how much stress sufferers were causing their parents and carers. Then it was pointed out how much it cost the authorities to look after the sufferers. Then stories appeared, highlighting the criminal acts committed by the sufferers. Andy had had to write his fair share of articles on the subject; when he couldn't find any criminality committed by Down's syndrome victims, Paul Draper would order him to make something up. This propaganda campaign went on for seven years before the authorities deemed Down's syndrome sufferers eligible for voluntary euthanasia. Three years later, they were put under a compulsory euthanasia order.

The conversation stalled so Andy began speculating on his predicament. Did the police really think he was behind the murder or murders, or were they trying to frame him? After a moment's reflection, he reckoned in either case, Armstrong would have at least tried to extract a confession out of him. No, he had been locked up to stop him from prying into the murders.

The cell was unheated and Andy was feeling the cold, so he paced up and down what little space there was to keep warm. After a couple of hours, the door opened and the constable brought a tray with a bowl of soup and beans on toast, but no cutlery apart from a spoon.

"You commies always go on about sharing, so you'll have to share supper," said the constable. "Deegan, you'll get your clothes back in the morning."

"Can we have a knife and fork for the beans on toast?" said Andy.

"Sorry, no. Regulations."

Andy placed the tray on the bed between himself and Phillip Chapman.

"You first," said Andy.

Chapman took a spoonful of the soup and raised it to his lips, spilling most of it on his shirt.

"Let me help," said Andy. He started feeding the man his soup. Given it looked like in the past, most of Chapman's food had ended up on his shirt rather than inside his stomach, Andy let him have nearly all the soup, just leaving a couple of spoonfuls for himself. They shared the beans on toast a bit more equitably, but Andy still let Chapman have the larger share.

Andy didn't think Chapman was a stool pigeon. His Parkinson's certainly wasn't faked, but he still could have been planted to learn something from Andy. He seemed to be the type, individualistic, the sort that wouldn't join activities organised by the Fascists, which the police liked to pick on when making their arbitrary arrests.

The meal, miniscule as it was, revived him a bit and staved off the cold for a few minutes. It was a lot later when the constable returned to collect the tray. He brought a couple of blankets with him.

"It's bedtime now," said the constable. "I'll see you in the morning at slopping-out time. You'll have to decide your bed sharing arrangements yourselves. No funny business, mind you. Chapman, I've got some good news for you; you'll be freed in the morning. We can't release you now, as it's nearly curfew, so you'll have to accept our hospitality for one more night. Sleep well, goodnight. " The constable took the tray and left.

They agreed that Philip Chapman would have the bed for the first three hours and Andy the floor underneath, then they would swap. The blanket was dirty and smelly so Andy was loath to cover himself with it. Instead, despite feeling cold, he lay on the floor and wondered how Jane would be reacting. He often worked late and couldn't get home because of the curfew, so it wouldn't be until the morning before she would start getting worried.

Andy couldn't get to sleep. First, the cold kept him awake then Chapman's snoring. Andy's watch had been removed so he didn't know when the three hours had passed. He supposed Chapman had a watch but he had covered himself with the blanket and was sleeping soundly. Andy didn't want to wake him up.

In the morning, Andy was ordered to take the bucket out of the cell and empty it in the toilet at the end of the corridor. He was given a couple of minutes to wash his hands and face but was given no opportunity to shave. Then, Chapman was allowed to wash. When he returned, he let Andy have the use of the bed and finally, the cold forced Andy to cover himself with the dirty blanket. Shortly, the cell door opened and the constable appeared again.

"Chapman, you'll be out as soon as the Chief arrives and signs the release form," said the constable. "Now, blankets please."

"How come?" said Andy.

"Regulations; bedcovers are for night use only," said the constable. "You'll be having breakfast soon and we don't want to get any food soiling our blankets."

The blankets could hardly get filthier, thought Andy; reluctantly, he handed his to the constable. Shortly, Andy and Chapman shared a breakfast of scrambled egg on toast and a mug of tea. When the tray came to be collected, Andy finally got his clothes back, minus his shoelaces, belt and his pocket contents. He dressed then dozed off on the bed, after asking Philip Chapman to wake him up after three hours.

It was a constable, a different one whom Andy hadn't seen before, who roused him.

"Deegan, you're being released," said the constable. "It seems you have friends in high places. The Chief wants to see you now."

"Surely you mean me," said Philip Chapman. "Your colleague said I'd be freed today."

"Change of plans, Chapman," said the constable. "The Chief decided that now that Mr Deegan is being released, there will be room for you to stay with us after all."

This brought home to Andy just how arbitrary Chapman's arrest had been. The police had been prepared to free him just because the cells were full. Andy felt a bit bad about the situation; his "friend in high places", whoever that might be, had secured his freedom at Chapman's expense.

The constable led Andy back to the interview room and left him alone. Andy wondered what the constable meant by friends in high places; he certainly didn't know of any, apart from Paul Draper, and he didn't think he'd be pulling strings for him. After a few minutes, DCI Armstrong arrived carrying a small black plastic bag.

"You're free to go," DCI Armstrong said. "Your personal items are in the bag."

DCI Armstrong left the room, leaving the door open. Andy checked the contents of the bag; everything had been returned, including the photos of the four evangelists.

On his way out, Andy was asked by the duty sergeant to sign a form.

"Can I get a lift back home?" asked Andy.

"Don't push your luck," said the sergeant.

Chapter 21

Andy wondered why he had been released. He didn't believe Armstrong had a sudden change of heart. He didn't think the police officer had just come across evidence that showed Andy was innocent. He was still convinced that Armstrong was involved in some sort of cover up and had wanted to keep him locked up but was overruled.

But by whom? Someone in a senior position of authority, surely. Could the murders be part of some sort of positioning for power within the regime? Could those opposed to the murders be gaining the upper hand and so engineered the release?

The people who overrode Armstrong didn't do so just because they thought it was wrong to keep an innocent man locked up. No one senior in the regime would have any qualms about that. They ordered Andy's release because they wanted him to find out more about the murders.

Should he carry on looking? If there was a conflict within the regime, whose side should he be on anyway? He knew nothing about the factions, if indeed they existed. But he supposed if there was a power struggle, it might be better to be on the side of those that released him. However, continuing could get him into more danger if the Armstrong faction gained the upper hand.

"What happened last night? Why didn't you phone?" said Jane as soon as Andy got back home.

"I got arrested by Inspector Armstrong and spent the night in the cells."

"So you've carried on with your murder investigations?"

Andy nodded then told Jane about finding out the identity of Charlotte and his visit to the Left Hook Boxing Club.

"You'll stop now."

"I can't. This is too important; it's much bigger than the Darent brothers' case. Besides, I've got someone high up on my side, someone who can pull rank on Armstrong."

"Can't you just leave it for a couple of days?"

Andy wasn't sure about that. He really had the bit between his teeth regarding the case now that a mysterious figure had got him released from his police cell. He glanced at Jane; she had that look, both upset and angry, but more upset than anything. He was aware he had one day less to find a job but right now, he really needed some sleep.

"OK, I'll do that."

Andy then went to bed. When he woke up, he phoned Paul Draper on the off-chance he had had a hand in his release; if so, he might be willing for him to return to work at the *Daily Citizen*. He had no such luck; Paul Draper's secretary had refused to put Andy through.

*

The next day, a Saturday, was Cup Final day. Andy was an Arsenal supporter and in the normal course of events, he would have got a ticket for the match, but this year, it clashed with his mother-in-law's birthday. So that morning, the whole family set off to Chingford to see Jane's parents, Carl and Hannah Coleman. Andy would be in the driver's seat on the way out and Jane on the return leg. They drove along the North Circular Road, which was full of traffic; people doing their Saturday morning shopping, Andy supposed. At one point, they were within a few hundred yards of Wembley Stadium, where the Cup Final would be taking place later that afternoon, although both Jane and Andy were diplomatic enough not to mention it.

It was near Finchley, about three quarters into their journey, when Andy thought he was being followed by a red Austin-Healey Sprite. The sports car was never directly behind him; there were always one or two intervening cars between them. Maybe his imagination was getting the better of him. After all, it was a busy road and it was not unusual to drive from one end of London to the other on it. Nevertheless, Andy decided to try to shake the Sprite off; he adjusted his speed so that he would cross a traffic light just as it was turning from green to amber. At one such light, the Sprite continued after the light must have turned red, but finally, Andy lost the Sprite when an intervening car stopped at a traffic light that Andy managed to drive past. Shortly after crossing the River Lea, they left the North Circular Road and drove the last couple of miles into Chingford. The Colemans lived in a quiet residential road with detached mock Georgians on either side, on the outskirts of town, close to the edge of Epping Forest. The whole journey had taken nearly two hours. As Andy parked the car, a red Austin-Healey Sprite drove slowly past; he was able to get a glimpse of the occupants – two middle-aged men in grey suits.

"Goodness, that's quite a shiner you got there, Andy," said Carl Coleman as soon as he had opened the door.

Andy's jaw still hurt from DCI Armstrong's punch, but it was his right black eye that was more visible. Andy briefly explained how he received it.

They had lunch, Hannah Coleman opened her presents, and they all went for a walk in Hawk Wood, apart from Carl, who stayed behind to clear up. They got back just before three. Jane and Hannah went upstairs to have a mother-daughter chat while the children played in the garden. Meanwhile, Andy and Carl opened a couple of cans of Long Life and sat down to watch the football on television.

As this was the centenary anniversary of the FA Cup, the proceedings started with a cavalcade, showing all past cup winners with their team flags. Men dressed in knickerbockers, caps and sporting mutton chop whiskers represented the earlier victors. The television camera's focus switched to the Royal Box, occupied by The Leader and Lady Mosley. The King and Queen normally attended the Cup Final and the fact the Royals weren't present meant that the King had to be seriously ill and not just suffering from one of his "colds".

Andy wondered if Britain would have been any different if George VI had still been King, which if it wasn't for a tragic accident, he would have been. In 1941, on a goodwill tour of Australia, the plane carrying King George VI and Princess Elizabeth crashed into the sea; their bodies had never been found. At the time, there was some talk of making Margaret Queen under a Regent. Princess Margaret, then aged 10, had remained in London with her mother during her father's and elder sister's Australian tour. But Sir Oswald Mosley, by then in a powerful position in Britain, although still not Leader, leaned on the Archbishop of Canterbury and other establishment figures to declare King Edward VIII's abdication in 1936 null and void and bring him back. In 1936, King Edward had been forced to abdicate and accept the new title of Duke of Windsor because the British establishment was not prepared to accept his fiancée, Wallis Simpson, as future Queen as she was a divorcee. However, now that in 1941, the British Government was prepared to accept Wallis as Queen, the Duke of Windsor agreed to be King again. Consequently, the Duke of Windsor, King George's elder brother, was reinstated as King Edward VIII.

Arsenal was playing Leeds United. The Arsenal side wore red shirts with white sleeves, white shorts and red socks, whereas the Leeds team were all in white. Andy thought how much easier it would be to follow the game on colour television.

The game didn't get off to a good start; within a minute, McNab got booked for fouling Lorimer.

"What a useless referee," said Andy. "It's obvious McNab was going for the ball and Lorimer forced the foul."

"I suppose it's because this happened right in front of The Leader's box," said Carl. "The referee just wanted to show him how strict he is."

"More likely The Leader is a Leeds supporter," said Andy. "And the referee knows it."

The game seemed to be going Arsenal's way, and 15 minutes into the game, there was a tense moment when McLintock fired a powerful shot at the Leeds goal, only to be saved by their goalkeeper. Andy and Carl finished their beers and opened a second can.

However, for the rest of the first half, Leeds had possession of the ball. Despite this, Arsenal won a corner about half an hour in. Armstrong took the corner, which was caught by Arsenal's Alan Ball. He would have scored a goal if the ball hadn't been intercepted by Reaney for Leeds. It was the excuse for a third beer. Five minutes later, Leeds were awarded a free kick 25 yards from goal. Lorimer took a shot that was intercepted by the Arsenal goalkeeper Barnett then lost. For a heart-stopping couple of seconds, Andy and Carl watched the ball trickle inches past the goalpost. It was a close shave.

At half time, a Blackshirt band playing *Greensleeves* marched into the stadium. An open-topped truck, carrying what looked like a hoist attached at one end, followed them, and a Black Maria followed at the rear of the procession. The truck stopped at the kick-off spot and the band ceased playing. Two prisoners were escorted out of the Black Maria onto the truck, which had been converted into a mobile gallows; their hands and feet were bound and a noose put round each of their necks.

Executions sometimes took place at football matches, but never at cup finals, because of the presence of royal dignitaries. Today's hanging was an exception, presumably because of the King's absence. The men were rather unlucky, thought Andy. He was familiar with the case; two 17-year-old youths had been caught committing a homosexual act. They were unlucky in that only a month earlier, the minimum age for capital punishment eligibility had been lowered from 18 to 16. Our youth is maturing earlier, The Leader had said, so this fact must be taken cognisance of in our laws. The teenagers had been caught in the act by one of the boys' stepfather. Andy couldn't understand how a parent, albeit a stepfather, could shop one of their own children, but Paul Draper had thought it very public spirited of the man, and had said so in a leader column that he had written for the *Daily Citizen*.

As was the custom at such events, each of the condemned men would be given a two-minute interview with a BBC reporter, which was transmitted live.

"Would you like to take this opportunity to apologise to the whole of society for your heinous crime?" the reporter asked the first youth.

"I don't want to die," the boy sobbed.

"How does it feel knowing that in three minutes, you will be dead?"

"How banal can you get?" Andy shouted at the television. "Why doesn't the man step on the gallows, put the noose round his own neck and tell us himself?"

The boy continued crying and gave the same answer, "I don't want to die," to all the remaining questions.

The reporter moved on to the second youth, who seemed much more composed.

"Do you have any regrets?" the BBC reporter asked.

"Only that as a Leeds United supporter, I won't live to see my team thrash Arsenal," the boy replied.

The reporter paused and glanced at the Royal Box. For a moment, Andy thought he was going to ask The Leader to postpone the execution until after the match. But it looked like the reporter had second thoughts and wanted to keep his job, so he continued interviewing the youth.

After the reporter finished, the executioner, who had been sitting in the back of the truck, stood up. He was dressed entirely in black and wore a balaclava with holes just for his eyes and mouth. He gave a thumbs up sign and the Blackshirt band started playing the National Anthem.

At that moment, the television camera switched to the Royal Box. The Leader stood to attention and removed his cap; the spectators around him followed suit. It was The Leader himself who had decided that the National Anthem should be played at executions: he wanted it to be the last sound the condemned would hear. Television viewers were spared seeing the trap door open as the camera remained focused on The Leader and his entourage. As soon as the music finished, he clapped then sat down and continued chatting to Lady Mosley and his aides. Shortly, the camera switched to the mobile gallows that was now leaving the stadium, with the two bodies just faintly visible, dangling from the end of their respective ropes. The Blackshirt band was now in the rear, playing Cliff Richard's *Congratulations*.

From start to finish, the execution had taken less than 10 minutes. In a way, Andy was impressed with the efficiency of it all. This was something the Government could do well; after all, it had a lot of practice.

The second half of the match resumed. Leeds got their goal eight minutes in, after Clarke headed a cross shot in from Jones. There were no more goals after that but Andy and Carl conceded that Leeds played better. In the last minute, Jones tripped over Barnett and dislocated his left elbow; he was carried away on a stretcher. Andy and Carl opened their fifth cans to commiserate on Arsenal's one-nil defeat.

It was soon time to go; they all gathered in the hallway to say their farewells. Jane was last to leave, climbing down the stairs from the first floor, clutching a handkerchief to her cheek, followed by Hannah Coleman.

"Why does Mum always cry when she sees Grandma?" said Karen when Jane was out of earshot.

"Well, it's not that often we get to visit each other."

"Why don't Grandma and Grandpa come to us then? They never do," said Karen.

As the children headed to the car, Carl tugged at Andy's sleeve. "You're going to have to tell them," he said. "Sooner, rather than later."

"I know, I know," said Andy.

Chapter 22

Andy and Jane Deegan didn't have three children. Their fourth and last child, Adrian, was born when Jenny and Karen were four and Harry just two. When Adrian was nine months old, he was diagnosed with Down's syndrome. At the time, sufferers were eligible only for voluntary euthanasia, but Andy knew that euthanasia would become compulsory in due course. A sympathetic doctor signed a fake death certificate for Adrian and Jane's parents offered to take him in. At first, the children kept asking about Adrian, being told he was away with relatives or in hospital, then that he had passed away, but eventually, they forgot they ever had a younger sibling. All this time, Adrian had been confined to an upstairs bedroom, only being allowed into the garden for short periods when it was dark outside. Adrian was now five and Andy and Jane were well aware he could not be hidden in this way for very much longer.

The morning after the Cup Final, Andy made the decision to continue his investigation into the evangelists' murders. He thought the risks to himself and his family had been lessened by his release, although he intended to steer clear of DCI Armstrong and his subordinates. He explained all this to Jane, adding that as a journalist, he couldn't just let go of the story.

"It's not about journalism," said Jane. "It's about you having to prove yourself. You're still trying to earn that Military Cross."

She was right.

Andy had spent most of his three years' National Service in Kenya. The apartheid system pioneered in South Africa had been extended throughout British colonial Africa. Kenya had been split fifty-fifty into white and native zones respectively, despite whites only accounting for three per cent of the population. Furthermore, the white zone had the most productive land, both from an agricultural and mineral point of view. This state of affairs, combined with forced evictions of natives from the white zone, caused resentment among Africans, which led to a low level, but continuous, insurgency. This took the form of terrorist attacks on military and economic targets, individual white settlers, but mostly against other Africans working for the authorities as policemen or interpreters.

In the course of his posting, Andy was involved in a number of these evictions. Typically, troops would surround a village at dawn, and through an interpreter, the inhabitants were given an hour to gather their belongings and clear off. Then, to discourage the natives from returning, the village would be torched. Many National Servicemen refused to take part in such evictions. Although a few objectors faced a firing squad as an example to others, most spent three years in a military prison before being dishonourably discharged. Andy wasn't one of these objectors; he felt uncomfortable about the evictions, but said and did nothing.

After a white farmer had been murdered in his home outside the town of Nyeri, Andy's platoon had been ordered to go after the perpetrators. They were believed to number about three or four and were hiding in the forests on the lower slopes of Mount Kenya. The platoon was driven to the end of a dirt road and from there, they progressed on foot. They spent three hours climbing through terrain that was both swampy and steep, before they reached the forest. An hour into the wood, they walked straight into a trap; instead of just a few terrorists, they were confronted by over 100. In just a few seconds, half the unit, including their commander, Lieutenant Clark, was dead. Seeing they were outnumbered, the remainder of the platoon retreated down the mountain. They were chased by the terrorists, who picked off the slower members one by one. The platoon had lost their radio operator in the initial skirmish, so the survivors couldn't call for reinforcements. The retreat turned into a rout, as the men abandoned their packs and started running. By the time the swamp was reached, only Andy was left. This was the steepest part of the route but at least it was downhill; every few seconds, a bullet would whistle close by. After a couple of minutes, the shots stopped; his pursuers had given up the chase.

It was dark by the time Andy reached the base in Nyeri. In the morning, two military policemen arrived in a Land Rover and drove him to the barracks in Nairobi, locking him in a cell. He was sure he would face a court martial, swiftly followed by a firing squad. For the next two days, he faced a series of interrogations and he gave the same account of what had happened. Andy saw no point in lying; the Army would surely return in force to the scene and quickly establish the facts in any case.

On his final visit to the interrogation room, he was met by two new men. One was a brigadier in uniform, the other, a middle-aged civilian in a pinstripe suit. The brigadier read a statement through clenched teeth. "We have established the facts of the Mount Kenya action of 25 November 1954. A force of over 100 well-armed terrorists surrounded Lieutenant Clark's platoon. Exchange of fire commenced and did not end until all the terrorists had been killed or had fled. Corporal Deegan is the sole survivor of said platoon. He is being recommended for the Military Cross."

"Congratulations," said the civilian, extending a hand. He managed an attempt at a smile, while the brigadier looked rather uncomfortable, sucking his teeth and avoiding eye contact with Andy. The civilian had to be someone senior in the Government, or at least acting on their behalf, as he seemed able to pull rank on the brigadier.

The authorities had decided to turn a disaster into a propaganda victory. They needed a hero and decided to choose the living Corporal Deegan, rather than the dead Lieutenant Clark. Andy really had no choice but to play along in this charade; the alternative was almost certainly a firing squad.

*

It was over seventeen years since Andy's Kenya experience, but it was why he wanted to keep going with the four evangelists' murders. He was trying in part to live up to his reputation as a hero, a reputation that only he, Jane and his parents knew to be completely undeserved. It wasn't just the Kenya episode; it was the praise he earned for his Darent brothers' scoop too. He had only gone ahead and reported it when he knew there was no danger to himself.

Andy started with the National Physical Laboratory; it was the nearest Government establishment to the boxing club. He met with the personnel manager, a Mr Stonehouse, who confirmed that Bob Thomas, Gavin Baker, Frank Parker and Max Kitson were not employees and, no, he didn't recognise anyone in the photographs.

Next, he decided to try the Ministry of Defence Research Station, located just a few hundred yards away. He wasn't sure what to expect there or whether they would even let him in. And if they did, surely they would know that four of their men were missing and would have made their own enquiries.

A 10-foot high chain-linked fence topped with coils of barbed wire surrounded the complex. There was just one entrance; a guard post stood just in front of the fence. Behind was a barrier that could be lifted to let cars through. Andy had gone past this place dozens of times over the years. Normally, the guard post was occupied both day and night; but today, there was no one there. Puzzled, Andy walked past the guard post, crossed over the barrier and moved into the compound. The site consisted of three buildings, two single-storey barrack-like huts and a three-storey building that looked more like a country house than an office. He tried to control his nerves; although there was no one to stop him, he was clearly trespassing on Ministry of Defence property. He attempted to open the door to one of the huts; it was locked. But he was able to get a good view through the windows; the inside was empty, apart from half a dozen stripped beds. He supposed this must be the guards' dormitory. The second hut was also locked but through the windows, he could make out a small kitchen, dining area and some sort of mess room. Again, only the main items of furniture remained; all the fittings had been removed. It was clear neither hut was being used at the moment.

The main building was a three-storey red-bricked Georgian country house. There were about half a dozen windows on each floor. These were all identical; white-framed and their height twice their width. At the centre of the ground floor was a porch with two white stone Doric columns. A neoclassical white stone pediment was positioned above a black oak door. Andy pressed the doorbell and could hear it ringing inside, but after a minute, no one had come to the door. He half-heartedly turned the handle, expecting the door to be locked, so was surprised when it opened. He was struck by the complete silence inside as he explored the ground floor. He moved through a reception room, a kitchen and two sitting rooms, all sparsely but elegantly furnished. He supposed the offices and scientists' laboratories were all upstairs.

He headed up a staircase to the first floor and turned into a corridor with three rooms on each side, all with their doors shut. He opened the first door on the right; it was dark inside, as the curtains had been drawn. It took him a moment to make out the end of a bed. Adjusting his vision was done at the expense of his remaining senses; Andy didn't hear the footsteps creep up behind him. In one second, his arms were seized and pinioned behind his back; in the next moment, a cloth was placed over his mouth. He smelled a sickly odour, felt increasingly light-headed and queasy then, within seconds, passed out.

Chapter 23

Andy came round gradually; he felt nauseous, very thirsty, and his vision was blurred. He was slouched in an armchair and handcuffed. He was in a sitting room, to his left were thick drawn curtains, and opposite was a sofa, on which he could make out two male figures.

"Give him some water," said one.

The other man left the room and returned a minute later with a glass of water that he offered to Andy. He drank it in one go and immediately felt a little better and his vision became clearer; the two men were in their 30s and wore grey business suits with white shirts and red ties. One was short, plump and slightly balding, the other, tall and slim.

The shorter man stood up. "Who are you and what were you doing at the research station?"

"Who are you? And why am I in handcuffs?" Andy responded.

"I'll be asking the questions," said the short man. "You were caught trespassing on a restricted Army site, a serious offence. We are responsible for Ministry of Defence security. It's in your interests to cooperate if you want to stay out of trouble."

Andy told them everything.

The tall man left the room. The short man sat back on the sofa. "Relax and don't try anything funny. We are armed." He pulled out a pistol from inside his jacket, pointed it in Andy's direction for a few seconds then put it back.

Andy took in his surroundings; it was an elegantly furnished room. He was sitting in a Queen Anne armchair and his guard was ensconced in a matching pink velvet Chesterfield sofa. A white shag-pile carpet covered much of the floor, and photographs of The Leader and Lady Mosley were fixed to the walls. This was obviously a sitting room rather than an office, but there were no indications of the sort of work that must go in the building.

Andy could hear the tall man making phone calls from an adjoining room, but he couldn't make out what was being said. After an hour, he entered the room, nodded to his companion and they both left. On the way out, Shorty said, "We'll be back soon. Remember what I said."

Five minutes later, they re-entered and Shorty immediately removed Andy's handcuffs. "My name is Roy," he said.

"And I'm Oliver," said his taller colleague.

Roy continued, "I said earlier we are responsible for security here. But we're not just guards. We work for British Intelligence; State Security, to be precise. The Bushy Park site is, or rather was, a chemical weapons research facility. It was infiltrated by a spy ring; we found out about them, but the agents escaped before we could apprehend them. We shut down the station and moved the personnel to a new site. We caught four of the agents and had them eliminated; they were lab technicians and just foot soldiers in the spy ring."

"These were the men who were members of the boxing club and whose bodies I had discovered?" Andy was not at all happy dealing with these individuals. They had drugged him, pulled a gun on him and threatened unpleasant consequences if he did not cooperate. However, he was curious where all this was leading and decided to hear the men out. Besides, he really had no choice.

"Exactly," said Roy. "Their leader is scientist Dr Mary Brown and unfortunately, so far, she has managed to elude us. Her real name is Marie Brun, a French Canadian working for the Americans, and we very much want her alive. About four weeks ago, she was supposed to meet her American handler at Victoria Station, but we intercepted him shortly before the planned rendezvous and interrogated him. By the time he'd confessed and we had arrived at the station, she was gone. We want you to help us find her."

"Why me?" said Andy. "And who has been behind Thames Valley Police's attempts to warn me off the case if it wasn't you? Not to mention my getting fired."

"We're guilty on both counts, I'm afraid," said Roy. "We did at first think your sleuthing would just get in our way and complicate matters. So we leaned on the police, had a quiet word with your boss, and when that wasn't enough, got Detective Chief Inspector Armstrong to have you thrown in jail. What made us change our minds is hearing that you had found the names of the lab technicians at the boxing club. By now, we expected to find Dr Brown ourselves, but we haven't. So we need all the help we can get; that's why we asked Inspector Armstrong to release you. You're obviously a very resourceful individual; you've got so far with all the obstacles that have been put in your way that you might just be the person who could find Mary Brown. So will you help us?"

Andy was in two minds over this offer. On the one hand, he felt he ought to do his bit in catching a foreign spy. On the other hand, he felt really angry having to work for people who had caused him such grief and who had been prepared to harm his family. But in the end, Andy realised he had no choice; if he refused, he probably wouldn't leave the room alive.

"Yes, I will help. I do have one question though. The four men had all been whipped. So they had all been interrogated before they were eliminated?"

"No, they were not whipped by us," said Oliver. "We use more sophisticated methods in our interrogations. They were all S&M aficionados. I know The Leader regards that sort of thing as good for character building, but I don't see the attraction myself."

"There is one more thing you need to know," said Roy. "This centre carried out research into amnesia-inducing drugs. More than that, they have produced prototypes that are believed to work. Some samples are missing and we believe Mary Brown may have the drug with her. It's possible she may have injected herself with the drug when her contact failed to turn up."

"Why would she want to do that?" asked Andy.

Roy replied, "If she's convinced she's going to get caught and reveal United States' secrets under interrogation, an amnesia drug might be preferable to the old-fashioned potassium cyanide suicide pill. Although I would have thought losing your entire memory is not a much better fate than a quick death. Anyway, the point is that you may be looking for a Mary Brown who has absolutely no idea who she is, let alone that she's a scientist and a spy."

"In that case, she's not going to be of much use to you when she's caught," said Andy.

"We should be able to swap her for one of our agents currently serving a long prison sentence in the United States," said Oliver. "Détente hasn't stopped us spying on each other, but the climate is more favourable for negotiating spy exchanges. There's one more detail. Should she, for any reason, have failed to meet her handler at Victoria Station, there was another rendezvous to fall back on. It was a pub in Kings Road, Hackney. We put the place under surveillance of course, but there was no sign of her."

"This may sound like a stupid question," said Andy, "but did you put her home under surveillance in case she returned to pick up papers or contact someone in her spy ring?"

"Not a stupid question at all. Because of the irregular hours worked at the centre, all employees are required to live in Teddington within one mile of the site. Indeed, a few, including Mary Brown, actually lived at the site. That's why we were at the centre when you paid us a visit."

Andy was given a photograph of Mary Brown.

"She's five foot four inches, of medium build, and has blue eyes and medium brown hair, which she may of course have dyed, since she's given us the slip," said Oliver.

They spent a few more minutes discussing details then Roy handed Andy a piece of paper with a telephone number on it. "We'll have no problem contacting you if we need to. But if you want to get in touch with us, phone that number. I suggest you phone every afternoon at five with a progress report, but contact us at any other time if you have news or run into any difficulties."

"We'll need to use a password whenever we communicate with each other," said Oliver. "Any ideas?"

"How about *forget-me-not*?" said Andy.

"Yes, you will use that to identify yourself to us," said Roy. "We will use *Cordelia* as a password to identify ourselves to you." He glanced towards Oliver and both men left the room again.

Andy sat, trying to take this all in. The silence was broken by the men's murmuring next door and the distant sound of a siren outside. He looked at his watch; it was just past 11 o'clock so he had been detained for over 12 hours.

Shortly, the men came back in again. "We'll give you a lift home now," said Roy, "but we've moved you from the research centre to one of our safe houses, which we want to remain secret. We won't drug you again but you will need to be blindfolded."

A hood was placed over his head and Andy was led away. He went down one flight of stairs and out into the open. He was guided some 20 yards, and then helped into the back of what he thought was a van. The van sped off, took a right turn, and drove for a couple of minutes before coming to a stop at what Andy assumed were traffic lights. The vehicle moved slowly for a few seconds then stopped again. They kept crawling then stopping for what seemed like 10 minutes, before they could accelerate and keep a steady speed for much of the journey. They slowed down for the last few minutes, with more breaking and turns, before coming to a final stop. Andy was assisted out the van and positioned next to a tree, and told to count to 20 before removing his hood. He did just that and when he took his hood off, he could see a white Bedford van taking a left turn but he couldn't make out the registration number. He looked at his watch; the journey had taken about 40 minutes and he was now just 200 yards from home.

Chapter 24

Although he knew he had no choice, Andy continued to feel uncomfortable about his new mission.

Was Mary Brown really an enemy?

The only country Britain was still officially at war with was Free Britain, but their leader, Winston Churchill, had died seven years ago, and the Free British forces now only consisted of a few retired admirals on Bermuda. As a consequence, the Free British were not regarded as a serious threat to the Mosley Government, although they were the target of a lot of hostile propaganda. For 25 years, the United States was considered the main enemy, although we were never at war during that period. But President Nixon's Berlin visit three years before had changed things. It was the start of détente and the US was portrayed by the regime in a much more favourable light. Diplomatic relations had been established and the new US ambassador, Charles Lindbergh, seemed to have formed a great personal rapport with The Leader. But the Mosley Government was a regime that had detained Andy's father for 14 years, had arbitrarily thrown him in jail, and had threatened his son. It eased his conscience a bit to know that no one was going to be harmed in this operation. All that would happen to Mary Brown would be repatriation home and an end to her spying career.

But what if State Security were planning to kill her after all?

What also bothered Andy were his growing doubts about the State Security version of events.

Were the murdered men really spies? Why would one try to contact him?

Surely, it would have made sense to keep them alive, as they might have known something about Mary Brown's contacts or where she might be hiding. It seemed too much of a coincidence that all four men were into S&M. After all, Charlotte had reacted only to one of the photos.

And what about Charlotte? She was, after all, Superintendent Pauline Young; did she have a police rather than a dominatrix role in all this?

Another doubt he had was "Why me?" State Security would surely have a pool of trained agents they could call on to do the job. It wasn't as if he had specific knowledge or skills that made him useful to them. There was also something else that was nagging him about this whole business, but he couldn't put his finger on it.

*

In the morning, Andy headed straight to Victoria Station. He asked at all the ticket counters, cafés and kiosks at the station if Mary Brown had been seen on the 7th or 8th of April, and showed her photo. More than four weeks had passed since then, so unsurprisingly, he drew a blank. The station served much of South London and South East England, so if she had taken a train, she could have gone to any number of places. One possibility was that she had a safe house to go to, but that could be anywhere on the railway network. She may have tried to flee the country, but she wouldn't have had as many options. Trains ran to Gatwick Airport, as well as to a number of Channel ports, from Ramsgate to Weymouth.

She would need documentation, probably forged, and tickets to leave by air. But if she had sufficient funds, she could probably leave the country by sea, even without documentation. She was a French speaker, so France seemed a plausible destination. He resolved to check out all these possibilities later.

Although, Andy mused, all this assumed she hadn't taken her amnesia drug. If she'd lost her memory, she would have no idea where to go, unless she had written something down before taking the drug and even then, there was no certainty she would find the instruction or make sense of it. On reflection, he didn't think she would write anything down; after all, the whole point of taking the drug was to prevent her would-be captors learning anything from her, including where she was heading or whom she was going to meet.

So what would she do upon finding herself in Victoria Station and remembering absolutely nothing?

Andy decided to ask around a few local hotels. If she had money and if it was late in the day, she might have checked into one. None of the hotels recalled a Mary Brown or someone like her spending the night.

At five, Andy phoned his State Security handlers, gave a report, and they agreed he should go to Hackney next. The Bull at the end of Kings Road seemed a strange place for a rendezvous. The pub was very small; it would be overcrowded if there were more than a dozen customers in the main bar at any one time. He thought that if spies were to meet here, their presence could be recalled and there was a risk their conversations could be overheard. The décor was seedy: tatty green upholstered benches and a worn blue carpet. In the back was another room with enough space for a pool table and piano. The bar and pool room were both empty, except for a barmaid behind the counter. She didn't recognise Mary Brown's photo; she spoke to someone in a room behind the bar marked "private" and a burly man in his 50s emerged. He introduced himself as the landlord and no, he didn't recognise Mary Brown either. The couple only employed extra staff on Friday and Saturday nights, and as Mary Brown would have been at the pub on a Monday or Tuesday, one of them would have been present.

Andy left the pub and worked his way down the street, knocking on each door in turn. At number 28, a woman in her 20s opened the door. Andy introduced himself and showed her Mary Brown's photo.

"Oh yes, I do remember her. It must have been about four weeks ago," said the woman.

"Where did you see her and what was she doing?"

"She came knocking on my door, just like you. But the funny thing is, she was actually looking for a Mary Brown. There are no Mary Browns on this street; but there is, or rather was, a Mavis Brown at 54. So I told her to try there. But Mavis Brown was in her 80s and died in hospital a week ago."

Andy thanked the woman and left. He was puzzled by Mary Brown's behaviour; he didn't see any point in going to number 54, so he decided to head home.

When he got to Twickenham, he decided to drop in at the Queen's Head for a pint. Over his Samuel Smith's, he tried to work out what could have happened. It looked like she had taken the amnesia drug. But she had found her way to Hackney. She must have waited at the pub for quite a while for her contact before taking the drug. But the bar staff were quite sure she hadn't been there.

Maybe she had poked her head inside for a few moments, saw her contact was not there and then waited outside. But why would she look for a Mary Brown? Maybe she had something that could identify her such as a passport. But wouldn't she have got rid of it before taking the drug? Maybe she thought there was a greater risk of being arrested for not carrying identification. But then, her card or passport would have her home address, which is in Teddington, so she would have headed straight there. Maybe all she had was some kind of receipt with her name included, hidden in a pocket, which she had forgotten to throw away before taking the drug.

It was all very puzzling.

Andy wondered what she might do next, having found out there was no Mary Brown on that street. He tried to put himself in her shoes and work out her next move. He couldn't think of an answer by the time he finished his pint and left for home.

Outside the pub, he bumped into Michael Roberts, walking his black Labrador. Unlike Andy, who was sporting a single black eye, Michael Roberts was nursing two. Andy had felt guilty about his role in getting Michael Roberts arrested, so he was relieved to see that he had been released.

"Mr Roberts, am I pleased to see you," said Andy. "I heard about your arrest; some nonsense about your dog's name. Can I buy you a drink?"

For a few seconds, Michael Roberts looked suspiciously at Andy, then he said, "Why not? I'll have a pint of Red Barrel."

Michael Roberts sat next to a terrace table while Andy brought him his beer and another pint of Samuel Smith for himself.

"The police told me if your dog's name is Morris, with two r's, you'd be in a lot of trouble. So it must be Maurice, spelt with the one r," said Andy.

"Oh no, you're wrong there. It's Morris, with two r's," said Michael Roberts.

"How come? What exactly happened at the police station?"

"After questioning about how I found the body, the police wanted to know how I spelt Morris's name. I sensed a wrong answer could get me into some sort of trouble, so I refused until I could see a solicitor. Well, that got me a black eye, and I was locked in the cells until I would agree to the spelling test. I was kept there for two days without food or water. I could have sat there for a lot longer but I was worried how Morris was being treated. So I gave in and wrote down Morris's name. I was then told I would be subjected to positive ancestry vetting; this would take at least nine months, during which time, I would be held in remand."

"That's terrible. Just because of your dog's spelling," said Andy.

"I asked why and was told that many Jews have first names of Morris, with the two r's. I then told the police that Morris was not my dog's first name but his surname. That's when I got my second black eye; the cops thought I was being funny. I pointed out that William Morris, the car manufacturer, wasn't Jewish. Not only that but he was also an early supporter of The Leader. What got me out I suppose was the fact that my previous dog was called Carruthers. After all, have you heard of anyone with a first name of Carruthers? The police checked with my neighbours and Morris and I were released."

"The experience wasn't too distressing for Morris, I hope," said Andy.

"No, he was well treated. Properly fed and exercised. My black eyes were the only ill effects, but they're healing up nicely. I got a lot of stick with children calling me panda. 'Ever seen a panda walking a dog?' they would shout out when they thought I was out of earshot. Mind you, you've got a nice shiner yourself. Courtesy of Twickenham Police, I suppose?"

"No, mine is thanks to the Windsor Police. The case of the body you discovered was taken over by them and I got a bit too nosey. I got the black eye only a couple of days ago, so it's going to look worse before it gets better."

Andy was about to buy Michael Roberts a second pint when a group of Blackshirts arrived on the scene, collecting for one of their charities. The customers at the adjoining tables put down their drinks, got out their wallets and looked for change, but Michael Roberts just stared at his empty glass.

"I'd drop a coin in, however small, if I were you," said Andy. "The Blackshirts sometimes film their collection activities, and those who don't donate can find themselves in trouble."

A Blackshirt approached their table and shook his collection box.

"What's this in aid of, may I ask?" said Andy.

"You may," said the Blackshirt. "It's our *Knuckledusters for the Boys in Black* campaign. The plan is to provide a knuckleduster to every new Blackshirt recruit. At the moment, we have to purchase our own weapons to defend ourselves from the vicious attacks by Communists and their liberal sympathisers."

"A most worthy cause," said Andy, dropping in a two-pence.

"Makes a change, I suppose," said Michael Roberts after the Blackshirts left. "It's usually the Salvation Army that comes round collecting, just when you've settled down for a quiet pint."

Chapter 25

"Is it OK if I use the car today, Jane?" asked Andy.

"Well I was thinking of driving down to see Mum and Dad. Why do you need it?"

"I have to go to the Salvation Army offices in Hackney. It's a rather long journey by tube." Andy had already told Jane that the search for Mary Brown was the latest development in the four evangelists' case.

Michael Roberts' mention of Salvation Army fundraising in the Queen's Head the day before had given Andy an idea: if Mary Brown had taken the amnesia drug and found she had nowhere to spend the night, she could well have turned to the Salvation Army for help. So his plan was to ask at the Salvation Army offices nearest to Hackney before trying others further afield.

"Tell you what, I'll drive you down," said Jane. "It's not exactly on my way, but I'm supposed to be at my parents at 12 so there's plenty of time. You'll have to go back by tube though."

They left after dropping the children off at school, heading down the A4 towards the centre of London. Ten minutes after leaving the school, they hit a traffic jam. For the next quarter of an hour, they drove at a snail's pace. Andy began to wish he had taken the tube after all. Then a sense of déjà vu crept up on him, although he couldn't pinpoint what it was that he had experienced before.

"Jane, there's something strange about this very moment in time. I feel I'm experiencing something that has happened in the past before."

"Well, we have driven along this road before."

"No, it's not that."

"A traffic jam? Nothing unusual about that."

"Maybe it was. I just can't place it."

"It will come to you."

"There must have been an accident ahead," said Jane. A few minutes later, an ambulance passed in the opposite direction with its siren on. "What did I say?"

It dawned on Andy what he felt he was experiencing for the second time. It was the night when he was driven, hooded, from the safe house. The same stops and starts just after they'd set off. A few minutes before they'd left that night, he'd heard a siren, but didn't recognise it at the time. He was quite sure now it was an ambulance siren. So there had been a traffic accident near the safe house, and a serious one at that.

Was it just standard procedure or was there a specific reason that State Security didn't want Andy to know where the safe house was?

He was sure there was something not quite right about this whole operation, but he couldn't fathom exactly what. He thought it might help if he knew where the safe house that he had been taken to was. There can't be too many serious traffic accidents around eleven o'clock two nights ago, about forty minutes' drive from home. If the safe house was in the middle of the countryside, there's just a chance he might locate it. Of course, he couldn't rule out the possibility that he hadn't been moved from the Bushy Park research facility at all, and while hooded, he had been driven round in circles.

Five minutes after the ambulance passed, the traffic got going again, although Andy didn't manage to see any signs of an accident. There were no further incidents and shortly after 10 o'clock, Jane dropped him off at the Salvation Army offices on Mile End Road. He introduced himself to the receptionist and asked if she'd heard or seen anything about Mary Brown.

"We do have a Mary Brown with us, Mr Deegan, but she's staying with one of our officers. Captain Hawkins is out at the moment, but she should be in at one this afternoon. I suggest you come back later and speak to her."

Andy thanked the lady and left. He had nearly three hours to kill, but he had an idea how to make use of the time. He asked a passer-by where the nearest library was and headed straight there. He made a beeline for the reference section. He looked at both the current and previous day's editions of newspapers local to London and the Home Counties. There were a couple of accidents reported, but there was no mention of any injuries. The papers he looked at only covered parts of Central and East London and the eastern Home Counties, so he got hold of a reference guide and made a list of all newspapers within 60 miles of London, together with contact phone numbers. He then found a telephone booth and made his calls. There were just two accidents around that time requiring hospitalisation in or near London: one in Stevenage, the other in Slough. He ruled Stevenage out as being too far; there was no way you could drive home from there in less than 40 minutes, especially as there was at least a 10-minute delay caused by the accident. He made a note of the Slough accident address, Wellington Street. He then went back to the library and looked at a map of Slough. Wellington Street was just a quarter of a mile from Kilmorey Close, the street where Superintendent Pauline Young, aka dominatrix Charlotte, lived.

Could the safe house where he was held actually be Charlotte's home? Or was Slough just a coincidence?

Whether he was held at Charlotte's or not, he was sure she was in some way involved in this business. He would have to bring this up next time he spoke with his State Security handlers.

Andy had a quick lunch at a nearby café then went for his meeting with Captain Hawkins. He introduced himself as a journalist then, showing the photograph, asked about Mary Brown.

"What is your role in all this, Mr Deegan?" she asked suspiciously.

Andy gave the cover story provided by the State Security men. "Mary went missing a few months ago. She's not married so her brother, Robert, reported her disappearance to the authorities. Robert was concerned that after two months, the police had got nowhere so he turned to me. He is an acquaintance of mine and he thought that with my journalism background, I could help out as a sort of private detective. So here I am."

Sally Hawkins was silent for a minute then took a closer look at the photo. "Yes, that's her. She's staying with me at the moment. She's completely lost her memory. Did you know that?"

"No, but it does explain why she's been missing for so long," Andy lied.

"Well Mary is out fundraising today," said Sally, "but she'll be back at my place later in the evening. Her brother could come to pick her up then. What did Mary do by the way?"

"She's a scientist."

"Her identity card has her as a gardener, although we didn't think she had green fingers," said Sally.

State Security hadn't told Andy anything about this. But he didn't want Captain Hawkins to doubt his cover story so he had to think on his feet. "I think she's a plant scientist of some sort, which may explain having gardener on her card."

"Funny that, she told me she had no interest in science when I took her to the Science Museum. Mary's memory loss was so complete that there was very little she was able to tell us about herself. We knew she had an Uncle David and that she spoke French."

Andy managed to close the meeting, getting her address and confirming that Robert Brown would collect Mary later that evening.

He had made real progress and felt that State Security should know immediately rather than wait for his regular five o'clock call, so he would phone right away. As he searched for a telephone kiosk, he looked back on his meeting with the Salvation Army officer. A couple of things puzzled him. First, there was the gardener business. Of course, Mary Brown being a spy could well have had a forged identity card, declaring her profession to be a gardener. But Andy wondered why she would have a card with just gardener as the falsified entry; why not a card with a forged name?

There were also those remarks about Mary Brown not liking science. Then it clicked what had been bothering him since his meeting with State Security. It was the Ministry of Defence Research Station he had trespassed onto. There were no signs that it ever was a scientific research laboratory. There were no workbenches or lab pedestals. He tried to think what there might be in a laboratory: shelves, racks for test tubes, chemical storage cabinets and fume cupboards. There were none of those in the building. In fact, it looked like the interior of a small country house; more like a State Security safe house.

And then there was the involvement of Charlotte. But, above all, his biggest concern was the fact that finding Mary Brown had been so straightforward; State Security could have easily done it themselves.

Did they even try?

Because of his mistrust of State Security, he was prepared to tell them he had found her, but not where, at least not until they had answered his misgivings. He decided against phoning from the area in case his call could be traced, so he took the tube back home.

At the entrance to Mile End Station, he saw an *Evening Standard* poster with the headline "Goebbels Arrested", so he bought the paper. Although the story made the front page, there was almost nothing to report. He had been arrested at his Berlin home in the early hours of the morning and was now helping the Gestapo at their Prinz-Albrecht-Strasse headquarters. End of story. There was no mention of the reasons for his arrest.

Andy phoned from a kiosk near home. He could tell it was Oliver who answered, but nevertheless, he gave the password, *forget-me-not*, and got the reply, *Cordelia*.

"I've found Mary Brown."

"Where is she?"

"Before I tell you, I need the answers to some questions."

"Go ahead," said Oliver.

"Superintendent Pauline Young, who has a side-line as a Slough dominatrix by the name of Charlotte, is involved in all this. Isn't that so?"

A long pause followed. "Anything else?"

"Mary Brown is not a scientist and the Ministry of Defence Research Station where we first met doesn't do any scientific research," said Andy.

This time, the pause was even longer. "I think we had better meet," said Oliver. "Where are you now?"

Andy told him.

"We'll pick you up in half an hour."

Chapter 26

Sally Hawkins was home at six that evening. Her meeting with Mr Deegan had been a lot to take in. At first, she had thought he was a police detective, but after hearing him out, she was convinced of his account, apart from the scientist bit, which puzzled her a little. Over the years, Sally had come across scores of police detectives at the hostel, so she reckoned she could spot one fairly quickly.

She felt both pleased and a little sad at the news regarding Mary Brown. She was pleased that at last she'll be back with her family. Being in familiar surroundings might help her recover her memory. But Sally was sad that she was losing a potential recruit; in time, Mary would have made an excellent Salvation Army officer. *If her memory problems prevented her from taking up her science again then maybe that will still be her path.* Of course, Mary was more than just a potential recruit; she had become a dear friend. *Would they still remain friends?* She lived on the other side of London so they wouldn't be seeing each other that often. *But would Mary be a different person once she had recovered her memory?*

She made herself a cup of tea and switched on the television. The news was just finishing, but she managed to catch that the King had a cold again. She was worried about him: this must be the tenth cold he'd caught this year, and he hadn't been seen in public since the German leader's visit a month earlier. She thought he must be seriously ill and, since he was in his late 70s, this could be an illness from which he might not recover.

Not long after she'd finished her tea, the doorbell rang. A policeman and two civilians stood outside in the rain. One of the civilians was about 50, the other in his late 20s, but both were dressed in identical grey suits, white shirts and grey ties. The older man introduced himself as Detective Inspector Burrington and the younger as Detective Constable Larkin.

"We would like to see Mary Brown. We believe she is staying with you," said Burrington.

"Is she in some sort of trouble?" asked Sally.

"No, she hasn't done anything wrong. We just want to talk to her," said Burrington.

"Well she's out fundraising at the moment. She won't be back until 10 o'clock."

"You don't mind if we wait inside? This wretched rain doesn't show any sign of stopping," said Burrington.

Sally wasn't too happy about this but managed to mutter, "Come in."

Detective Inspector Burrington nodded towards the policeman. "You can go now, PC Connor. Thank you."

Burrington and Larkin followed Sally into the living room. She made the men some tea and they all sat in silence watching a David Attenborough programme about wildlife in the Kenyan Masai Mara park.

Sally wasn't sure whether to believe the detective's assurance that Mary was not in trouble. If she was, she couldn't defend herself because of her memory problems. Sally wondered if the detectives knew about Mary's amnesia, and whether she should tell them. She reasoned that it might get Mary into trouble, even if she wasn't before. She wasn't officially employed by the Salvation

Army and had been with Sally well over a month, and so could be arrested under the Workshy Act. On the other hand, the detectives would very quickly learn that Mary had a memory problem as soon as she got home. On balance, she thought it best to be level with the men.

"You do realise that Mary Brown is suffering from complete memory loss."

"Yes, we know," said Burrington. The men remained silent and continued to watch scenes of crocodiles attacking wildebeest as they tried to ford a river.

Surely, the detectives didn't just want to question Mary if they knew about her amnesia, Sally reckoned. *They must be planning to arrest Mary.* She wondered if the earlier meeting with Mr Deegan was not a coincidence. Maybe it was Mary's brother, Robert, who was in trouble. What should she do? She couldn't think of a plan, but she wanted to at least warn Mary and tell her not to come home tonight. That would give her some time to think of what to do next. But how could she tip off Mary? It seemed just as impossible as trying to warn the wildebeest about the crocodiles. Then she had an idea.

"I need to pop out for a few minutes," said Sally. "I'm short of bread. There's a shop just round the corner that's open till eight." The men murmured their assent and Sally collected her purse, shopping bag and umbrella, and had just opened the door when Detective Constable Larkin grabbed her umbrella.

"Let me carry this for you," said the detective.

Sally agreed without a fuss; she didn't think the men would let her out of their sight. It was less than a 10-minute walk to the shop; there were no customers inside and in a couple of minutes, she had bought her loaf. Outside the shop was a telephone kiosk. "I need to make a call," she said. "I'm supposed to be at a meeting shortly. I'm going to have to cancel it."

"Don't you have a phone at home?" said DC Larkin.

"It's not been working for the last couple of days." Sally knew this wasn't true, but the detective couldn't disprove her. Even if the phone rang as soon as they got back home, Sally could claim it just fixed itself.

"Go ahead then."

Sally entered the booth while the detective stood outside. She dialled a number and got through straight away. "Is that William Booth College?" she said, her voice barely above a whisper. "It's Captain Hawkins from Mile End. Could someone put Mary Brown up just for tonight?"

Chapter 27

The van in fact arrived within 20 minutes. Only Roy was inside. Andy was told to go in the back and put a hood on. This time, the journey took just fifteen minutes; he was led out of the van and escorted to a ground-floor room, just one minute's walk from the van. The hood was removed and Andy took in his surroundings. The room was much larger this time; it had a bright, airy feel and was nicely furnished with a cream-coloured three-seater sofa, four matching armchairs, and a light brown mahogany grand piano in the corner. Oliver was seated in one of the armchairs. In the centre of the room was a coffee table with a telephone resting on top. Behind the sofa stood a white bookshelf, filled with copies of Shakespeare, Dickens and volumes of the *Encyclopaedia Britannica*, but no other indication of the owner's reading tastes. In fact, there was nothing personal in the room at all and, as before, the curtains were drawn, although this time, it was definitely light outside.

Oliver gestured to Andy to take a seat. Roy picked up the phone and dialled a number. He just said, "He's here," then put the receiver down.

Oliver then started talking. "There have been some aspects of this case that, for security reasons, we haven't been able to divulge to you. But someone very senior in the organisation, who for obvious reasons can't meet you face to face, will shortly call and tell you everything. We can't tell you his real name but he's known as Casper."

They all sat in silence for another three minutes, which seemed much longer for Andy. The phone rang;

Roy picked up, listened for a few seconds, and handed Andy the receiver.

"Is that Andrew Deegan? This is Casper. Nice to speak to you." The voice sounded tinny and was obviously disguised. "I hope you're sitting comfortably, Mr Deegan, because you're about to get a history lesson."

Andy sank back in his chair. "I'm ready. Do continue".

"Well, you're aware of the Australian plane crash of 1941, in which King George VI and Princess Elizabeth were killed?"

"Yes, I am."

"At the time, Lloyd George was Prime Minister of Britain, having signed a peace treaty with Nazi Germany the previous June. Winston Churchill had set up a rival government-in-exile in Canada. Although Australia recognised the Lloyd George administration, there was widespread support for Churchill in that country. To make sure Australia stayed with us, Lloyd George sent the Duke of Kent, a keen supporter of peace with Nazi Germany, as Governor in October 1940. But just to make additionally certain that Australia didn't go over to the Churchill camp, in February 1941, Lloyd George sent King George on a goodwill tour of the country. To ensure the whole Royal Family didn't set up a pro-Churchill court in Australia, Lloyd George insisted that the Queen and Princess Margaret remained in Britain; that way, the King and Princess Elizabeth were sure to return."

"Where is this leading to, Casper?" asked Andy.

"There was no plane crash. The aircraft, on a flight from Perth to Adelaide, was hijacked and landed on a makeshift airstrip next to a disused mine in the Australian desert. The occupants were secretly flown to Britain in a waiting plane and placed under house arrest. The original aircraft, with its occupants now removed, was blown up and the wreckage covered with the desert's sand. The pilot, who was in on the kidnap plot, gave his location to Adelaide Airport as over the Great Australian Bight, before issuing a distress call then switching off the plane's radio. The Navy and Air Force spent weeks searching the sea for the wreckage, which of course was never found. The kidnapping was engineered by Sir Oswald Mosley, at that time, Home Secretary, to ensure the Duke of Windsor returned to the throne as Edward VIII."

"Why would he want to do that?" asked Andy.

"After the elections of May 1941, the British Union of Fascists found themselves leading a coalition government with part of the Labour Party. They needed a crisis to be given emergency powers. The crisis came easily enough. Home Secretary Mosley had ensured the BUF had disproportionate coverage in the newspapers and in the BBC. He also had his men counting the votes, which amounted to quite blatant ballot rigging. So the ensuing protests and General Strike came as no surprise. The Leader had to be sure to create a situation in which the King would grant emergency powers. He hadn't been certain whether King George VI would cooperate, but he was sure he could rely on his older brother, Edward, Duke of Windsor, to do so. The Duke of Windsor, known as David to family and close friends, was both a personal friend and politically sympathetic to the BUF. So the whole plan was to get the Duke of Windsor on the throne. King George died several years later while still under house arrest in a secret location, but his daughter is still alive."

"She was held in the Bushy Park safe house?" said Andy.

"Exactly, Mary Brown is none other than Princess Elizabeth," said Casper.

"But why keep her and the King captive," said Andy. "Surely it would have been better, from The Leader's point of view, to have had them killed?"

"I can only speculate what had been going on in his head. Maybe he thought the royals could in future be used as some sort of bargaining chip. The Leader is an aristocrat first and a Fascist second. That may have been the reason behind the decision to keep them alive. Of course, very few in the regime knew about this. Even her guards didn't know the Princess's identity, although they may have guessed. In any event, to ensure this, security guards who were single men without family ties, the sort that once might have joined the French Foreign Legion, were eliminated after a few years' service and replaced."

"The fact you're telling me all this means you don't approve," said Andy.

"Not just for sentimental or compassionate grounds, but for hard-headed political calculation, if you let me explain. Many influential people in Britain feel it is time for regime change. Leading industrialists want to end our protectionist economic policies and go for free trade. The Army top brass wants to end our colonial wars. Even some in the regime feel that way. The Leader is getting on, he's 75 and there's no obvious successor. William Joyce is 10 years younger but is hated by the rest of the leadership. So some of us inside the regime have decided to get rid of Mosley and restore democracy."

"Surely our European friends, especially the Germans, might object to this and react rather forcibly."

"Even a year ago, that would have been true. The fact is that all European regimes are moribund, run by aged leaders with no obvious successors. Spain's Franco is nearly 80 and Italy's Mussolini is 88. And Germany is on the verge of civil war now that Hitler's gone. There's a power struggle between Heydrich, Goebbels and Speer, none of whom are young anymore. The Wehrmacht and SS are at each other's throats. I don't think Germany will be indulging in any foreign adventures at this moment in time.

"Let me continue with our plans to get rid of Mosley. Because we are effectively planning a Palace coup, it is important for us to have some sort of legitimacy. Releasing Princes Elizabeth and making her existence public may not itself give sufficient underpinning to our coup, but the news of the Princess's house arrest and the death of her father after 10 years of captivity would fatally undermine Mosley's legitimacy, despite the support he receives from King Edward."

"Would people believe you?" said Andy. "Would she be recognisable? After all, it's more than 30 years since she was last seen in public, and then she was still a child. She might be thought of as an impostor, especially with her memory problems, a bit like the Russian princess in that Ingrid Bergman film."

"Anastasia. Yes, we are well aware of that. But something happened that solved that problem, yet forced our hand at the same time. Two months ago, an Australian prospector stumbled upon the wreckage of the 1941 airplane carrying King George and Princess Elizabeth. It won't be long before it becomes public knowledge that no bodies could be found near the wreckage. This would support our assertion that the

Royals were moved to a waiting plane, flown to secret house arrest in England, and the original aircraft then blown up. But the discovery meant that we had to act fast. The Princess was in great danger, as Mosley could well decide to kill her to get rid of the evidence, as it were.

"So we had to free the Princess first before toppling Mosley. She was allowed a short walk in the grounds of the safe house with one of her guards every evening after dark. That's when we struck, overpowering the guard with chloroform, as we did with you. The plan was to smuggle her out of the country to Canada until the coup was over. But then we ran into a problem."

"What happened?"

"Scientists at the Buchenwald medical research centre in Germany have developed an amnesia-inducing drug. It has been extensively tested on inmates of the adjacent concentration camp. Memory loss is total. Some prisoners, having being given the medication, would even embrace SS guards after being told they were their brothers. Any side effects disappear after a day or two, and the patient's memory makes a full recovery after a couple of months. British Intelligence had earlier been given samples of the drug and it was decided to regularly inject the Princess with it in order to make her easier to control. The drug takes effect a few hours after injection, usually inducing the victim to fall asleep then wake up with the amnesia. We found out that the Princess had been injected just before her walk with her guard.

"We gave the Princess a fake identity card and she was escorted to Victoria Station by Roy, who you've met. They made their way to a waiting room where shortly, the Princess fell asleep from the effects of the drug. They were supposed to meet another of our agents who had aeroplane tickets to Canada and forged Canadian passports for himself and the Princess. The couple would then travel by train to Gatwick Airport and fly out of the country. The agent was supposed to arrive by eight o'clock that morning; unfortunately, Roy had to be at a State Security meeting at seven-thirty. This was an important briefing and one at which he could not be late, so at ten-past seven, he left the sleeping Princess, whom Roy reasonably assumed wouldn't move in the next hour. Leaving her alone was a weakness in our plan, but we had been forced to act quickly by the Australian discovery. For security reasons, we have kept the numbers involved in this plot to a minimum. The agent had come down all the way from Scotland by sleeper and his train was delayed by two hours. By the time he arrived at Victoria Station just after 10, the Princess was gone.

"We looked but of course, we couldn't use the resources of State Security or the police. That is why, in due course, we turned to you for help."

"What about the four dead men whose photographs I had received and who trained at the Teddington boxing club? Presumably, they weren't spies."

"No, they were all guards. One of them sensed that he would be in serious trouble after the abduction and did a runner. He, of course, contacted you later. A State Security special operations squad was sent to the safe house, interrogated the remaining guards and, convinced of their innocence, had them eliminated. State Security too was acting under pressure and had to quickly dispose of the bodies. But in case the police or journalists like you got too nosey, they decided to create a false trail. State Security knew that one of the guards, a Bob Thomas, regularly visited a dominatrix – Charlotte in Slough. They also knew that Charlotte was a senior policewoman with Thames Valley Police. So the remaining guards had whip marks inflicted upon them and their bodies dumped in Thames Valley Police's area of operations, so that no other police force would get involved. The beauty of the State Security plan was that not only did it provide a false trail but that Thames Valley Police, as soon as they had established a link with Charlotte, would do everything to cover the matter up."

"This is exactly what DCI Armstrong tried to do," said Andy. "So he was responsible for my harassment?"

"Mostly, yes. But State Security noticed you were a bit too persistent, so they threatened your son. They also engineered the business with Mrs Fox and her missing husband. And they persuaded your boss to have you fired."

It was becoming obvious to Andy that Casper had to be someone senior in State Security. "Who arranged to get me released from DCI Armstrong's police station?"

"Charlotte. What State Security didn't know was that Charlotte was one of us. Charlotte, or rather Superintendent Pauline Young, is an excellent policewoman. She should have been Chief Constable by now, and feels quite rightly betrayed by the regime. It was their decision to implement the 'family friendly working policies' directive that caused her career to stall. As I'm sure you know, this directive bans married women from employment and single women can only be employed in the most junior positions. Single women who had already reached positions of some seniority were able to keep their rank, but were banned from further promotion. Superintendent Young saw this as a betrayal of Fascist principles. Leading suffragettes had been at the forefront of the BUF in its early days. About a quarter of the activists had been women and both The Leader's wives had played a prominent role in the movement.

"Superintendent Young is one of those rare police officers who has never assaulted a suspect. She only enjoys inflicting pain where the recipient is a willing participant. This accounts for her dominatrix side-line. As soon as she heard that Armstrong had had you locked up, she ordered your release and in turn, informed us. Since then, we've kept a close eye on you."

"It was her house that I was taken to after I was overpowered in Bushy Park," said Andy.

"Yes, it was risky to stay there too long so we took you to Superintendent Young's home."

"Why the cock and bull story about Mary Brown being a scientist and a spy?"

"At that point, we weren't sure if we could trust you. We were aware that you weren't a Party member and that had damaged your promotion prospects. We knew about your father's internment. So that background should have made you sympathetic to our cause, but we didn't want to take any chances. We knew you were a good journalist and were impressed that you had found out the guards' names and the safe house, despite all the obstacles put in your way. So we thought you had a good chance of finding the Princess, and it seems we were right. But now that you've found the holes in our cover story, we've decided to trust you and be straight with you. We can't afford to play any more games as we believe with every day that passes, the Princess is in greater danger of capture by the regime. And this time, it will mean death, not house arrest. So, Mr Deegan, are you with us?"

It was a lot for Andy to take in. The story seemed incredible; so outrageous that it was not something one would make up. He tried to find flaws in what he had just been told and couldn't find any. The man, Casper, had to be telling the truth. This time, Andy had no problems taking sides: Mosley had to go, and the sooner the better. He didn't think he would be just replacing one Fascist leader with another; once news about the fate of the Royals became public, Fascism would be finished forever.

Andy gave his assent and told Casper all about his meeting with Sally Hawkins.

"Good," said Casper. "We'll pick Mary Brown up later this evening. I may need to contact you again. You will use your existing password and I will use *Anastasia*. I think it's best for security reasons we continue to refer to our VIP as Mary Brown, at least until she's out of the country. Thank you and goodbye."

Andy handed the phone to Roy, who had a few words with Casper. Roy passed the phone to Oliver who muttered "Yes" a few times then put the receiver down.

Five minutes later, the plotters gave Andy a lift home in their van; this time, he didn't have to wear a hood.

Chapter 28

Mary had been a few days at the Salvationists' William Booth College and had settled into a routine. She would have breakfast with Sally Hawkins then travel to Denmark Hill by bus. The first time she went with Sally, but now she managed the journey on her own. She felt she was gaining more confidence as she learned about the world around her. She knew The Leader ran the country and that the King kept on having colds, although Sally had said in hushed tones, she thought he was much more seriously ill. She felt confident to chat to other bus passengers, but occasionally got stuck whenever the talk was about events that had happened more than a month previously.

Mary was assigned to a company based at the college. The company would start with hymns inside then would go out on the streets with their brass band and collect from people going about their shopping. Around six o'clock, they would have supper at the centre, with time for a short rest before going out on a pub tour, selling their newspaper, *The War Cry*. Then she would head back to Hackney, arriving around 10 o'clock in the evening.

So far, this had all gone on without incident. That evening, she was collecting with Lieutenant Speight and they had entered the George and Dragon. Inside was a group of about 20 Blackshirts who, by their raucous banter, looked as if they had been drinking some time.

"Hello. What have we here?" one of them spoke out. "Ladies who think they're soldiers."

"Fucking do-gooders," a voice from the crowd muttered out loud.

One Blackshirt tore a copy of *The War Cry* from Mary's hand. "Seditious crap. We should perform a citizen's arrest."

"Which one's the colonel and which the general?"

"Maybe they're both field marshals."

"Then we should salute them. How do they salute each other?"

"I'll show you a Salvation Army salute," said one Blackshirt, putting down his pint of beer. He then punched Lieutenant Speight in the face, causing her to drop her copies of the weekly and her collection box and stumble back onto an empty chair.

"A perfect right-hook, if I may say so, sir," said the publican, while the Blackshirts cheered. He then turned to Mary. "Ladies, leave immediately. I don't want trouble in my pub."

"But they're the ones causing trouble," said Mary.

"Out!" shouted the barman, pointing at the door.

Mary helped her colleague to her feet and they left the pub to the sound of jeers from the Blackshirts. Mary could see her friend's nose was bleeding.

"Are you all right?" said Mary. "We should call the police; that was outrageous behaviour by the Blackshirts."

"I'm fine. We are not going to call the police," said Lieutenant Speight.

"Why not?"

"Mary, you still have a lot to learn. If you are assaulted by one of these gangsters for whatever reason and you report the incident to the police, you will be charged with provoking a Blackshirt, which is a serious offence."

"But that's wrong."

"It's just the way it is," said Lieutenant Speight. "You know, when the Blackshirts were founded back in the '30s, their hierarchy was modelled on ours. But those young thugs in there wouldn't know that."

They decided to cancel the remainder of their pub visits. Normally, they would return to headquarters with their takings, but as these had been lost at the George and Dragon, they headed to Lieutenant Speight's home. She assured Mary she could take care of herself, so Mary decided to go straight back to Sally Hawkins' house.

Mary arrived just before nine o'clock, an hour earlier than usual. She rang Sally's front doorbell, even though she had a spare key. She waited a minute but there was no reply, so she let herself in. "Sally," she called out as she moved down the hallway. She entered the sitting room and could see Sally slouched in an armchair with her back to Mary and facing the television, which was still switched on. "Sally, wake up. Are you all right?"

She stepped round to face Sally and was horrified to see her bulging but lifeless eyes and her protruding tongue.

CHAPTER 29

Mary screamed and tried to look away but, like iron filings to a magnet, she was drawn to Sally's grotesque death mask of a face. She stood in stunned silence for a minute. Then she heard the sound of clapping coming from the television; it was a game show. She switched the set off and wondered what to do next. She supposed she should call the police, but then she recalled what Lieutenant Speight had said about them earlier. Maybe it was a crime to report a crime, and even if it wasn't, she'd be in trouble with the police. They would suspect her of the murder of course, and during interrogation, would quickly find out about her memory problems. That would make them even more suspicious.

She had to get away from here, but she had no idea where to go or what to do next. She gathered her few belongings in a shoulder bag and left. She ruled out going to the Mile End Road hostel; she would be asked why she couldn't stay with Sally. For the same reason, she dismissed going to Denmark Hill. She walked around aimlessly for a while, trying to think of her next move. She heard a clock chime 10; she realised she had to find a place to stay before the midnight curfew. Then she recalled something Sally had told her; the major railway stations in London were exempt from the curfew laws to allow for the possible late arrival of trains. She would head for Victoria Station. This time, she didn't have to walk, she had enough money for the tube fare.

On the train, she wondered who could have killed Sally. She didn't think it was a burglary gone wrong. There were no signs of the premises being searched, no drawers opened and their contents upturned. Besides, there was nothing in Sally's house worth stealing; her television set was probably the most expensive item and that hadn't been touched. Then Mary remembered the scene in the sitting room; on the coffee table, there had been three cups, which had been recently drunk from. Sally had had at least two visitors with whom she was happy enough to offer refreshment. Mary didn't think Sally had any enemies. It couldn't have been a jealous lover.

Could it have been the Blackshirts?

The business at the George and Dragon had shown that the Salvation Army wasn't popular with them. But killing a member for no reason seemed extreme. Maybe there was a reason, but Mary couldn't think of one.

Mary arrived at Victoria Station well before curfew and spent the night on the same waiting room bench where her present life began.

She managed to get only a little sleep, so was feeling quite tired the next morning. She was still at a loss as what to do next. She remained in the station until lunchtime, feeling both tired and hungry, but it was the tiredness that was by far the stronger sensation. She really needed a good sleep, then she might be able to think more clearly. She checked the contents of her purse; she had nine pounds and four shillings. Sally had been giving her pocket money for some time now and Mary had managed to save most of it.

Mary left the station and enquired at a few cheap-looking hotels. One, the Thames Hotel, offered a single room for four pounds and nineteen shillings a night. She checked in, paid in advance for one night, went to her room, laid down on the bed and within a minute, fell asleep.

Chapter 30

"Hello." Andy sounded as groggy and half-asleep as he felt.

"Is that Andrew Deegan?"

"Speaking. Do you realise what time it is? Why are you calling at this hour?" Andy glanced at his alarm clock; it was five o'clock in the morning.

"I'm sorry, this can't wait. It's Casper. Could you confirm you're Andrew Deegan?" It was the same tinny, disguised voice.

"*Forget-me-not.*"

"*Anastasia.* Mary Brown is still missing. We arrived at Sally Hawkins' house just after 10 o'clock last night. We knocked on her door; there was no reply. We waited for half an hour and then entered the premises. We found Sally Hawkins dead, strangled. We can assume the authorities did this. There was no sign of Mary Brown. We left the building but kept a watch on it until curfew in case Mary turned up late. She didn't. "

"Andy I want you to go and find Mary again. It looks as those who want to do her harm are closing in on her, so it's urgent you find her. Will you help?"

"Of course."

"Good. It might help if you posed as a copper rather than a journalist. At seven o'clock precisely, a courier will deliver a pass, identifying you as a police detective. I'll give you another phone number. Given the urgency, I want you to ring this number at noon, five in the afternoon then at seven in the morning. Of course, phone straight away if you have news." Casper gave the number, which Andy repeated then hung off.

"What's all that about?" Jane had woken up. Andy explained. There had been no more rows since the morning after his night in the cells. Indeed, since the evangelists' hunt had turned into a search for Mary Brown, Jane had become more accepting of his activities. He had kept her informed of every development, even revealing Mary Brown's true identity to her. He wondered if that had been the right thing to do; should matters go wrong and the authorities find out about his actions, would Jane's knowledge make her more or less safe?

He dressed, had breakfast and decided to go to the Mile End shelter as soon as his police pass arrived. On the dot of seven, as promised, an envelope was dropped in his letterbox. He could hear a motorcycle engine revving up. He opened the door but by the time he saw him, the black-clad rider had reached the end of the road. He opened the envelope and retrieved the pass, identifying him as Detective Inspector Christopher Howe of the Metropolitan Police.

He drove down to Mile End Road. On the car radio, he caught the eight o'clock news; the headline was the execution of Josef Goebbels. He had confessed to being an agent of the United States-based World Jewish Congress. Given his confession, there had been no need for judicial proceedings and The Führer, Reinhard Heydrich, had ordered his execution, which had been carried out during the night. The fact there hadn't been a trial, even a show trial, seemed to Andy that Heydrich was acting from a position of weakness, not strength.

The receptionist at the Mile End hostel was the same as the day before.

"I didn't manage to see Mary Brown yesterday. Is she in today?" Andy asked.

"As far as I know, Mary spends the day at our William Booth College in Denmark Hill, although she's lodging with Captain Hawkins. She should be in shortly so if you care to wait, you can ask her."

Andy decided not to tell the lady about Sally Hawkins' murder. "Does Mary have any close friends in Hackney, outside the Salvation Army?"

"I really don't know. You'll have to ask Captain Hawkins about that."

"Did Mary drop in here last night, on her way home?" asked Andy.

"No, she assists at William Booth College until quite late in the evening, so always goes straight back home afterwards. In fact, it's over a week since we've last seen her here."

"And when was the last time you saw Captain Hawkins?"

The lady was clearly puzzled by the question. "Just before six o'clock yesterday evening. She was on her way home."

Andy thanked her and left.

The receptionist at William Booth College was a slight woman, nursing an injured nose, who introduced herself as Lieutenant Speight. Andy showed his police pass and asked about Mary.

"Oh Mary! I did tell her not to contact the police. It really was nothing."

"I'm sorry. What are you talking about?" said Andy.

"Last night's fracas at the George and Dragon. It was just a misunderstanding. We're not in trouble about that, are we, Inspector?"

"No, this is a completely unrelated matter. But tell me what happened at the George and Dragon."

"Mary and I were selling copies of *The War Cry*. There was a group of Blackshirts inside and we forgot to ask their permission first. They were understandably angry about that and I received a well-deserved punch. But Mary, for some reason, seemed a bit upset by the incident, and said something stupid about calling the police. There really was no need."

Andy noted the fear in her voice and wondered if posing as a police detective was such a good idea. Most people would of course appear to cooperate, but there was the risk they could withhold important information.

"What did you do after the altercation?"

"We both went home. I live in the area and Mary went straight back to Hackney."

"What time was this?"

"About eight o'clock."

Andy thought she was telling the truth and yet, he had the feeling she was holding something back. Then he had a flash of inspiration.

"You're not telling me everything, are you? Somebody else has been asking, haven't they?"

The woman nodded. "Two men, plain clothes like you, except they didn't show any identification. They asked after Mary."

"When was this?"

"Just before midnight."

Andy thanked the lady and left.

Could Mary have been so spooked by the pub business that she decided to run away from the Salvation Army? In that case, where to?

If Mary had gone back to Hackney, she would have arrived between eight-thirty and nine. Andy knew Sally Hawkins had been murdered sometime between six, just after the last time she had been seen at the Mile End hostel, and ten, when her body had been discovered by Casper's men. Maybe Mary saw Sally's body, panicked and then fled.

Then who were Lieutenants Speight's visitors? Were they State Security or could they have been Roy and Oliver?

Another, more troubling thought occurred to Andy: could Mary have killed Sally Hawkins? Could she be a spy after all? Could she have been faking her amnesia? Or maybe she had recovered from her amnesia and recalled that her real job was being a spy. Could Casper and his sidekicks be members of the spy ring themselves? After a few minutes of reflection, he decided to go along with Casper's account of Mary Brown's history, but would keep the spy hypothesis as an alternative possibility.

Andy went to the George and Dragon and received confirmation of Lieutenant Speight's account from the barman. He asked about possible sightings of Mary Brown at shops and bus stops in the vicinity but got no leads. He then headed back to King's Road in Hackney where Mary Brown had first gone to from Victoria Station six weeks earlier. He asked residents if Mary had been seen since eight o'clock the previous evening. Again, he got no response. He made his way to Sally Hawkins' address and asked the neighbours if they had recently seen Mary.

It was mid-afternoon, as he was just three doors from Sally Hawkins' home, when two police cars and an ambulance arrived. The policemen, three uniforms and a plainclothes, together with two ambulance men entered the house. Andy decided it was best he left the scene and he headed back home.

Chapter 31

ACRA was a large room on the second floor of the Home Office headquarters in Whitehall. The room's name was the acronym for Action Cabinet Room A; here, members of Sir Oswald Mosley's inner, or "action", cabinet met. The Action Cabinet had just three members: Mosley himself, Home Secretary, William Joyce and Defence Minister and Deputy Leader of the BUF, Angus Bye.

One side of the chamber had windows that looked out on Horse Guards Parade and St James's Park, although the room's occupants rarely spent their time admiring the view. The remaining walls were decorated with a mixture of Union Flags, Fascist insignia, an obligatory portrait of The Leader, and paintings of historical figures, taken from the Civil Service's large archive. The room was once graced with a fine portrait of the first Duke of Marlborough, Winston Churchill's ancestor, but at the insistence of The Leader, this was replaced by a Goya of the Duke of Wellington.

Next to the doorway stood a man in a Blackshirt uniform, aged about 30, with his arms clasped behind his back. At six foot seven inches in height, with a fifty-two-inch chest and twenty-eight-inch waist, the guard was an intimidating presence.

In the middle of the wall, opposite the entrance, hung a huge mirror, and just a few feet away stood a round table of some six feet in diameter. Adjoining the table were six high-backed chairs; the chair facing the mirror and an adjacent chair were empty, but the remaining four were occupied. William Joyce and Angus Bye were joined by Philip Thompson, Minister of the Interior, and Jeremy Holroyd, Information Minister, who were not normally action cabinet members. The men were dressed in business suits with lightning flash badges attached to their lapels.

The guard barked "The Leader". The men stood up and gave raised-arm salutes. The Leader, Sir Oswald Mosley, dressed as a Blackshirt officer, strode briskly in, although with a slight limp. Following a few steps behind, dressed in a civilian suit, was Alistair Harper, Security Adviser to Oswald Mosley.

Mosley and Harper sat in their places first then the ministers lowered their salutes and sat down.

"Gentlemen, the first item on today's agenda is the situation with the King," said Mosley. "I regret to inform you that he is dying from throat cancer. Furthermore, we will have a constitutional crisis on our hands as he has no heir. I don't need to tell you how important the King has been to Fascist rule in the British Empire. Much of our legitimacy rests on his support." He spoke with a sonorous, affected, upper-class accent, laced with a slight Staffordshire burr. He was not one to indulge in small talk during such meetings, although he was proud of his ability to give four-hour speeches, entirely without notes.

"He should have adopted Gudrun Himmler when her father was assassinated back in 1944," said Joyce. He too spoke with an upper-class accent, but with a slow, nasal drawl and a barely perceptible Galway timbre. His manner of speech, together with a scar that ran right down his right cheek almost to his lips, exuded a sinister aura.

"Yes, that was a lost opportunity," said Mosley. "The Führer was keen on the idea but the King refused. But now that he is in such a poor state, it is imperative that we find a suitable successor and put maximum pressure on the King to agree to an adoption."

"There is something I'd like to bring up," said Joyce. "It's not on the agenda, but recent events make it important."

"Go on, but make it quick," said Mosley.

"I think this Action Cabinet should issue a statement, condemning the treachery of Josef Goebbels," said Joyce.

"Agreed," said Mosley. "Is that it?"

"Lady Mosley is a close friend of Frau Goebbels, is she not?" said Joyce. "Goebbels himself was best man at your wedding. Am I right?"

"Gordon-Canning was best man, as you well know," said Mosley.

The threat from Joyce was all too clear, Mosley reckoned. Joyce's voice had an even more menacing tone than usual. Of course, the Mosleys had been close to the Goebbels. His marriage to Diana had been held at the Goebbels' Berlin residence, witnessed by none other than Adolf Hitler himself. But then, Joyce had been an ally of Goebbels too, working at the Nazi Propaganda Ministry from 1939 to 1941. After Adolf Hitler's death, Joyce had cut his ties with Goebbels and had been a backer of Heydrich in the Nazi power struggle. Mosley had taken a "wait and see" line, maintaining good relations with Goebbels and Speer as well as Heydrich. With hindsight, that may have been a mistake. It didn't help that only the previous month, Diana had been a guest at the Goebbels' holiday home in Yalta, or whatever the Germans called the place nowadays. It could have been worse; when news of Goebbels' arrest was announced, Diana had wanted to fly to Berlin to plead his case, but the swift execution had put paid to that. Of course, the charge that Goebbels was a Jewish spy was nonsense, a complete fabrication. Something he couldn't say in public, not with Joyce on his back. The man had made an implicit challenge; he would have to watch him like a hawk, just in case he was planning a coup.

"We digress," said Mosley. "We shall move on to the Mary Brown case."

"My German contacts tell me that Heydrich set his hunting dogs loose on Goebbels," said Joyce. "A most fitting punishment for a traitor."

Mosley ignored the comment.

"Gentlemen, Harper will brief us on the fugitive spy, Mary Brown," said Mosley.

"Mary Brown has been staying with the Mile End Road branch of the Salvation Army for the last few weeks," said Harper. "She has been living with Salvationist Sally Hawkins."

"Traitor!" shouted Joyce.

Harper disregarded the remark. "Our men arrived at Hawkins' house yesterday evening and were told by her that Mary Brown was out fundraising and would arrive in a few hours. Our people stayed with Hawkins. She then went to a shop, escorted by one of our agents. Afterwards, she made a telephone call from a kiosk, telling our agent beforehand that she was going to cancel a meeting. She did not know that our agent could lip read. She telephoned the Salvationists' William Booth College and requested they put Mary Brown up for the night. On their return to Hawkins' house, the agents proceeded to eliminate Hawkins. She had, after all, committed treason, and our men had no further use of her."

"Quite right too," said Joyce. "We should eliminate all the Salvationists."

"We are not mass murderers," said Mosley. "We kill selectively and wisely. Continue."

"Our agents then went to Denmark Hill to find that Mary Brown had indeed been there earlier," said Harper. "The Salvationists had received the request to accommodate her but hadn't been able to contact her and believed she had gone back to Hackney. Our men returned to Hawkins' home; it was now past midnight and there was no sign of Mary Brown. We have lost her trail."

"Gentlemen, Sally Hawkins' death presents us with an opportunity," said Mosley. "We are going to hold Mary Brown responsible for her murder. This will no longer be a hush-hush search by our intelligence services; we can go public and use all of the forces of law and order to find her. "

"Joyce, you will direct the police in the search," Mosley continued. "Thompson, you will see that our intelligence services continue to give this top priority. Bye, you will ensure the Army assist us in this matter. Holroyd, you will make sure Mary Brown's crime is given prominence in all our newspapers, radio and television. I personally will lead our beloved Blackshirts.

"I will set up a command and control centre in ACRE. That's Action Cabinet Room E," Mosley said, for the benefit of Philip Thompson and Jeremy Holroyd, who were not members of the inner cabinet. "ACRE will have secure telephone and teleprinter links to the respective police, State Security and Army control centres. All information they receive will be immediately duplicated to ACRE. All of us round this table will have 24-hour access to ACRE and we will be able to direct our forces accordingly. We've talked long enough, now is the time for action."

Mosley stood up and gave a raised-arm salute. All the men seated at the table stood up, saluted and left the room. Mosley sat down and looked at the large mirror facing him. At 75, he was still good-looking, he thought. He reckoned the face staring back at him was at least 15 years younger. Maybe he could do without the cap. He took it off and observed he still had a fair amount of hair, although now grey. And he had that distinguished moustache. The man in the mirror could still seduce women, he concluded. He had one rule, however: all his mistresses had to be upper class and married. Back in the '40s, he had had an affair with Magda Goebbels. Diana, who was one of Magda's closest friends, and who must have known, didn't object, but he wondered if Diana's subsequent affair with Heydrich was retaliation. Enough reminiscing, there was tonight to think about; just which lady should he invite for oysters in his study?

Chapter 32

Mary woke up and looked at her watch; it showed six-thirty but she wasn't sure if it was evening or morning. She got up and looked out of the window; she could see a street with shops and offices. It was light outside but there was little traffic so she supposed it was morning. She had slept for over 15 hours. Although she felt refreshed by her rest, her overwhelming sensation was now hunger: she hadn't eaten for 36 hours.

The hotel didn't provide breakfast, so she decided to go to Victoria Station and get something to eat at one of the cafés there, thinking that they should be open, even at this hour. She walked down to the hotel's entrance lobby and handed her key to the receptionist, who was reading a magazine. He looked up, took her key and went back to his magazine without saying a word.

At the station's entrance, she did a double-take at the sight of a newspaper stand poster. The headline screamed out in bold capitals: "*SALVATION ARMY MURDER: HUNT FOR MARY BROWN.*" She froze in her tracks and was barely aware of the travellers arriving at and leaving the station.

She was shaken out of her trance by the cry of a newspaper vendor: "Sally Hawkins murder. Read all about it."

She could see a photograph of herself, which took up half the front page.

She did an about turn and headed back to her hotel. She was just yards from the entrance when she decided not to go back in. She didn't have enough money for a

233

second night and she didn't see the point of going back just for a few hours until her check-out time. There was also the risk the receptionist would learn about the news and inform the police.

She walked along the street in which her hotel was located but she could see more newsagents ahead so she turned into a quieter side street. She wandered aimlessly in the neighbourhood until she reached a bridge over the River Thames. To the left, she could see the Houses of Parliament and Westminster Abbey about a quarter of a mile away; she had been there with Sally a few weeks earlier. A police checkpoint had been set up halfway between her and the Parliament buildings. She wasn't going to go that way. She could go either right and follow the river embankment or continue over the bridge. She took the bridge. On the other side were more checkpoints ahead and to the right of her; she could only go left along Lambeth Palace Road.

Just a minute later, she got the second shock of the day. Outside what she supposed was Lambeth Palace was a huge poster of her Uncle David. She took a closer look and saw that the portrait was that of the King. She had seen many pictures of the King, which were all recently taken and showed him as an elderly man in his 70s. But this one showed a man in his mid-40s who looked just like her Uncle David.

She could feel the fog that had covered her memory lifting; it was as sudden as those days when fog turns to mist and then to bright blue sunshine in a matter of minutes. It was the same with her memory; in just a few moments, everything came back to her.

Uncle David *was* King Edward VIII. Next to King Edward's portrait was one of Archbishop Cosmo Lang.

Both of these posters must have been put up at the time of King Edward's coronation in 1941. The Archbishop had been strongly in favour of his abdication in 1936, so the 1941 Government must have put great pressure on him to perform the coronation. The posters just outside the Archbishop of Canterbury's Lambeth Palace residence were a constant reminder to the Archbishop and his successors just who the boss was in matters between Church and State.

Childhood recollections first rushed to fill the vacuum created by her amnesia. She had bitter-sweet memories of Uncle David. As a child, she had always looked forward to his frequent weekend visits to Royal Lodge in Windsor. But after the abdication, she never saw him again and she knew he had been in her parents' bad books.

Then she recalled the hijacking and her house arrest; memories she wished could have stayed forgotten. There was still a bit of a mist shrouding that period, but a few events were coming to the fore. She had met Sir Oswald Mosley twice during her long house arrest. The first time was on her 18th birthday; Sir Oswald gave her a Corgi puppy as a present. The second time was after her father, King George's, death. Sir Oswald came to offer his condolences and left her a signed copy of his autobiography; she never read the book. During her imprisonment, she had never seen Uncle David, who she now knew had been crowned King Edward VIII for a second time, so she assumed he had known nothing about it.

She recalled earlier, happier times before the war when, together with sister Margaret and their governess, Crawfie, they travelled incognito by underground to Tottenham Court Road Station to have tea at the YWCA. However, they were eventually recognised and crowds started to gather round them, so their detective had to call for a car to take them home.

The hoot of a car horn shook her from her reverie. She could go on reminiscing all day; in the here and now, she was Mary Brown and in great danger. She carried on walking in the direction of Waterloo Station; standing too long in front of the posters might draw attention to her. She was sure King Edward would offer her protection but she would need to find out if he was at Buckingham Palace or Windsor. Even if he were at Windsor, she could get there easily. There was a train to Windsor from Waterloo Station; it was nearby and she should have enough money for the train journey.

But though she was sure the King would take her in, she quickly realised there was little chance she could get past the guards and checkpoints. She had a better idea. She was in the centre of London, after all; she could go to an embassy and ask for asylum. Obviously, it couldn't be an embassy with too friendly relations with Britain, such as Germany or France. Even a neutral country's embassy was risky; they may not believe her story and decide to hand her over to the authorities. Diplomatic immunity wasn't usually granted to common criminals, especially murderers such as Mary Brown.

She knew relations between Britain and Australia and Canada were cool, so their embassies would be a good place to ask for asylum; she also thought she could convince their ambassadors about her story. She knew a lot about Canada and Australia; her parents had told her all about their 1939 Canadian tour, and she herself had been in Perth, Australia in 1941, just before her abduction. But she didn't know if these countries even had diplomatic representation in Britain. A few hundred yards short of Waterloo Station, she came across a phone booth and saw it had a telephone directory inside. She checked if there were entries for the Australian and Canadian Embassies. She was in luck; both countries were listed. The Australian Embassy was nearest; it was only a 10-minute walk away on the Strand on the other side of the river. Just to be sure, she phoned and was told the embassy was indeed on the Strand and was open that day.

Mary headed for Waterloo Bridge, which she would need to cross to get to the Embassy. She was halfway across when she spotted a police checkpoint on the far side. She turned and went back; she would try crossing the river by the next bridge, Blackfriars. She had only walked past Waterloo Bridge for a minute when a couple of Army trucks passed her and stopped just a few hundred yards in front of her. Soldiers immediately jumped out; they took positions across the road while two officers started checking the papers of both motorists and pedestrians.

Mary was trapped; she was surrounded by checkpoints and had nowhere to go. It was all the more frustrating because the Australian Embassy and safety was so close, just a short distance away on the other side of the river. But in her predicament, it might as well have been on another planet. At that moment, she felt a tug on her sleeve; it was a shabbily-dressed man in his 80s.

"Come this way. I'm sure Miss Brown could do with a cup of tea."

Chapter 33

Andy had woken up early; it was a quarter to six. He tried to go back to sleep but found he couldn't, so he quietly got up and went to the kitchen. He made himself toast and coffee and switched on the radio as he started his breakfast. The shipping forecast was just finishing and the news shortly followed: *This is the six o'clock news. A nationwide search is underway for Mary Brown, wanted for the murder of Salvation Army member, Sally Hawkins.* The next five minutes of the report were taken up solely with the details of the murder and descriptions of Mary Brown.

A minute after the news had ended, Casper phoned.

"Mary's not just on the radio," Casper said. "She's on the television and front pages of all the newspapers, together with photographs of her. It's even more urgent you find her. She cannot go unrecognised for more than a day or so, especially as the authorities will certainly be setting up extra checkpoints all over the city. What was your plan for today?"

"Yesterday, I looked around Denmark Hill and Hackney without any leads. I think Mary saw Sally's body and panicked, and tried to get as far away from the Salvationists as possible. Given her amnesia, I think there's one other place she might have gone to – Victoria Station. It's where she was reborn, as it were. So I'll start looking there."

"That makes sense," said Casper. "The photographs of Mary in the press have her wearing a beige coat. Has your wife a black coat?"

"I think so."

"Bring it with you. As Mary has medium-length brown hair, you should go to a theatrical supplies shop and get a red-haired lady's wig, preferably shoulder length. Again, report any progress directly to me. When you find Mary, and you will find her, Andy, take her somewhere safe, south of London. A small bed and breakfast, say. When you've done that, go back to London and tell no one of her whereabouts, and that includes Roy and Oliver. Instead, ask them to take you to meet me."

*

For a moment, Mary wasn't sure what to do or whether she could trust the man. On the other hand, he could have easily gone to the checkpoint and reported her, or he could have shouted to other pedestrians that the fugitive Mary Brown was among them. But he didn't. Mary decided to accept the man's offer.

"Come this way," the man gestured. "My name's Derek."

She followed Derek back towards Waterloo Bridge then down some steps to a spot under the bridge where a group of about 20 men, all in their 80s, were assembled. Some lay in sleeping bags, or on mattresses wrapped in dirty, threadbare blankets. One was darning his socks, while a couple sat on the pavement, playing draughts. About half a dozen were huddled around a fire, while a smaller group were seated on packing crates by a stove, on which a kettle was placed, and were sipping from their mugs. The only item of furniture present was a large, solidly-built table, on which lay two heavy-duty sewing machines, a few cans of glue, brushes, zips, and an assortment of ladies' and gentlemen's shoes and a couple of handbags.

"Tom, some tea for our visitor." Derek spoke to the man who seemed to be in charge of operating the stove.

Mary accepted the tea thankfully, even though she could see it was made with a well-used teabag, and came without milk or sugar. She was even more grateful for the single digestive biscuit that was offered; for a short while, it eased her pangs of hunger.

"You're wondering why we've taken you in?" said Derek. "Do we always offer hospitality to murderers on the run? Well, we don't, but we know you're no murderer, Miss Brown. People like that poor Sally Hawkins get done in all the time, but the powers that be don't bother to make it front page news or set up police checkpoints all over the place. The cops and Blackshirts do set up roadblocks, checking everyone who passes, but this time, they're only stopping and questioning middle-aged women. So we know you're an enemy of the Fascists, and that makes you a welcome visitor."

"What are you doing here?" asked Mary. She cast her eye over the sleeping bags and old mattresses. "Surely you'll all be arrested under the Workshy Laws."

"We're safe from that point of view; the Workshy Acts don't apply to us. You see, we're all pensioners; except that we don't get a pension."

"Why's that?" asked Mary.

"We're all veterans from 1940. We saw action in Norway or Flanders."

"Surely you're all too…" Mary broke off, realising she was about to make a rather impolite remark.

"Too old to see action in 1940, you were going to say. No, we're all in our late 60s, except Tom, who's 72, and saw action in 1918 too. Living like this ages you very quickly. Mosley promised a 'Land fit for Heroes' for all ex-service personnel. At first, he kept his word. On reaching 65, all ex-servicemen received good-quality, free housing and double the standard state pension. Then, three years ago, the German government objected; it didn't have a problem with the Great War veterans receiving pensions, but the 1940 servicemen were a different matter. The Germans said it was anti-European to honour men who had fought against the Wehrmacht, which had shed so much blood to unify Europe. Mosley lost no time in acting. We were given 24 hours' notice to leave our homes, our pensions were stopped, and we soon used up any savings."

"But you don't have to live like this," said Mary. "Surely you can stay at a shelter."

"We did to begin with," said Derek. "I was with the Salvation Army for a month before the Blackshirts arrived and turfed us out."

"But where do you get your food from?"

"We run a small cobblers and shoeshine business, which helps us get by. We go out into the streets, offering to clean shoes and take in the odd shoe or handbag repair. People are quite generous, you know; when they realise we're veterans, they often pay above the asking price for our services. We just need to keep an eye out for cops or Blackshirts when touting for business, and scarper as soon as we see them."

"What happens if you fall ill?" said Mary.

"Some doctors will take a look if we get sick, but if it's something serious, the hospitals refuse to treat us. But that's enough about us. You can stay here as long as you want and you should be safe; the police wouldn't think of looking here."

Chapter 34

Andy drove to Victoria Station and started looking in the waiting rooms and cafés. He hadn't really expected Mary Brown to still be there, so wasn't too disappointed when that search came to nothing. Next were hotels in the area. He wasn't too hopeful about this either; surely, any hotel staff would have heard the news and would have immediately reported Mary to the police if she had been staying with them.

It was noon by the time he entered the Thames Hotel. A receptionist with a surly demeanour looked up from a copy of *Titbits*.

"Oh yes, she stayed here last night," said the receptionist on being shown Mary's photograph.

"Is she still with you?" asked Andy.

"No."

"Did she tell you where she was going when she settled her bill?"

"She didn't settle her bill."

"So you reported her to the police," said Andy.

"There was no need to. All our customers have to pay in advance. Is there anything else?"

"What time did you last see her?"

"Just before seven this morning. She gave me her key and hasn't been back since."

Andy thanked the man and let him go back to reading his magazine. He returned to Victoria Station, found a booth and phoned Casper.

"Mary was last seen at the Thames Hotel in Victoria at seven this morning," said Andy.

"Can you just hold for a few minutes?" said Casper.

Casper had been in ACRE just half an hour earlier. He was one of only six, all members of the extended Action Cabinet, who was allowed access to the room at any time of day and night. He had taken a list of sightings of Mary Brown that had been reported to the police. The list included the time and location of every observation; the last one had been at 11 o'clock that morning. There were nearly 300 entries, but his job was made easier by the list being ordered by time of sighting. He narrowed his search to reports after seven o'clock and located not too far from Victoria Station. Someone had seen her walking near Lambeth Bridge at eight o'clock. Another report had her seen with tramps under Waterloo Bridge at nine o'clock. There was a record of her in the Limehouse area, about three miles away, at ten-thirty. She could have got to Limehouse from Waterloo in an hour and a half if she had walked, less if she had taken public transport. But there had been no sightings of her along any possible route. This made Casper think there was a chance Mary didn't stop by the tramps just to ask directions, but had stayed with them.

He thought it was worth investigating anyway. The police didn't know that Mary had stayed at the Thames Hotel so wouldn't give the Waterloo Bridge sighting priority. They would most likely work through the list in order, visiting each location reported. With luck, they wouldn't have got to Waterloo Bridge yet. He picked up the receiver.

"Andy, I want you to go to a tramps' squat under Waterloo Bridge straight away. Mary might be there; you must hurry."

Andy got there in less than 10 minutes, parking his car just 200 yards from the bridge. The squat was not what he expected; it was part workshop and part sleeping quarters, which seemed to be a mixture of cardboard boxes, mattresses and sleeping bags. There were more than a dozen old men there, but although they were dressed in rags, there was an organised air about the place. They were sleeping, cooking, drinking tea or working, repairing shoes, apart from one who was seated on a soapbox, chatting with a woman. Andy was in no doubt as to her identity.

"Mary Brown?" said Andy.

The woman looked up but said nothing. The men stopped what they were doing and six of them formed a shield between Andy and Mary Brown.

"I've come to collect you," said Andy. "We were supposed to pick you up at a Victoria Station waiting room six weeks ago, but you had gone. Do you remember that?"

"Don't believe him," said one of the men.

"I do," said Mary. "And where are you taking me?"

"Canada. You have relatives there; they'll help you with your memory problems." Andy spun the line he had been given by Casper.

The vagrants surrounding Mary tightened their cordon, while others dropped what they were doing and glared at Andy.

"Don't go!" shouted one.

"Stay here," said another.

"This is a trick," said the tramp who had been talking to Mary. "He's from the police, come to arrest you."

"Would I come alone and unarmed to do that?" said Andy. "You can search me." He raised his arms.

For a few seconds, the men were undecided about taking up Andy's offer. The silence was broken by a shout. "Cops! Over there."

Four armed police were heading towards them from the north side of the bridge. They were about 200 yards away, walking briskly. The way south of the bridge was clear.

"You've no choice, Miss Brown," said the tramp. "You have to trust the man."

Mary gave a brief nod.

"This way," said Andy. "Walk, don't run."

The walk to Andy's car took just two minutes, but every second seemed like a minute to him. Andy opened the boot of the car and made sure Mary put on her coat and wig unobserved. He drove in a south-westerly direction towards Wimbledon. He'd driven less than a mile when, at Vauxhall, he came across a police checkpoint; all cars were being stopped. Andy rolled down his window.

"Papers," barked a police constable.

Andy showed him his police identity card. "I'm off duty now; just finished a shift. And that's the missus," he said, nodding in Mary's direction. It was a heart-stopping moment. If the policeman asked to see her identity card, they would be finished. There hadn't been enough time to produce a card for the Princess with a new identity and a photograph of her in a red wig. The policeman looked at Mary for a moment and satisfied, waved them on.

"My name is Andy." He was wary of giving his surname. He assumed Mary remembered nothing before waking up in that Victoria Station waiting room. "Your relatives were all given exit visas for Canada many years ago, but you were given yours only last month. A representative of the Canadian Government had all the papers and, because of your memory problems, was going to accompany you out of the country when you disappeared. You will meet him later. For some reason, the authorities think you've murdered Sally Hawkins, which does complicate things."

Mary at first wanted to tell her rescuer that her amnesia had cured itself, but then had second thoughts.

Did this Andy really know who she was? Would he act any differently if he didn't and now found out? If she was caught again by the authorities, would it help her if it was believed she still had amnesia?

Finally, she decided not to admit that her memory had returned until she was out of the country.

"I'll be seeing my relatives again. That will be nice," said Mary.

Chapter 35

The six men assembled in ACRA sat in their usual places; the same Blackshirt guard kept watch. Apart from one exception, the furniture and fittings hadn't changed in years; the previous day, the mirror had been replaced by a three-foot square photograph of The Leader, taken 30 years earlier.

"Brief us please, Harper," said Oswald Mosley.

"A woman matching Mary Brown's description was seen among tramps under Waterloo Bridge," said Alistair Harper. "She had been invited by one of the tramps to join them a few hours earlier. The vagrants are veterans of Churchill's war. Because we believe they could become a source of trouble, our intelligence services have always kept a stool pigeon among the men. He phoned the police about Mary Brown."

"I told you so," said William Joyce. "We should have shot the lot of them. We're now paying dearly for the decision to spare the tramps. Besides, it would have been more humane to get rid of the men than let them live in squalor."

"Comment overruled," said Mosley. "Continue, Harper."

"Unfortunately, the police didn't know of the informer's role in the security services so did not give the report top priority. By the time the police did arrive at the scene, the woman had gone, accompanied by a man who had arrived a few minutes earlier to pick her up."

"You fucked up, Joyce," said Mosley. "See that heads roll. Next time, it will be yours."

"But the police can't be held responsible if the intelligence services didn't tell them about their informer," said Joyce.

"Shut up," said Mosley. He turned to Philip Thompson, his Minister of the Interior. "Thompson, my remarks apply to you too. Harper, continue."

"We have a description of the man who left with Mary Brown. Clearly, he had been tipped off about her being with the vagrants. This happened just over an hour ago; we've had no further credible sightings since."

"Gentlemen, we are going to have to ratchet this up a level," said Mosley. "I want an immediate 24-hour curfew throughout Greater London. All public transport is to cease in the city, as well as any flights out of the country. This is to be strictly enforced." Mosley turned to Jeremy Holroyd, his Information Minister. "Holroyd, I want you to make sure the public, through continuous radio, television and newspaper reports, are informed that Mary Brown is a spy. Furthermore, the public should now be told that in addition to Sally Hawkins' death, she is responsible for the murder of four of our security service men. She is a dangerous terrorist and a reward of £100,000 is offered for information leading to her death or capture. Dismissed," said Mosley. The men all stood up, gave raised-arm salutes and got ready to leave.

"Harper, don't go just yet," said Mosley.

After the other men had left the room, Mosley turned to Alistair Harper. "There's something I don't understand. How could Mary Brown's contact have known she was with the vagrants? There's no evidence this was a pre-arranged meeting place. The lead could only have come from someone within the police."

"I was thinking the same, my leader. But there's another potential source for the tip-off. That's from within this very room. All of us round this table have full access to ACRE and could have seen the report of that particular sighting of Mary Brown."

"A rather disturbing possibility that had occurred to me too," said Mosley. "Keep a close eye on my ministers; do whatever is necessary, even tap their phones."

"Including Joyce?" said Harper.

"Especially Joyce."

Chapter 36

Andy Deegan and Mary Brown drove past two more checkpoints as they continued their journey through the South London suburbs. The police didn't bother to check their papers; they just waved them through when they could see Andy's passenger didn't fit their description of Mary Brown.

They continued along the A24 as far Leatherhead. For a moment, Andy thought of putting Mary up with his parents. Very quickly, he rejected the idea; he didn't want to put them at risk. Besides, Casper had specified a modest hotel, south of London. Andy reckoned he was still too close to London, so decided to drive on to the next town, Dorking. He stopped at the two-star Hill View Hotel in the centre of town.

He asked for the best double room, introducing himself as Inspector and Mrs Howe, an off-duty police detective on a short break with his wife. He paid upfront for one night. The bedroom was a modest affair; the king-size bed took up most of the space. There wasn't even a wardrobe, just a tiny alcove with a few coat hangers. The bathroom was at the end of the corridor, which was shared with three other bedrooms.

"I'm sorry about the room," said Andy. "But it was the best on offer."

"That's all right," said Mary. "It's better than the place I stayed at last night."

"I've got to go back to London now to meet your contact. He'll pick you up later this evening. In the meantime, you mustn't leave the hotel; in fact, it's better to stay in your room."

"How will the contact identify himself? After all, the authorities are looking for me too."

Andy wasn't sure if he should reveal Casper's name. Besides, he didn't know if Casper would actually collect Mary himself. He thought it best to come up with a password that, besides Mary, he would only reveal to Casper. "He'll identify himself using the password *Succession*."

Andy left, telling the hotel receptionist that he'd been recalled back on duty but hoped to return before curfew. He switched on the radio as he drove back towards London. It was the Jimmy Savile show on Radio 2. Suddenly, the music stopped and there was silence for a few seconds. Andy was about to tune into Radio 4 when the radio sprang to life again.

This is a special announcement. Please listen carefully. The Leader has declared a 24-hour curfew throughout London in connection with the escaped spy and terrorist, Mary Brown. The fugitive is aged 46, is of medium height and has brown hair, and was wearing a beige overcoat. She was last seen accompanied by a fair-haired man in his late 30s or early 40s and about five foot ten inches tall. A reward of £100,000 is offered for information leading to Mary Brown's capture. The curfew will start at three o'clock and will take effect throughout Greater London. Citizens are required to remain at home or in their place of work. If driving, stop immediately and take shelter in the nearest public building. All public transport will stop at the nearest bus or train station and passengers must remain at the station's premises until further notice. I repeat: the curfew starts at three o'clock and will be rigorously enforced. Any violators will be shot.

The message over, Jimmy Savile started wittering on about how wise The Leader was, how important it was to follow his instructions, how The Leader was a good friend of his, and that he, Jimmy Savile, would be sleeping over at the BBC studios because of the curfew. Andy switched the radio off. He was relieved that Mary Brown was described as brown rather than red-haired and, although his own description was not far off the mark, the authorities still didn't have a name for the male accomplice. It was now a quarter to three; there was no way he could get back home before curfew. He was near Leatherhead, so he'd stop by his parents after all and ask if they would put him up for the night.

He was there 10 minutes later; he didn't have much explaining to do as they too had heard the curfew announcement. First, he phoned Jane.

"Jane, its Andy. I'm with Mum and Dad. I can't pick up the children because of the curfew. You do know about it?"

"Yes, I heard about halfway through an interesting new fishcake recipe on *Woman's Hour*. There wasn't enough time to collect the children even if I could get a taxi immediately. I phoned the school straight away. Miss Miller said the children could stay overnight; there was no food for supper, but she said she was quite accomplished at the piano and had a good selection of Fascist marching songs to keep the pupils' spirits up."

"That's Miss Miller for you," said Andy.

"How long is this supposed to last?"

"Officially 24-hours, but in practice, until Mary Brown is caught, which in principle is indefinitely.

However, just imagine the chaos this is causing; for starters, just about every school in London has children who can't go home. They'll have to lift the curfew soon, at least for a couple of hours."

Andy tried Roy and Oliver's number next. It was Roy who answered.

"Casper wanted you to take me to him in a certain eventuality," said Andy. "That eventuality has occurred, but we do have the problem of the curfew."

"So you've found Mary Brown," said Roy. "Don't worry about the curfew, we can get round that."

Andy gave Roy his address and Roy promised to be there within a couple of hours.

In fact, it was just over an hour before the doorbell rang, but it was Oliver rather than Roy at the door. He had arrived in a white marked police Triumph 2000, driven by a uniformed constable.

They drove through the London suburbs at great speed. The streets were clear of both civilians and traffic. There were numerous checkpoints manned by police, Blackshirts or the Army but they were quickly waved through. At one point, they came across a line of half a dozen cars with their driver's doors left open. Opposite each car, on the pavement, lay a body face-down with blood running from its head. Nearby, a couple of armed Blackshirts were having a cigarette break.

"They obviously didn't know about the curfew; should have had their radios on," muttered the constable.

Near the city centre, they drove past a restaurant, outside of which were a few more bodies; all shot with multiple bullet wounds.

"We saw the same outside a café on the way out," said Oliver. "It looks like some cafés and restaurants only heard about the curfew at three and immediately closed down and ordered their clientele out. The forces of law and order happened to be outside and shot the customers."

High stakes were involved here, thought Andy. Normally, curfew violators spent a few nights in a police cell, or if they were repeat offenders, ended up at one of the labour camps. This was the first time Andy had seen anyone shot for breaking a curfew.

They arrived at a 12-storey office building at Millbank, on the Thames embankment. Oliver showed his pass at the entrance and an official frisked Andy. Andy knew that this was State Security headquarters, although even that information was officially classified. As he had long suspected, Casper had to be a senior intelligence officer.

They took a lift to the top floor and Oliver led Andy into an office. It was a large room with standard issue Civil Service metal desk and filing cabinets, but with a few additions that indicated the rank of its occupant. The office was fitted with a deep-pile, grey-green carpet. Behind the desk was a high-back, leather swivel chair. On the desk itself there were no papers, just a telephone, intercom and what looked like a framed family photograph. A black leather sofa was placed alongside one of the walls. On one side of the sofa stood a cocktail cabinet, while on the other stood a small table, upon which was placed an ice bucket, from which the neck of a bottle of wine protruded. A safe was set into one of the walls, while on the other hung an oil portrait of The Leader.

The room's sole occupant was by a windowsill, watering some potted plants. The man put down the watering can, turned to face Andy and held out his hand.

"Casper. Nice to meet you, Andy, take a seat." Casper stood at six foot two, was about fifty years old, dark-haired with streaks of grey, and dressed in a well-cut Savile Row pinstripe suit. He spoke with a public school cut-glass accent, quite different to the scrambled speech Andy had heard over the phone.

Andy sat down by the desk opposite Casper, while Oliver stood behind by the door.

"Care for some champagne?" said Casper.

Andy nodded and was offered a glass. He noted the label on the bottle, Dom Pérignon. This didn't come cheap, so he surmised that Casper must be near, if not at the top of the organisation.

"Your family well? Not caught out by this curfew business, I hope," said Casper.

Andy took a sip and explained how the children had been forced to stay at school.

"What a bind. Look, Andy, sorry to be a bore, but I need to have the details of Mary Brown's whereabouts pronto. We have to move fast, especially since the authorities are pulling out all the stops. *Carpe Diem*, you know."

"I need to have your password before I can give away such sensitive information," said Andy. There was something about Casper that made him feel uneasy.

"There's no need for that formality now that we've met in person. Oliver here can vouch for me, as he can for you."

"I'm sorry, I must insist," said Andy. "Just to put my mind at rest."

"Very well then, it's *Cordelia*."

Andy relaxed a bit. "She's in a two-star " He stopped himself short. "You've given me Roy and Oliver's password. You've got your own."

Casper was silent for all of 10 seconds. "I've forgotten. Look, Andy, we really don't have time for these games. *Tempus fugit*."

Andy felt a knot tighten in his stomach and a bad feeling spread throughout all his senses. This was not Casper. It wasn't just the password; he had other misgivings that up to now had been suppressed. There was the peppering of sentences with Latin; in all his telephone conversations, Casper had never used a single Latin quote. Then why hadn't Roy picked him up after he had phoned him? He had said he would pick him up in person; not that it would be either him or Oliver.

"I'd like to see Roy in person," said Andy. "If he can vouch for you as Oliver does then we can proceed."

There was a silence that lasted about 15 seconds but seemed a lot longer to Andy. "Casper" let out a sigh and spoke over Andy's head to Oliver. "It was worth a try."

Andy knew for sure he had been betrayed by Oliver and he was now in the tightest spot he'd ever been since his National Service Mount Kenya debacle.

Chapter 37

"Andy, you don't need to know my name," said Casper's imposter. "I am a senior officer in British intelligence and my job is to catch traitors such as Mary Brown and Casper. All the forces of law and order are looking for the spy, Mary Brown. You know where she is; withholding that information is itself a treasonable offence. You're obviously a patriot; your Military Cross proves that. Why would you want to betray your country? Now where is Mary Brown?"

Andy remained silent.

"There'll be no repercussions for you if you cooperate now. Oliver was one of Casper's men until he saw the error of his ways and came over to us. Now he's a valuable member of my team. I'm offering you the same terms, Andy; you can work for us. What do you say?"

Andy said nothing; this time, the silent pause was a little longer.

"We can make life very unpleasant for you if you do not cooperate. A treason trial and concomitant death sentence will come as a relief to you."

There was another silent pause.

"Very well, have it your way," the intelligence officer sighed. He then pressed an intercom on his desk. "John, B2 here. How's the wife? It's a boy, how nice. Shame about the cricket; about time we beat the Blackshirts. Look, John, I need an interrogation slot now. Room 103, that's fine. I'd like a couple of assistants too. Experienced and not afraid of the sight of blood please. The new boy last week threw up all over my suit. Thank you, that's really appreciated. Regards to the good wife."

B2 paused then spoke to Andy. "My offer still stands. You can recant at any time, but we may have difficulty employing a cripple."

Shortly, the door opened and Andy turned to see two men enter; both were in their twenties, over six foot, and heavily-built rugby types.

"Drink up," said B2. "I don't like decent champagne going to waste."

Andy took a sip then one of the assistants slipped on a pair of handcuffs.

B2 stood up. "I'd like you to come, Oliver. You don't have to come inside the interrogation room if you find it distressing. You can stay outside if you like; but I do need you close at hand."

Andy was overwhelmed by a sense of foreboding. The thought of the unpleasant fate that was in store for him made him feel physically weak at the knees. The two assistants hauled him to his feet and firmly gripped each of his elbows.

They all left the office and took a lift down to the basement. Andy wondered if all the talk from B2 was just bluff; an attempt to put psychological pressure on him and that there would be nothing like the serious torture B2 had implied. Andy thought he could cope with a few slaps around the face, but he was not sure how much pain he could take. The lift doors opened to a reception room of sorts; a guard in commissionaire's uniform sat behind a desk, reading *Sporting Life*.

"Good afternoon, Fred, any tips?" B2 asked.

"Newbury, two-thirty on Saturday, sir. I'd put my money on Juggernaut; eleven to one odds."

"I might wager a fiver myself," said B2. "You've always proved right so far."

B2 showed his pass and Fred opened a door opposite the lift entrance. It led onto a long, cold and dimly-lit corridor. At first, it was silent, then Andy could hear muffled sounds coming from some of the rooms either side of the corridor. Then he heard a scream, followed by more silence, then a long, moaning sound. He wondered if these noises were for real and not just tapes being played, which had been previously recorded by some actors. Nevertheless, the fear that had started at his knees spread throughout Andy's body. He could feel his pulse race and his breaths getting shorter.

The first door to the left had a "*Robing Room*" sign above the entrance.

"I don't want a repeat of last week," said B2 as he entered the room.

The rest of the party waited outside.

"You'll talk in the end," said Oliver. "They always do. Tell us where Mary Brown is and B2 will be true to his word and give you a position in intelligence. You've got the makings of a good agent; you won't need much in the way of training. Think about it."

"What made you betray Casper?" said Andy. "Was it reward money, fear of getting caught, or was it just ambition?"

Oliver didn't answer; he just gave a shrug.

B2 emerged from the robing room, dressed like a hospital surgeon. He wore a long green gown, blue overshoes, a cap and mask, and cream-coloured vinyl gloves. Andy gave an involuntary shiver, from fear and not from the cold. B2 led the group down the corridor, stopping at a door that had a red light above it. B2 knocked and the door was shortly opened from within.

The inside reminded Andy of Charlotte's chamber at Chastisers, except there was a "client" present; opposite, a naked man, facing the wall, was strapped to a St Andrew's Cross. His back, posterior and thighs were criss-crossed with bloody welts. Facing the visitors were two men who had hung their suit jackets on chairs and had rolled up their sleeves to just above their elbows. They each held a bullwhip.

B2 pulled down his facemask. "Good evening, gentlemen. Any progress?"

"We've got to 60, but still no confession, sir."

"Jolly good show," said B2. "I'd stop at a hundred if I were you then put him on the rack. The old methods are the best," said B2 addressing the visitors as they left the chamber.

Andy quickly put aside any ideas that the talk of torture was all bluff; it was obvious that B2 was prepared to use extreme methods on Andy. Could he take 60 lashes, let alone the rack? He didn't think so.

They entered the next occupied room; opposite were two imitations of Robinson Crusoe, sitting slouched against the wall but held in place by chains. The men wore dirty, torn shirts and ragged trousers, and were barefoot. They had shoulder-length hair and beards that reached their chests, and both were skeletally thin. The floor was covered in faeces and puddles of urine.

The man on the left slowly lifted a hand to his mouth and tried to say something. The second prisoner was completely still; Andy then realised that it was actually a corpse. It could only have been a couple of seconds before he was struck by the overpowering stench of the decomposing body and he quickly became extremely nauseous. It was Oliver, however, who actually managed to throw up over B2's gown. B2 gave Oliver a withering look then pulled his mask up.

They swiftly left the room and proceeded down the corridor. Andy was now feeling very shaken; part of him still hung on to the slim hope that this was all bluff. Maybe the reason he was being given the guided tour of the torture chambers was because B2 was going to use more psychological methods. But why? In his state, Andy just couldn't think straight at all.

Room 103 had a green light over its door and they entered. In the middle of the chamber was a large table, about eight-feet square, with straps hanging at each corner and at intervals along each side. Hanging from or lying on shelves were assorted tools you might find in a workshop: scissors, knives, meat cleavers, hammers, drills, saws and axes in all sizes.

"Strip him to his underpants," said B2 as soon as the door was closed. The two assistants did not undress him in the normal manner, but with the help of large scissors and knives, ripped off his clothes. The men then rifled through his torn clothing.

"Anything?" asked B2.

"Only this," said one of the assistants, handing B2 Andy's fake police identity card.

"Well, well, Detective Inspector Christopher Howe," chuckled B2. "Impersonating a police officer is a criminal offence. But we'll let you off that if you let us know where Mary Brown is."

One of the assistants punched Andy in the kidney and he doubled over in pain. The men pulled him to his feet, but he couldn't stand up straight because of the pain in his back. His handcuffs were removed and he was strapped to the table, the stretched position continuing to cause pain in the small of his back. Andy could feel his heart racing and his was sweating, despite the chill.

B2 took his pulse. "190, that's far too high. We don't want you dropping dead from a heart attack, at least not until after you've told us where Mary Brown is. Let's try something to help you relax."

B2 moved to the corner of the room and put a cassette in a player. Andy recognised the music as Mozart.

"The *Sull'aria* duet from the *Marriage of Figaro*," said Andy.

"Very good," said B2. "You're not making my job any easier you know. This is the first time I'll be interrogating someone who knows his Mozart. Such a waste."

"I saw the opera at Covent Garden years ago when I was a student," said Andy, hoping to keep the conversation going in order to delay the inevitable.

"I saw it only last summer at Glyndebourne, most civilised," said B2. "Excellence, that's what defines Fascism. Promoting excellence in our racial policies and being ruled by a leader of the highest calibre, of course. But also, promoting excellence in culture; a lower-middle-class chap like you Andy can now afford to see Mozart and Wagner at the Royal Opera House. It wouldn't have been possible under Churchill; if that lot were in power now, they would have us listening to Jazz.

"Do you really think it would be better if Casper's lot got in?" B2 continued. "He'd invite all Churchill's cronies back to run the country; men who have been sunning themselves on Bermuda for the last 30 years, and who have no idea what Britain is like now. Think what we have achieved: full employment, a free health service, Jewish influence eradicated, and streets safe to walk in. You should know that. As a crime reporter, you had hardly any crime to write about. All that would be lost if Churchill's lot took power."

B2 took his pulse again. "We can start. *Veritas odit moras*. For the last time before you're permanently damaged, where is Mary Brown?"

It occurred to Andy that his captors may not be aware of Mary Brown's true story.

"You do know that Mary Brown is Princess Elizabeth," said Andy. "She survived the 1941 plane crash and The Leader has held her under house arrest ever since." Andy couldn't tell from B2's expression whether he knew this, but the assistants looked puzzled.

"He's losing his marbles," said B2. "This often happens in the course of interrogations, although not usually so soon. Hold him down."

B2 pulled up his facemask, fetched a pair of pliers from a shelf and pulled Andy's big toenail off.

Andy gave a yell; the pain was intense but lasted only a few seconds before subsiding. Then, within a minute, it returned, overriding the pain in his kidney. But despite the agony, his wits were returning to him. He thought of a way to buy some time.

"She's in a two-star hotel in Hindhead." Andy had stayed in the village, some 15 miles south-west of Dorking, a few years earlier.

"Go on," said B2, pulling down his mask.

"She's booked into the Three Counties Hotel."

"Room number?"

"Seven."

"Address?"

"On the high street."

"How far from the train station?"

"Hindhead doesn't have a train station."

"The name of the nearest pub?"

"Dog and Whistle."

"The name of the hotel?"

"I've already told you. The Three Counties hotel."

"Under what name is Mary Brown booked under?"

"Mrs Howe, wife of the police detective."

"How far is the Dog and Bone pub from the hotel?"

"Dog and Whistle. About 200 yards."

"He may be telling the truth," said B2. "He's answered promptly and consistently; he's certainly been to the place."

"If you are lying, Andy, you'll be begging me to torture you."

Andy wondered what B2 meant.

B2 turned to Oliver. "Oliver, check out this Hindhead hotel. And have his family brought in, just in case he has been telling us fibs."

Andy felt the blood rush from his face. It was clear what B2 had meant about begging to be tortured; they were going to work on his family.

"Meantime, how about a cup of tea?" B2 spoke to the interrogation team.

The party left the room, leaving Andy alone strapped to the table; shortly, the Mozart cassette came to an end and in the silence, Andy could hear his own heartbeat and heavy breathing.

Andy wondered how much time he had bought. His captors could phone the Hindhead hotel and be told there was no Mrs Howe staying and they would be back in five minutes. If he was lucky, the hotel might refuse to give a guest's name over the phone, in which case, the authorities would need to send some men from the local police down to the hotel in person. That would give him an hour at the most. Time to think of an explanation that would convince B2 that he hadn't been lying and why at the same time, there was no evidence that he and Mary Brown had been to Hindhead. Right now, he couldn't think of a convincing story. Andy knew that very soon, all would be lost. It was no longer a question of how long he could hold out under torture; there was no way he was going to let these bastards harm Jane or the children.

A few minutes later, a man entered the room; he was just as elegantly turned out as B2, and had the same height and build. But he was dark-haired, rather than B2's salt and pepper, and looked a few years younger than his torturer.

"Andy, I'm Casper," said the newcomer.

"Your colleague has tried that one already."

"Does *Anastasia* convince you? Andy, I know that Oliver betrayed you, us, I should say. Roy arrived at your parents' house to collect you, only to be told that someone fitting Oliver's description had picked you up five minutes earlier. Roy didn't give Oliver your whereabouts, so someone must have tipped him off. We don't know who yet. Look, Andy, I knew there was a mole in my cell and it had to be Roy or Oliver. I knew as soon as the regime sent its agents to Sally Hawkins just hours after you told us that Mary Brown was staying with her. That's why I wanted you to reveal Mary Brown's latest whereabouts only to me in person. Am I making sense?"

Andy still had niggling doubts about the man. This Casper did know the password, but maybe the regime could have caught the real Casper and tortured the password out of him. But what the man said about Oliver did make sense. In the end, he felt he had no choice but to trust the man. Andy had run out of options, yet he was being offered the possibility, however slim, of a way out. Within the hour, B2 would have got Mary Brown's whereabouts out of him in any case. But if this man was Casper, he might have enough time to move Mary Brown to a new hiding place.

"Yes, you do make sense," said Andy.

He gave Casper details of Mary Brown's hotel in Dorking, the password to use when meeting her, and told him about the Hindhead diversion.

"I'm going to give you a sedative now," said Casper. "B2 can't interrogate you while you're asleep so it should give us a few more hours' time. Of course, he may well give you an antidote, which will cause you to wake up with a headache. When your interrogators return, try to hold out as long as you can. Each minute's delay improves the odds I'll get Mary Brown safely away."

He moved to the shelf behind Andy, picked up a hammer and, with a single blow, struck Andy unconscious on the back of the head. "Sorry about that, my friend." He patted Andy on the shoulder, turned and left the room.

Andy woke up from a nightmare. He had been drowning in icy rapids with his head constantly banging against submerged rocks. As he regained consciousness, he saw one of B2's henchmen, standing with a bucket of water.

"You've been a naughty boy, Andy," said B2. "Very naughty. Who did this to you?"

"Did what?" Andy had a thumping headache and couldn't think straight.

"Never mind that. One last time – where is Mary Brown?"

The mention of the name made Andy more alert; he realised why he was in that torture chamber, strapped to a table. He had no idea how long had passed since he had talked to Casper; it might have been a few minutes or a day. The fact that B2 was still asking about Mary Brown at least reassured Andy that Casper had not been an imposter.

Turning to Oliver, B2 asked "Any news of the wife and brood?"

"They should be here shortly, half an hour at the most," said Oliver. "We picked the wife up easily enough, but the children were overnighting at their school because of the curfew. They were playing hide and seek and the boy happened to be hiding rather well."

"We can't wait that long," said B2. He picked up an electrical drill and plugged in it. He pressed it for a couple of seconds; Andy's teeth hurt just from the high-pitched sound.

"German-made, Siemens, state of the art," said B2. "You'll need to hold him down hard," he addressed the assistants.

"Do you mind if I go outside?" said Oliver, who had turned very grey.

"You really are a mummy's boy, Oliver," said B2. "Yes, go if you must. This calls for Wagner, no less," he said, inserting a cassette into the player.

As soon as Oliver had closed the door behind him, B2 pulled up his mask, switched on the drill and to the accompaniment of the *Ride of the Valkyries*, started drilling in Andy's right kneecap.

Andy screamed and almost immediately managed to shout out "Dorking." B2 stopped the drill and brought Oliver back into the room. Andy told B2 the truth this time, while Oliver made notes. Andy not only felt physical pain, but also the pain of humiliation; under serious torture, he had held out for all of two seconds.

"I don't believe you," said B2, after Andy had finished.

B2 then resumed drilling Andy's right knee. With Andy's screams getting louder and more desperate, he drilled Andy's remaining knee cap then his ankles. By the time he started on Andy's shoulders, his screams became feebler and turned to a mixture of moans and whimpers. B2 asked again and Andy replied with the same, true, story.

"He's telling the truth," said B2. "See that he receives medical attention."

The interrogators left the room and Andy was alone again, barely conscious of *Wotan's Farewell to Brünnhilde*.

Chapter 38

Andy lay in a stupor, barely aware of his surroundings, but all too conscious of the pain throughout his body. He had vague recollections of a doctor bandaging his wounds and refusing to give him a painkiller, explaining it would send him to sleep and B2 wanted him awake in case a further interrogation might be necessary. Afterwards, he had been moved to a new cell, just 10 feet square, and empty apart from a mattress on which he'd been placed.

The cell door opened and a woman entered: it was Jane and she'd been crying.

"Oh God, you look terrible," she said, barely holding back her tears.

"Thanks," Andy mumbled. "Have they mistreated you? "

"They've been quite correct, so far."

"What about the children?"

"They're being looked after in the staff restaurant upstairs. Look, Andy, I need you to sign these divorce papers before your ex—," She stopped in her tracks and started crying again.

"My what?" said Andy. Then it dawned on him. "My execution," he finished the sentence for her.

Once B2 had finished his work with the drill, Andy had sensed that he wouldn't leave the place alive. His injuries were too severe for him to be seen in public. He supposed he was still living because Mary Brown hadn't been caught yet. It must mean that Casper had reached her in time.

"But why the divorce? I'll be dead in a few hours in any case. What have I done?"

"It's nothing to do with your affair with Alice Greengrass," said Jane.

"What affair?"

"When the hotel phoned me about your scarf a few weeks ago, they mentioned you shared a room with Alice Greengrass."

"It was just a one-night-stand. It wasn't even—"

"As I said, it's nothing to do with that. The divorce is best for the children and for me too, to be honest. As a traitor, the Government will confiscate your entire estate and your children will be denied an education, and could only be employed in the most menial jobs. As a widow of a traitor, I'd be denied both employment and the right to remarry. If I divorce you first, these problems disappear."

This did make sense to Andy, although he couldn't see why B2 would allow Jane to see him. He signed the papers, although it was a struggle with the excruciating pain in his shoulder and elbow.

"Do you think Mary Brown got away?" said Jane, once Andy had returned the signed documents.

"I think so. Casper must have met up with her in time."

"Where were they going to next?"

"I don't know," he said.

It then dawned on Andy why B2 had let Jane in to see him. It was precisely to get the answer to that last question. It also meant for sure that by the time B2's men had reached the hotel, Mary Brown had gone.

But why was Jane cooperating with B2?

Maybe he had put pressure on her, although she had said she was being well treated.

Maybe she had been working for B2 for some time. She can't be one of the regime's agents; she was never with them, politically speaking.

Then the penny dropped.

"You told Oliver, the intelligence officer, I was with Mum and Dad this afternoon, after I'd phoned. You shopped me, didn't you? But why? "

"They found out about Adrian. If I didn't cooperate, he would have been entered into the euthanasia programme. I'm beginning to sound like them. Adrian would have been murdered, that is. I had no choice."

Jane started crying again, then she knelt and gave Andy a hug, but he winced from the pain.

"Goodbye," he croaked. He felt more sorrow than anger.

Jane nodded, got up and knocked on the door. It was shortly opened and B2 stood in the doorway, now dressed again in his Savile Row pinstripe suit.

"Well?" B2 said.

Jane shook her head.

They both left the cell; the door slammed shut and Andy was alone again.

*

Casper left London in his ministerial Rolls Royce, driven by his chauffeur, Unsworth. He had taken a risk seeing Andy Deegan. Of course, in his position, he had access to State Security headquarters, but he still might be asked what he was doing there. He had thought of giving Andy sleeping pills but he would have been toast if someone had seen him entering the interrogation room. By using the hammer on Andy, he could claim he wanted to question him and got angry with his lack of cooperation and so banged Andy's head on the table, unintentionally knocking him unconscious. He was still worried about the security risk of him seeing the Princess, so as soon as they reached Leatherhead, they stopped by The George Hotel. Casper told Unsworth to have a good meal on expenses; he would return later that evening. Then Casper drove himself to the Hill View Hotel in Dorking.

He was a bag of nerves as he entered the lobby; this was a critical moment in the whole mission. It would be a disaster if the Princess wasn't there. He was also concerned the Princess wouldn't believe he was her rescuer, and would refuse to go with him.

He tried to appear calm when he said to the receptionist, "I'd like to see Inspector Howe please."

"He's gone out but I think Mrs Howe is in."

"Could I see her?"

"Upstairs, room three."

His nerves returned when he knocked on the door. It was opened by a middle-aged lady with red hair, but he had no doubt it was the Princess.

"I'm Andy's friend," said Casper.

"Andy said something about a password."

"*Succession.*"

The lady smiled and said, "You're taking me to Canada."

Casper could finally relax a little.

There were more checkpoints, even after Dorking, as the curfew had now been extended to all areas within a hundred miles of London. He was concerned the police or

Blackshirts manning the checkpoints might be suspicious of a minister driving his car without a chauffeur. But the sight of the Rolls Royce with its lightning flash pennant and a glimpse of Casper's identity card meant he was quickly waved through with smart raised-armed salutes and no questions asked.

He had been waiting for this moment all his adult life, and the next few hours would lead either to success or total disaster. There would be no second chance; he had taken far too many risks in the last few days. First, he had passed on information to Deegan that could only have come from ACRE. And now, he had arrived at the Dorking hotel in person to collect the Princess; the manager might well provide the authorities with a reasonable description of him. In turn, the authorities would connect his Dorking visit with his call on Deegan in State Security headquarters earlier that evening.

Casper was not a Johnny-come-lately opponent of Fascism. The democratic opposition had in fact recruited him nearly 30 years earlier. Mosley had closed down the universities when he had come to power; he had argued they were a hotbed of Communism and Liberalism, besides which, he had not been to university himself and saw no need for anyone else to do so either. However, three years later, following a thorough purge of professors and the banning of certain subjects such as politics or economics, The Leader decided to reopen the universities. So when Casper went up to Oxford's Brasenose College to read mathematics, he was three years older and more mature than his peers; in particular, he had already learned to keep his political views to himself. In so doing, he was off the radar of the intelligence services. One person to whom Casper did convey his political opinions was his girlfriend, Shirley, who had a relative in the opposition. At the end of his first year, he was contacted by them and was asked to become an opposition sleeper.

The long-term plan was to enter Government or the armed forces, work his way up, and then subvert the regime in some way when in a position of power. This meant becoming active in Fascist politics and joining the BUF and the Brasenose Blackshirts. It also meant ending his relationship with Shirley, who was on the intelligence services watch list. This double life was, at first, stressful for Casper; it was particularly distasteful for him to join fellow Blackshirts in their beating up of students who had expressed democratic views. After university, Casper joined the Government, working his way up to a position where he was now a member of the ACRA committee. He had married Harriet, the daughter of a senior Fascist, and they had a son, Graeme, who was now 15 years old. He was well off, with a town house in Belgravia, a country home in West Sussex, and he could afford to send Graeme to Eton.

For most of his career, Casper's work for the opposition had just been an annual meeting with his minder and the occasional leaking of sensitive information. He had only learned of the Princess's house arrest the previous year, and he immediately informed the opposition of this and they set about planning a rescue attempt. It soon became clear that he would have to take an active role in this. A year earlier, he had serious doubts about what he was doing; he had achieved so little for the opposition and if anything, he had done his bit to prop up the regime. But today, all going well, the result of 30 years waiting would be the collapse of Fascist rule in Britain.

Some 10 miles from Portsmouth, he heard a news item on the radio. Previous descriptions of the fugitive spy, Mary Brown, may be incorrect; she was last seen wearing a red wig. Clearly, Andy had finally talked and the regime had been to the Hill View in Dorking and had asked the hotel staff about their female guest.

He turned off the main road and drove into the grounds of Cherrytrees, the country house of fellow conspirator, Rear Admiral Magnus Forster-Brimacombe. Casper had the backing of a number of senior officers in the armed services for his coup. They were now ready to act, once he made the first move. To ensure his co-conspirators didn't get cold feet or, worse, betray him, he had seen to it that each one had implicated himself in an anti-regime act. For Rear Admiral Forster-Brimacombe, that act would be the providing of shelter to the Princess.

Forster-Brimacombe opened the door himself; his domestic staff had all been given the evening off. Casper introduced the Princess to him and they were led into a drawing room. Sitting in an armchair, nursing a whisky and soda, was William Ross, supposedly naval attaché at the Canadian Embassy, but actually an intelligence officer. Casper had arranged for him to come down to Cherrytrees earlier in the day.

"How much time do we have?" said Casper.

"Just under three hours," replied William Ross.

"You'll have to disguise the Princess again," said Casper.

"That's no problem; we're experts at that sort of thing," said William Ross.

"I have to go back to London now," said Casper. "Mosley is calling for meetings several times a day at short notice, so I have to be there. I'll need some sort of message when the Princess is finally out of the country so I can start the coup."

"How will we know the coup's started?" asked Forster-Brimacombe.

"There'll be an announcement on the BBC of The Leader's death, arrest or resignation. It will be as simple as that," said Casper.

Casper agreed on a message with William Ross then he left.

Chapter 39

The cabinet members sat in their usual places in ACRA. A cassette player was placed in the middle of the table and, because it was seven o'clock in the morning, each of the participants had been provided with tea, coffee, orange juice and toast.

The Leader, Sir Oswald Mosley, opened the proceedings. "Before Harper informs us of the latest on the hunt for Mary Brown, I'd like to say a few words. After our last meeting, Harper pointed out to me that there could be a traitor in this very room. Alas, he has been proved right."

There was silence as the ministers stopped their chewing and sipping, followed by a few synchronised gasps.

Mosley turned to the guard. "Bring in the witness," he said.

The guard opened the door, took a step out into the corridor, and repeated the command.

A few minutes later, a dishevelled, pale and terrified-looking man entered the room, escorted by two more Blackshirts. The guards pushed their prisoner into position, just five feet from the table and facing Mosley.

"Where's your salute man, have you no manners?" Mosley barked.

"They broke my shoulder so it's too painful," said the witness.

"They what?" Mosley raised his voice then slammed a fist on the table. "Are you accusing the authorities of mistreating you? Making such an allegation is a very serious offence."

"No, of course not. I mean, I broke my shoulder," the man stammered. "I slipped in my cell; it was most careless of me."

Wincing, he slowly raised his right arm in a half-salute.

"You have a statement to make?" said Mosley.

"Yes, my leader."

"Proceed."

"My name is Nicolas Gibson and I am the manager of the Hill View Hotel in Dorking. Yesterday afternoon, a man calling himself Inspector Howe checked in with the terrorist, Mary Brown. The man then departed, leaving the terrorist alone in her room. Around eight o'clock in the evening, another gentleman arrived at the hotel, asking to see Mary Brown. He then left with her. He looked important, like a senior civil servant or something, and I was a bit curious with all the comings and goings so I looked to see where they were off to. They got into a Rolls Royce, with a flag on the front, and drove off."

"Would you recognise that man if you saw him again?"

"Yes, your leadership."

"Is he in this room?"

"Yes, my leader."

"Could you point out him out?"

Gibson raised his left arm and pointed at Alistair Harper.

"Have you anything to say, Harper?" said Mosley.

"This is absurd," said Alistair Harper. "I've been raising heaven and earth to catch the traitor, Mary

Brown. You know that. It's his word against mine. Surely, you accept the word of a senior Fascist over that of a hotel receptionist."

"Why would the witness lie?" said Mosley.

"He's been questioned under duress," said Alistair Harper. "If he had had a red-hot poker thrust in his sensitive parts, he would have confessed to being Winston Churchill. It's obvious I've been set up to deflect attention from the real traitor."

Mosley turned to Gibson. "We may need you to appear as a witness before a special tribunal; after that, you'll be dealt with. Harbouring a terrorist is a very serious crime."

"But I didn't know, I—" started Gibson.

"I've heard enough," Mosley interrupted. "You could have listened and paid attention to the many Government broadcasts concerning the terrorist. You failed in your duty as a citizen."

He turned to the guards. "Remove this creature."

After Gibson had been led away, Alistair Harper said, "This is not evidence."

"Maybe not," said Mosley. "You saw Andrew Deegan in his cell at State Security headquarters yesterday, is that so?"

"Of course, as soon as Minister Thompson informed me that State Security was holding an accomplice of Mary Brown," said Alistair Harper. "You've given me plenipotentiary powers regarding national security, so it was my duty to see if I could glean any more information from Deegan."

"And did you glean anything from Mr Deegan?"

"No, he said nothing."

"Minister Thompson, I'd like you to take the floor, please," said Mosley.

Thompson placed a tape in the cassette player. Only then did its significance dawn on Casper and he realised he was finished.

Thompson continued, "We record all interrogations at our intelligence headquarters. Mostly as training material for junior members of staff, but sometimes, as aide-memoirs in on-going investigations. The tape was left running after B2's interrogation of Deegan; Harper arrived only a few minutes later so we have a recording of his visit."

The tape was played. There was no mistaking Alistair Harper's voice and Andy Deegan clearly revealing Mary Brown's hiding place as the Hill View Hotel.

"So Harper, or should I call you Casper, you gleaned nothing from that meeting." Mosley paused to let the other members of the Action Cabinet absorb the shock. "You realise, of course, you cannot leave this building alive. But I'm prepared to offer you a deal. If you reveal where Mary Brown is right now, as soon as we have apprehended her, I will give you a bottle of your favourite whisky and a pistol. In your suicide note, you may write about the pressures of your job and not having enough time with your family. Furthermore, you will receive a funeral fitting a senior Fascist. Your family will be unmolested and your son will be allowed to remain at Eton; in fact, the Government will continue to pay his fees.

"On the other hand, if you do not cooperate," Mosley continued, "the consequences will be most unpleasant for you and your family. You mentioned a red-hot poker earlier, but I understand our chief intelligence interrogator is a dab hand with an electric drill."

Under the circumstances, it seemed a reasonable offer to Alistair Harper; he didn't think Mosley would renege, given the deal was made in the presence of all the members of the Action Cabinet. But the truth was he didn't know where Mary Brown was at that moment. He hadn't received word that she had been either smuggled out of the country successfully or that the operation had failed. He had to stall for as long as he could. He wondered how many members of the Action Cabinet knew the true story of Mary Brown; if they were to learn of it now, they might just turn against their leader.

"Mary Brown is in fact Princess Elizabeth," said Harper. He then gave a summary of the 1941 royal flight hijacking and the King and Princess's house arrest. He looked closely at the expressions of his fellow cabinet members; it seemed that only Mosley and Joyce had known about the royals.

"Poppycock," said Mosley. "Absolute fantasy."

The meeting was interrupted by a knock on the door; a Civil Service messenger had a communication for Security Adviser Harper from the Admiralty. As the messenger handed Harper the note, Mosley snatched it. He glanced over the contents then read out aloud:

"*From Canadian ship Newfoundland. Many thanks to United Kingdom Leader, Navy and people of Plymouth and Portsmouth for their warm hospitality. We have enjoyed our visit to England but now a new day begins and it's time for us Canada geese to be heading home.*"

"Odd turn of phrase, Canada geese," said Mosley. "But your goose is cooked, Harper, if you don't confess everything."

"What is meant by the message," said Harper, "is that Princess Elizabeth is on a Canadian warship, heading for North America. She left Portsmouth eight hours ago, at midnight, so is now in international waters. In four days, she will arrive in Canada and the world will know what you did to her and her father. It will be over for you, Sir Oswald. No regime can shrug off the crime of regicide; for that is what letting King George die under house arrest amounts to. Think of Oliver Cromwell, Danton or Robespierre."

Mosley stood up and walked over to another smaller table, on which an intercom was positioned. He pressed a switch. "Sir Quentin, I'd like to see you in ACRA immediately please."

Just two minutes later, Permanent Secretary to the Action Cabinet, Sir Quentin Danvers-Mutton, entered the room. A silver-haired man in his 50s, he was dressed in standard Civil Service dress of short black jacket, black waistcoat, striped grey trousers and a lightning flash armband.

Mosley handed Sir Quentin the note. "I'd like you to confirm the latest position of the Newfoundland. It is a matter of the greatest urgency."

Sir Quentin left the room with as brisk a pace as his dignified position would allow.

"The woman can't prove she's the Princess," said Mosley. "We could argue she's an impostor and the story of house arrest pure fiction."

"I don't think so," said Harper. "Firstly, she'll be joining her mother and sister, who would very quickly spot a pretender. Secondly, there's the recent discovery of the 1941 plane wreckage. It won't be long before the Australians announce that the King and Princess's bodies were not found among the wreckage, so giving more proof that they were abducted."

The occupants of ACRA sat in silence; nevertheless, the tension was all too palpable. Philip Thompson, the Minister of the Interior, mopped his brow with a handkerchief, while Jeremy Holroyd, the Information Minister, fidgeted with his collar. Mosley was lost in his thoughts, staring at his hands, which had been placed on the table, and every now and then, casting a hostile glance towards Harper.

Sir Quentin returned 10 minutes later and confirmed that the Newfoundland had left Portsmouth at midnight, heading for Canada, and would now be some 80 miles south-west of Plymouth in international waters.

"You do have a way out, Sir Oswald," said Harper, as soon as Sir Quentin had left the room. "You were kind enough to offer me a deal earlier on, so let me return the favour. I want you to sign this resignation statement." Harper pulled out a sheet of paper from his inside jacket pocket with a flourish. "It will take effect immediately and you will grant me full executive powers. You can give ill health or a wish to retire as an excuse. You will also invite the BBC to this very room, from which you will broadcast your resignation to the country. In return, there will be no mention of the Princess until she arrives in Canada. That gives you four days to pack your bags and depart for a country of your choice. Once news of the Princess is announced, public opinion would leave me no option but to have you arrested and charged, so there is no alternative to exile. This really is a good offer. The only other option is to rule for a few more days then be overthrown on far less favourable terms. What do you say, Sir Oswald?"

"My leader, is this true about the Princess and King George?" Interior Minister Thompson could not hide the nervousness from his voice.

Mosley remained silent.

"Why were we not informed, my leader?" Information Minister Jeremy Holroyd snapped his pencil in two.

Mosley did not reply.

"Say something, Sir Oswald." Deputy Leader Angus Bye's voice was increasingly shrill.

Mosley was silent for another minute before he replied, "I'm afraid Harper's assessment is right; we can't survive this. Much of our legitimacy has been thanks to us being seen as committed monarchists, but this episode will fatally weaken our royalist credentials. We're finished, I'm afraid. I suggest we vote on this."

"Very well," said Harper. "But before the vote, let me point out that the four-day grace offer applies to all members of this cabinet." Harper took a sip of orange juice. "Those in favour of The Leader's immediate resignation, please raise their hands."

All the cabinet members except Mosley and Joyce raised their hands.

"Those against," said Harper.

Only Joyce raised his hand. For the first time that Harper could remember, Mosley had abstained from an Action Cabinet decision.

"The ayes have it," said Harper, thrusting the resignation letter towards Mosley.

"Don't sign," Joyce blurted out. "We can still ask Germany to get one of their submarines to sink the bloody ship."

"I don't think that's a serious option, Joyce," said Mosley. "It would mean war with Canada and her allies."

"You know what the problem with you is, Mosley," said Joyce, "you're not a full-blooded National Socialist. You never were; you loved your aristocratic chums too much. When I learned about the Royals' house arrest back in 1942, I urged you to shoot the bitch and her stuttering father. We would have none of this trouble now if you'd followed my advice. Then there was the business with the Jews. When we expelled them to Germany where they met their just deserts, you personally flew Israel Sieff to the Gestapo in your private plane. Behind your back, you were the laughing stock among the German Nazis when they heard about that. '*Did the British Führer think he was Moses?*' they'd say. Or '*Did the British Führer think the North Sea was the Red Sea?*' I once asked the Führer to have you replaced, as it was clear your Nazi credentials weren't up to scratch. He told me I should replace you myself if I felt that way. Well, better late than never."

Joyce stood up, pulled out a pistol from his jacket pocket and pointed it at Mosley. The tension in the room, already high, ratcheted up another notch. The Blackshirt giant of a guard stiffened and moved closer to the table. But his failure to act immediately showed he had not yet decided whose side he was on.

"You will not sign that paper, Mosley," said Joyce. "But you will sign a new resignation document, which I will present to you shortly, whereby all your powers will be transferred to me."

"You're crazy," said Mosley as he unscrewed the top of his pen.

Joyce pressed the trigger of his pistol, but only a click could be heard as the gun jammed. Before he could press the trigger again, a loud shot reverberated around the room. A second later, Joyce dropped his gun, and a second after that, a huge red stain spread across the front of his shirt. Just three seconds after the shot, Joyce fell back in his chair. The guard swiftly moved to Joyce's side then swivelled his chair so that he was no longer facing the table and fired a second shot in the back of his head. The Blackshirt turned to face Mosley and gave the last raised-arm salute ever seen in that room.

"At least we won't be forced to look at that dreadful scar anymore," said Mosley as he signed the paper.

Chapter 40

Ten days later. 29 May 1972.

The first cabinet meeting of the provisional government was held at 10 Downing Street. There were twelve participants; five had been released from prisons or labour camps, and three were members of various opposition groups who had come out of hiding.

As soon as they were all seated, Prime Minister Alistair Harper tapped a spoon against a glass. "I'm sure you have all heard the sad news of the death of King Edward, who passed away last night. I suggest we hold a silent tribute." The Prime Minister stood up and the remainder of his cabinet followed suit.

As soon as the two minutes' silence was over and they had all sat down, the Prime Minister continued. "Of course, a state funeral will follow; the exact arrangements are yet to be decided. Before we move on to today's agenda, there are a few things I would like to say. Sir Oswald Mosley has left the country for Ireland. I have ordered the release of all political prisoners and have lifted the ban on political parties and activities. The curfew has been abolished. Free elections will be held in a few months; the exact timing is the first item in today's agenda.

"This dramatic change in our country's political situation has come about in no small part to the brave actions of Andrew Deegan. He is recovering in St Thomas' Hospital from injuries received in the exfiltration of Princess Elizabeth. He is already a recipient of the Military Cross; in due course, he will be further suitably honoured. Finally, I would like to read the contents of a telegram that I propose to send to Princess Elizabeth in Canada: '*Your provisional and loyal Government invites Your Majesty to come to London to ascend the throne of Great Britain*'."

Author's Note

The seeds for this book were sown many years ago when I read Robert Harris's novel, *Fatherland*. In the book, he describes 1960's Germany following a Nazi victory in World War II. Although he made a couple of fleeting references to Britain, I wondered what Britain would have been like in that scenario. Ten years later and a thriller, *The Banker*, under my belt, *Succession* is my answer.

I picked 1972 as the year in which the story takes place for a couple of reasons. First, all the European dictators could still have been alive; Hitler and Mussolini would have been in their 80s, for example. Indeed, some of the historical characters mentioned in *Succession* were alive in 1972: Spain's General Franco, the Duke of Windsor and, above all, Sir Oswald Mosley. With all their leaders being so elderly, a German-dominated Nazi Europe would have been on the cusp of simultaneous succession crises.

Some readers may think that Princess Elizabeth would not have flown with her father as that would have broken the protocol that no two royals in direct lineage fly together. This protocol was introduced by Queen Elizabeth some time after her coronation in 1953. In fact Princess Elizabeth's first flight was with her father, King George VI, to Ulster in July 1945.

It now seems inconceivable that the socially liberal revolution that started in the 1960s would have occurred in a Nazi Europe. However, it is easy to forget that the Nazi and Fascist parties of the 1930s saw themselves as agents of progressive social change. For example, in 1934, women, including former leading suffragettes, numbered a quarter of the activists of the British Union of Fascists (BUF), a far higher proportion than in other British political parties. Mosley promised women a greater voice in the governance of the country. However, all this flies in the face of experience of Fascist and Nazi parties once in power. *Kinder, Küche, Kirche* (Children, Kitchen, Church) was how Hitler summed up the role of women.

Another example is the attitude towards homosexuality. There were many homosexual activists in the Nazi SA until the 1934 Röhm-Putsch, after which homosexuals were first purged from the Nazi movement then the wider homosexual community became increasingly persecuted. Mosley's position was common among the British upper class; homosexuality was tolerated, provided liaisons were discreet and did not cross class barriers. However, much of the BUF support came from the lower middle class, which had far more socially conservative mores. This leads me to speculate that in power, BUF treatment of homosexuals would have been no different to that of the German Nazis.

One area of social change would have been in the matter of euthanasia. The German Nazis introduced a euthanasia programme surreptitiously in the 1940s because they realised this clashed with German social and religious mores. However, had the Nazis still been in power in the 1970s, I speculate that euthanasia would have been openly practised. Decades of propaganda against targeted groups and a tighter, more Orwellian control of the population would have brought this about.

However, I think some aspects of 1970's culture, such as music and fashion, would have influenced even a Nazi Britain. The Soviet Union in that period provides something of a model. There was a thriving black market in jeans, for example, and there were a few state-employed pop groups, complete with Beatles' mop-tops. Of course, if an ordinary Soviet male dared to sport such a hairstyle, he would quickly find himself in a police cell, and would only be released after convincing the authorities he was not a Western subversive, and after receiving a free haircut.

As part of my research, I read two biographies of Oswald Mosley. The first *Oswald Mosley* by Robert Skidelsky is a not unsympathetic portrait, focussing on his economic policies. Skidelsky points out that Mosley was the first British politician converted to economist Keynes' ideas. *Blackshirt: Sir Oswald Mosley and British Fascism* by Stephen Dorril is a much more critical biography of Mosley, with more emphasis on his private life and his links with the Italian Fascists and German Nazis.

How and exactly when would Britain have become a Fascist country, allied to or overrun by Nazi Germany? Many historians believe that if Hitler had not agreed to German forces halting for 48 hours, just 15 miles from Dunkirk in May 1940 then the outcome would have been quite different. Instead of a successful evacuation, the entire British Expeditionary Force of some 300,000 men would have been destroyed or fallen into German hands. In the timeline below, I speculate that Hitler immediately reverses that halt order.

At the same time, the British War Cabinet, consisting of Prime Minister Winston Churchill, Lord Halifax, Neville

Chamberlain, Clement Attlee and Arthur Greenwood held several meetings discussing the possibility of suing for peace with Germany. Initially, Churchill was in a minority of one in arguing for continuing the war, but over a five-day period, he won over the remainder of the War Cabinet to his point of view. This is described in John Lukacs's book, *Five Days in London: May 1940*. I speculate that Churchill is outvoted and the War Cabinet decides to sue for peace.

The timeline below sums up the major events in my alternative history, starting with the halt order of 24th May 1940 and ending in 1971, just before the events described in this book. The first week is described in a lot of detail; I have used the same meetings detailed in *Five Days in London* but with different outcomes. I have also speculated that there still would have been a war in the Pacific between Japan and the United States. The overall duration and outcome of the war would not have changed, but individual battles may well have started and finished at different dates. However, to make the point that the Pacific War would not have been significantly different, I have used the actual dates and battles in my timeline.

Timeline 1940 – 1971

24th May 1940: 300,000 troops of the British Expeditionary Force (BEF), commanded by General Lord Gort, together with 200,000 men of the French 1st Army and Belgian Army, are surrounded by German forces in Flanders. The channel ports of Boulogne and Calais are besieged by the German 2nd and 10th Panzer divisions respectively. The allied strategy (Weygand Plan) has been for co-ordinated counter attacks on 21st May to link up French forces in the south with the Anglo-French-Belgian forces in the north. Although the BEF counter-attacked at Arras on 21st May, there was no move from the south, so since 23rd May, the BEF has been retreating towards the coast.

In the morning, General von Rundstedt, leader of German Army Group A, orders advancing forces to halt along the line Lens-Béthune-Aire-St Omer-Gravelines (the Aa Canal). The halt is opposed by General von Brauchitsch, Commander-in-Chief of the German Army.

However, the 1st Panzer Division has already established four bridgeheads east of this line, just 15 miles from Dunkirk, which is defended by just one BEF battalion and a few thousand French troops.

24th May 1940 - 12.30: Hitler meets von Rundstedt at his headquarters in Charleville. Hitler overrules von Rundstedt and reverses the Halt Order.

25th May 1940 - 08.30: 2nd Panzer Division captures Boulogne.

25th **May 1940 - 13.00:** 1st Panzer Division captures most of Dunkirk. Eight-hundred BEF and two-thousand French troops hold port and western suburbs.

25th **May 1940 - afternoon:** British Foreign Secretary, Lord Halifax, meets Italian ambassador, Giuseppe Bastianini, to discuss possible mediation. Italy is still neutral, although Mussolini has made it clear he is minded to shortly enter the war on Hitler's side.

25th **May 1940 - 17.30:** London. Defence committee meeting chaired by Prime Minister Winston Churchill discusses fall of Dunkirk. Port of Ostend is still in Belgian hands, but because the Belgian Army is on the point of collapse and cannot provide support, retreat of BEF to Ostend for evacuation by sea is not feasible. The only slim hope is reactivation of Weygand plan, namely a counter-attack by the French Army, situated along the Somme.

25th **May 1940 - 19.00:** Paris. French Comité de Guerre discuss suing for peace with Germany, using Italy as mediator. As France is bound by agreement with Britain not to seek a separate peace, Premier Reynaud will fly to London next day to meet the British.

25-26th **May 1940:** During the night, 300 wounded BEF soldiers are evacuated from Dunkirk by the Royal Navy.

26th **May 1940 - 08.00:** Three divisions of the German 6th Army (part of Army Group B) break through the gap between Comines and Ypres, so cutting off Belgians from the British.

26th May 1940 - 09.00: London. War Cabinet (consisting of Churchill, Halifax, Chamberlain, Attlee and Greenwood) discuss the dire situation of BEF. Also, being aware that the French regard the war as lost, they discuss a strategy in the event of a French surrender.

Halifax is in favour of a negotiated peace, provided that the independence of the British Empire is assured. Churchill wants to fight on, even if the BEF is destroyed and France surrenders. He argues that peace and security can never be achieved under German domination of Europe. Chamberlain's position is close to Halifax's. Atlee and Greenwood are undecided.

26th May 1940 - 12.00: Halifax meets the Italian ambassador again.

26th May 1940 - 14.00: The War Cabinet meets Reynaud and they discuss a joint peace approach to Mussolini. At 16.00, Reynaud leaves for France.

26th May 1940 - 16.00: The 10th Panzer Division captures Calais.

26th May 1940 - 17.00: Third War Cabinet meeting of the day. Churchill is against approaching Mussolini directly as it suggests weakness. All agree on a joint Anglo-French appeal to United States President Roosevelt to approach Mussolini regarding peace. Later that evening, the appeal is sent.

27th May 1940 - 05.00: In an attempt to relieve the BEF, the British 1st Armoured Division, stationed south of the

Somme, attacks Abbeville in force, but is beaten back with heavy losses.

27th May 1940 - 09.00: Forces of German Army Groups A and B meet at Poperinge, Belgium. The BEF is now cut off from the sea in a pocket around the towns of Lille and Armentières.

27th May 1940 - 10.30: Remaining French forces in Dunkirk surrender. The last 200 BEF troops had been evacuated the previous night.

27th May 1940 - 12.00: The Belgian Army surrenders.

27th May 1940 - 16.00: Mussolini rebuffs Roosevelt's offer. If the British or French want to talk to him, they should do so directly.

27th May 1940 - 21.00: French Council of Ministers, on hearing of Belgian surrender and Mussolini's rebuff, discuss direct approach to Mussolini, but first, will consult London on a joint approach.

27th May 1940 - 22.00: The War Cabinet discusses consequences of Belgian surrender and the worsening situation of the BEF. It is clear the BEF cannot hold out much longer. The War Cabinet is informed of Mussolini's rebuff.

28th May 1940 - 14.00: No French breakthrough along the Somme. After obtaining Churchill's permission, the BEF surrenders at Lord Gort's HQ at Prémesques, followed by a separate surrender of the 1st French Army at Lille.

28th May 1940 - 16.00: The War Cabinet meets. Halifax argues that better terms will be achieved now by negotiations arranged by Mussolini, who should be approached directly. If terms are too harsh, they can be subsequently rejected. Churchill disagrees, arguing it's best to fight on and that terms offered by Germany after a successful invasion of Britain would be no worse. Shocked by the BEF surrender, Chamberlain, Atlee and Greenwood all support Halifax's position.

28th May 1940 - 17.00: The War Cabinet adjourns. For one hour, Churchill addresses 25 members of the outer cabinet. The overwhelming majority support Halifax's position.

28th May 1940 - 19.00: The War Cabinet reconvenes. Churchill reluctantly concurs with Halifax.

28th May 1940 - 21.00: Churchill telegrams Reynaud, agreeing to a joint Anglo-French direct approach to Mussolini.

29th May 1940: Rome. Mussolini informs Marshal Badoglio and other military leaders of Anglo-French mediation requests. He will mediate but if a deal is not reached by June 5th, he will enter the war on Hitler's side.

30th May 1940 - 09.00: Mussolini invites leaders of France, Germany and Britain to a meeting in Stresa in Italy on 1ˢᵗ and 2ⁿᵈ of June 1940 to discuss general European settlement. The following pre-conditions are understood:

- Independence and integrity of British and French Empires to be respected with minor adjustments listed below.
- France to cede Alsace-Lorraine to Germany. Germany will maintain military bases in Dunkirk, Calais and Boulogne.
- France to cede Corsica to Italy.
- Britain and France to return former German African colonies to Germany.
- Britain to cede Malta and Gibraltar to Italy. Italy to have a place on the board of the Suez Canal Company.

30ᵗʰ May 1940 - 11.30: The War Cabinet meets to discuss Mussolini's offer. Churchill is in favour of rejection, but Halifax argues such terms were expected. Churchill is in a minority of one so agrees to accept the invitation.

30ᵗʰ May 1940 - 12.30: Churchill orders British fleet to sail for Canada. He also orders gold reserves worth £600 million ($2.4 billion) to be moved to Canada.

30ᵗʰ May 1940 - 15.00: Hitler accepts Mussolini's invitation on two further conditions. First, Churchill must resign: Lloyd George will be an acceptable replacement. Second, Reynaud must also resign: Marshal Pétain will be an acceptable alternative.

30th May 1940 - 17.00: The War Cabinet discusses Hitler's conditions. Churchill is prepared to resign, as he does not wish to be associated with such a humiliating surrender. Lloyd George is invited to be Prime Minister.

30th May 1940 - 20.00: Paris. It is announced that Reynaud has resigned and Marshal Pétain is the new Premier. Pierre Laval becomes Minister of Foreign Affairs. Mussolini's invitation is formally accepted.

30th May 1940 - 21.00: Lloyd George accepts the offer of Prime Minister but makes it clear that his first act will be to fire Chamberlain, whom he can't stand.

31st May 1940 - 12.30: London, Buckingham Palace. Churchill formally offers King George his resignation. Shortly after, the King appoints Lloyd George as Prime Minister. Rather than wait to be fired, Chamberlain resigned earlier in the morning.

31st May 1940 - 16.00: A temporary ceasefire throughout French front takes hold.

1st June 1940: Stresa, Italy. Leaders and foreign ministers of Germany, France, Britain and Italy meet for peace talks. Germany is represented by Hitler and von Ribbentrop, France by Pétain and Laval, Britain by Lloyd George and Halifax, Italy by Mussolini and Count Ciano. Hitler had insisted on Stresa as the venue, as it was the location of the failed 1935 Anglo-French-Italian anti-German Stresa Front conference. Indeed, Laval and Mussolini had been participants at that conference.

1st **June 1940 - 16.00:** Croydon Airfield, London. Churchill and his family leave Britain for exile in Canada.

2nd **June 1940 - 19.00:** Stresa. General European Settlement agreed and signed. The terms of the treaty were as outlined in Mussolini's invitation of 30th May, with the following amendments:

- Germany to have military bases along the entire Channel and Atlantic coasts of France.
- Germany to have possession of most of the British fleet, apart from a small number of ships stationed in South Africa, India and the Far East.
- Gibraltar to be ceded to Germany not Italy, but as compensation, Britain will cede Cyprus to Italy.
- Germany to have possession of half the French fleet, Italy the other half. France will be allowed to keep a small number of ships in Indo China.

2nd June 1940 - 23.00 BST/18.00 EST: Ottawa, Canada. Churchill denounces Stresa treaty and says he will form a government-in-exile.

4th **June 1940 - 09.00:** Under the terms of the Stresa treaty, Sir Oswald Mosley is driven straight from Brixton Prison, where he has been detained since 23rd May 1940 under Defence Regulation 18B, to Downing Street, where he is appointed Home Secretary.

4th **June 1940 - 12.00:** Individual ships of the British fleet are given names of German ports to which they should immediately sail. However, a large part of the

British fleet is either in or is close to Canadian waters and ignores the order.

5ᵗʰ June 1940: Lloyd George promises elections within a year.

6ᵗʰ June 1940: Canada. Churchill forms government-in-exile. It is recognised by Roosevelt, who thinks war between Germany and the United States is inevitable sooner or later, and it's better to have the British fleet loyal to Churchill in North American waters. The Churchill government-in-exile remains officially at war with Nazi Germany.

June 1940: The British Empire declares loyalty to the Lloyd George Government, however, the Dominions are split. South Africa is pro-Lloyd George. Canada and Newfoundland recognise the Churchill Government. Although Australia and New Zealand recognise the Lloyd George Government, opinion there is split. Ireland, which declared neutrality in September 1939, is pro-Lloyd George.

9ᵗʰ June 1940: The United States invades Iceland. The 4,000 British soldiers who occupied the island the previous month join the Free British Army being formed in Canada.

October 1940: The Duke of Kent succeeds Lord Gowrie as Governor General of Australia. This was supposed to have taken effect in November 1939, but was postponed because of the outbreak of war in September 1939.

November 1940: The Balkans are now either directly occupied or are in alliance with the Axis powers of Italy and Germany.

12th February 1941: King George VI and Princess Elizabeth, on a goodwill tour of Australia, are killed when their plane on a flight from Perth to Adelaide malfunctions and crashes into the sea. The Duke of Windsor is proclaimed the new monarch, King Edward VIII.

2nd March 1941: Former Queen Elizabeth and daughter, Princess Margaret, leave Britain for exile initially to Australia then to Canada.

1st May 1941: Elections are held in Great Britain. Mosley's British Union of Fascists (BUF) campaign on the promise that they will ensure all 300,000 British POWs still being held by Germany will be quickly returned home. Conservative, Labour and Liberal parties are split into pro and anti Stresa treaty factions. No party has enough votes to govern outright. The largest party is pro-Stresa Conservative and the second largest is the BUF. Ballot rigging is widespread, caused by Mosley using his position as Home Secretary to ensure BUF activists get to count the votes.

6th May 1941: The BUF forms a coalition government with pro-Stresa Labour, after attempts by pro-Stresa Conservatives to form a coalition fail. In the coalition agreement, the BUF commits to creating a National Health Service.

8th May 1941: Protest demonstrations and strikes against ballot rigging and result of general election take place.

9th May 1941: Strikes spread, although Communist-led trade unions refuse to join. Lady Mosley flies to Berlin to discuss repatriation of British POWs with Frau Goebbels.

11th May 1941: Germany invades the Soviet Union.

12th May 1941: British Communist-led trade unions join general strike.

13th May 1941: In view of the general strike, King Edward grants emergency powers for 30 days to the Mosley Government.

14th May 1941: Mosley forms an Action Cabinet, consisting of himself, Alexander Raven Thomson and Neil Francis Hawkins. All political activity is suspended.

25th May 1941: Final strike suppressed. Over 500 strikers have been killed and 80,000 interned.

1st June 1941: Britain joins Axis and declares war on the Soviet Union. By the end of the month, all British POWs in Germany have been returned home, apart from some 50,000 men who have been drafted into the Russian Expeditionary Force to fight in the Soviet Union alongside the Wehrmacht.

12th June 1941: In view of the state of war between Britain and the Soviet Union, the King extends indefinitely the emergency powers granted to Mosley. In the following weeks, political parties, other than the BUF, are outlawed, Parliament suspended and civil liberties curtailed. Britain is rapidly transformed into a Fascist state.

22nd August 1941: Mosley, under pressure from Nazi Germany to accelerate racist policies, appoints William Joyce as Home Secretary.

1st September 1941: The German Army captures Moscow.

9th September 1941: The Race Relations Act is passed. British Jews face restrictions similar to those of the 1935 German Nuremberg Laws.

17th September 1941: The German Army reaches Russian Ural Mountains.

29th September 1941: Last Russian division west of Urals surrenders. Germany declares the war in Russia won. Siberian and Central Asian parts of the Soviet Union are left unoccupied, but are too weak to offer further resistance. Shortly afterwards, Joseph Stalin is executed and is replaced by Lavrentiy Beria.

7th October 1941: Coronation of King Edward VIII by Archbishop of Canterbury, Cosmo Lang. Archbishop Lang had urged the King's abdication in 1936.

November 1941: Britain starts expelling foreign-born Jews.

2nd **November 1941:** Anglo-Japanese Non-Aggression treaty signed.

5th **November 1941:** Germany decides that the former Komi Autonomous Soviet Socialist Republic, renamed the Petschoragau, will become a reservation for all of Europe's Jews. The capital is the former Gulag town of Vorkuta, renamed Eichmannstadt in honour of the province's Gauleiter.

29th **November 1941:** German troops occupy Saudi Arabia.

30th **November 1941:** Saudi King, Ibn Saud, signs Saudi-German Petroleum Pact, whereby German oil companies will take over production from the Standard Oil of California company.

7th **December 1941:** Japan attacks United States fleet at Pearl Harbour.

8th **December 1941:** The United States and its ally, Churchill's Free British Government declare war on Japan. Free Britain also remains officially at war with Nazi Germany. Later, at a meeting with Roosevelt, a "defeat Japan first" policy is decided with the Free British Navy participating. The understanding is that after Japan is defeated, the United States will enter the war against Germany.

9th **December 1941:** Despite objections from its Governor General, the Duke of Kent, Australia declares war on Japan.

12th December 1941: Japan has occupied the entire South East Asian mainland. Under the terms of the Anglo-Japanese Non-Aggression Pact, Japan occupies Malaya and has control of Hong Kong and Singapore ports. In return, Japan recognises British Fascist rule over Burma and India.

25th December 1941: Free British and Canadian marines capture Bermuda and arrest the pro-Mosley Governor. He is allowed to finish his Christmas pudding. Over the next few months, all of Britain's possessions in the Caribbean come under Free British rule.

19th February 1942: Japanese bomb Darwin, Australia.

1st - 3rd May 1942: German invasion of Sweden.

4th - 7th June 1942: Battle of Midway. The United States, Free British and Australian Navies defeat the Imperial Japanese Navy attack against Midway Atoll in the South Pacific.

22nd June 1942: Germany invades Switzerland, despite Reichsmarschall Goering's objections. He had argued that the country should remain neutral "as a reminder of what a country run by bankers looks like".

23rd June 1942: During the previous night, Swiss troops transported gold from a number of banks to Alpine tunnels, which are then blown up. Later that day, 15,000 German paratroopers are dropped on the southern Swiss canton of Ticino in the largest airborne operation to date.

24th June 1942: Liechtenstein revokes its neutrality and joins the Axis.

25th June 1942: Rome. Mussolini, furious that Germany has occupied Ticino, which he regards as "his", orders Italian troops into Vatican City.

26th June 1942: Swiss Army surrenders at Brig. All of Europe, except Iceland, is either occupied by the Axis powers or is ruled by allied dictatorships.

1st August 1942: Italy and Germany swap territory. Ticino becomes part of Italy, while Alto Adige/South Tyrol is ceded to Germany.

7th August 1942: Start of the Battle of Guadalcanal in the South Pacific.

3rd September 1942: Germany. Goering is stripped of all titles, arrested by the SS, and interned at Flossenburg concentration camp, after it transpires that he has held a secret Swiss Bank account of over US $300,000,000.

October 1942: Deportation of British Jews to the Petschoragau begins. The final British Jews are expelled by March 1943. The very last Jews to be deported are industrialist and leading Zionist, Israel Sieff and his family, who are flown to Berlin by Mosley in his private plane.

14th November 1942: German Führer, Adolf Hitler, is awarded the Nobel Peace Prize in recognition of his efforts in unifying Europe.

9th February 1943: End of the Battle of Guadalcanal, resulting in victory for the United States and its allies against Japan.

May 1943: Nazi sappers complete the destruction of Moscow. Each year for the next few decades, a major Russian city is razed to the ground.

30th June 1943: Start of Operation Cartwheel, aimed at isolating the major Japanese forward base at Rabaul and cutting its supply and communication lines.

January 1944: Expulsions to Petschoragau cease. All of Europe's Jews have been deported.

25th February 1944: Reichsführer of the SS, Heinrich Himmler is assassinated by partisans in Warsaw. As a reprisal, his successor, Reinhard Heydrich, orders the execution of 100,000 Warsaw civilians and the destruction of the city.

20th March 1944: Operation Cartwheel ends with United States victory by the capture of Emirau Island.

13th June 1944: Invasion of Saipan by the United States. Capture of the island will enable the building of airfields, from which it will be possible to bomb Japan.

15th August 1945: Japan surrenders after the United States drops atom bombs on Hiroshima and Nagasaki.

Early September 1945: Australian troops and Free British Navy occupy Malaya, Singapore and Hong Kong.

16th September 1945: The United States gives Germany an ultimatum to withdraw all troops from Saudi Arabia by the end of the month. Germany complies and Ibn Saud signs agreement with US Arabian American Oil Company.

2nd October 1945: Washington. President Truman meets Churchill. The United States will not go to war with Germany as the major issue between the two countries – Saudi Arabian oil – has been resolved. US Public Opinion is against war with Germany and Truman does not feel bound by any private agreement between his predecessor, Roosevelt, and Churchill.

8th March 1946: Germany explodes an atomic bomb at its testing centre in Petschoragau. Over the next few decades, a nuclear arms race between the United States and Germany accelerates. The US leads in the race and puts Germany under great economic pressure. This is the start of the Cold War; however, Germany is bogged down by a partisan war in Poland and Russia, which lasts into the 1970s.

June 1948: First edition of Baedeker's *Guide to the Petschoragau* is published. The guide gives a figure of 600,000 for the population of the province, despite the relocation there of over 10 million European Jews.

25 March 1957: Treaty of Rome signed. European Union is formed to co-ordinate political and social but not economic policies. Signatories are the German Empire, British Empire, French Empire, Italian Empire, Turkey, Finland, Spain, Portugal, Ireland, Andorra, Liechtenstein and Monaco. All remaining European countries, except Iceland, have been annexed by Germany or Italy. Iceland remains allied with the United States.

20th April 1961: First manned German space flight.

5th May 1961: First American in space. Space race between Germany and the United States develops, with Germany consistently in the lead.

24th January 1965: Bermuda. Churchill dies aged 90. Free Britain comprises of just Bermuda and the Cayman Islands. Remaining British possessions in the Americas and South East Asia have become independent. Because of the difficulty in replacing their ageing crews, ships of the Free British Navy have been sold to Canada, Australia and the United States. Sir Oswald Mosley still leads a Fascist British Empire, with colonies in India and Africa, but unrest is widespread.

26th April 1966: Munich wins its bid for the 1972 Summer Olympics.

8th May 1969: Berlin. United States President Richard Nixon signs nuclear arms limitation treaty with Germany. His *"Ich bin ein Berliner!"* (I'm a Berliner) speech draws great applause from the assembled Nazi dignitaries. Era of détente begins.

17th June 1969: The United States breaks off diplomatic relations with Free Britain and recognises the Mosley Government. Charles Lindbergh is appointed US ambassador to London.

20th July 1969: First moon landing. Director of the German space programme, Wernher von Braun, is rewarded with an honorary SS rank of Oberst-Gruppenführer.

21st October 1970: Nobel Peace Prize awarded jointly to US President Richard Nixon and German Führer Adolf Hitler. This is the second time Hitler has been awarded the Nobel Prize.

11th Nov 1971: Berchtesgarden. Hitler dies aged 82. Of the Nazi Old Guard, only Joseph Goebbels, Reinhard Heydrich and Albert Speer are still alive. Amid rivalry between these three, Heydrich succeeds Hitler as Führer. There are also tensions between the Army and the SS. Many in the Army's command are well aware that despite having won the war, the average German is economically worse off than his Japanese counterpart, who of course lost his war. On the other hand, the SS leadership believes that ideology must trump economics.